THE BAD TUESDAYS

TWISTED SYMMETRY

THE BAD TUESDAYS

TWISTED SYMMETRY

Benjamin J. Myers

Orion
Children's Books

First published in Great Britain in 2009
by Orion Children's Books
a division of the Orion Publishing Group Ltd
Orion House
5 Upper St Martin's Lane
London WC2H 9EA
An Hachette Livre UK company

1 3 5 7 9 10 8 6 4 2

A catalogue record for this book
is available from the British Library.

ISBN 978 1 84255 645 0

Typeset by Input Data Services Ltd
Bridgwater, Somerset

Printed in Great Britain by
Clays Ltd, St Ives plc

The Orion Publishing Group's policy is to use papers that
are natural, renewable and recyclable products made from
wood grown in sustainable forests. The logging and
manufacturing processes are expected to conform to
the environmental regulations of the country of origin.

To Juliet

CHAPTER 1

Chess Tuesday had been stealing all morning. So had her brothers, Box and Splinter, but they had gone to a different part of the city. Splinter had said it was better that way. He had said that Chess wasn't safe to be with at the moment; not if she was being watched. She was thinking about this when she felt a push to her chest that knocked her backwards and onto the pavement, still holding the bag she'd been carrying.

'Shove off, street rat,' said a man who leant over her. By his overall she guessed that he worked in one of the shops she'd been passing.

I was shoving off, thought Chess. I was minding my own business. But she didn't say anything. She stayed crouching on the pavement.

She was kicked in the small of her back. It hurt and she twisted her neck to look behind and saw a woman holding a little girl by the hand and glaring. 'Go on,' the woman sneered. 'Shift, you filthy piece of rubbish.'

People were stopping to see what was happening.

This is too much attention, too many people watching,

thought Chess. Somebody kicked her right arm, just above the elbow.

She was frightened. Box or Splinter would have known what to do but she remained squatting on the floor, clutching the bag. A gobbet of spit hit her under her right eye. She wanted to strike back, to pick up bricks from the gutter and smash the shop windows but that would only have drawn more attention.

A needle of fear stabbed her chest. She didn't want the hunters to come.

Chess sprang to her feet as quickly as she could and ran away from the knot of people. They shouted after her but she did not look back.

'You must never look back,' Splinter had once told her. 'Not when you're running away.' She darted into a side street and up a fire escape, along a wall and down into a back alley. Then she headed for the wharf.

The wharf was a ramshackle heap of docks and warehouses that crouched on the riverbank beneath the city. Here, black tongues of water lapped at slime green quays and slid into dank tunnels where boats and barges had long since ceased to dock. Shrouded in mist and stinking of filth it was a place for tramps and bag ladies, for meths drinkers and drug addicts, for thieves and murderers.

This was where things came when they had nowhere else to go; when they had sunk below the jagged spread of the city and slipped through the sprawling slums of the Pit. The shifting mud banks and sluice gates draped with weed became the final resting place for bicycle wheels, bottles, mangled prams and the swollen dead, washed up by the dark waters of the river.

The wharf was also a place for street rats; the children with no homes, no families and no fear about stealing today what they would never get tomorrow. Hundreds of them hid here in gangs, slipping out of the tunnels and up into the noise and wealth of the city to steal what they could before vanishing back into the dark, wet places below.

In this world of rotting wood and crumbling brick where time was measured by the slow slap of water, they were safc. Safe from rain, safe from snow, safe from the hateful stares of honest city dwellers but most of all, safe from the hunters.

The hunters came with black boots, death's head badges, dogs and stun sticks to track and trap the street rats. They came whenever an infestation of rats had been located. They were part of the police, but a special part. They had their own detention units and unusual methods of interrogation. A street rat who was caught by the hunters knew that he or she would never see the wharf again. And nobody would see them again. The hunters were very efficient.

Box was better at fighting than any of the others in his gang and Splinter was cleverer so they had won for themselves a deep ledge built inside one of the tunnels. The lip of the ledge jutted out over the broad quayside and there was a recess at the rear where empty wooden barrels and boxes had been stacked, heaped with rust-stained ropes. The ledge was as smelly and gloomy and filthy as the rest of the wharf but because it was reached by a gantry about thirty feet above the water it was much drier. Here they lived with Chess and it was here that they would meet to consider the morning's takings.

Chess was the last to return. She was out of breath because she hadn't stopped running. Sweat prickled under her clothes. Even though the day was hot she wore a purple pullover. It was full of holes and so misshapen that the neck was almost as wide as the shoulders, and the sleeves hung down to her knees unless she kept rolling them up. Underneath she wore a T-shirt that had once been white but now was perfectly grey. Her jeans were torn over the knees and frayed at the ankles and had been for months. They were stiff with dirt. Her chestnut hair was thick and curly and had stuck flat to her forehead.

Her eyes were as brown as her hair and very big and she kept them on the cobbles over which her bare feet slapped. Some of the street rats watched her pass, eyes lingering on the bag that she was carrying. She wasn't frightened by the other gangs but she was frightened of what Splinter would do if she didn't have anything to show for the morning graft. She gripped the plastic bag more tightly.

Chess slowed to a walk but even when a cluster of bigger, older rats unfolded themselves from the innards of a burnt-out car they had scavenged, and turned to grin at her and say hello, she kept her eyes down and said nothing in reply. She was Splinter's sister: of course they were nice to her.

There were more than a hundred street rats in her brothers' gang but the only person that Chess looked for as she edged her way into the tunnel where they lived was Gemma. She had some chocolate for Gemma but she couldn't see her.

Chess stepped over legs and pushed round bands of squatting children. She walked past Pacer, Hex, Lynch and Jerky. They were her brothers' friends, which meant that her brothers didn't fight and argue with them as much as they fought and argued with everybody else. She heard them greet her and she mumbled a reply but she didn't look up until she came to the iron ladder that led to the ledge. Up there, above all the other street rats, were Box and Splinter.

Chess climbed the ladder and found her brothers inspecting their loot. Splinter, tall and thin, was holding up a ring. He studied it in the flickering light that was reflected from the river water and shimmered on the arched roof. He wore narrow, black trousers and a tatty, long-tailed morning coat that he had recovered from a bin. It was lined with pockets that he had sewn in himself. These contained a variety of useful items; string, matches, marbles, skeleton keys, a switchblade, a pencil. His long white hair was spiky with grime. He had pale blue eyes and sharp cheek bones.

'Good work, Box,' he said quietly. 'Did anyone see you?'

'Don't think so,' said Box, who sat with his legs dangling over the ledge. He wore ragged woollen trousers that were held up by braces and a blue and white striped T-shirt that was ripped. He was shorter than Splinter and stouter. His hair was black and tightly curled. Splinter called him 'fly head' because of his hair; he said it looked like a heap of squashed flies.

Chess dropped her plastic bag by Splinter's bare feet and sat down next to Box. Her legs dangled beside his, the air cool on their skin. They hadn't worn shoes for years and the soles of their feet had grown leathery and horn hard.

Splinter lifted the bag and looked inside, scowling. 'Chocolates,' he muttered, 'and bread rolls. And two apples. What use are two apples?' His hard voice reverberated against the tunnel walls.

Chess said nothing but dug her nails into the skin of her palms until the sharpness blotted out Splinter's glare.

'More use than one,' said Box. 'And anyway, Splinter, food's food.' Box stood up and rummaged in the plastic bag.

'All you ever do is stuff your mash. It's like you're half-boy, half-pig,' said Splinter.

'Yeah, well, you're all cretin,' replied Box, spitting on an apple and rubbing it on his grimy trousers.

'That makes me a hell of a lot cleverer than you. Pig boy.'

Chess said nothing. Eyes wide, she watched the pools of light shifting on the arches above her. She liked this. It was bright and clean and lifted her up from the ledge and the tunnel. It washed bad thoughts away.

She could hear her brothers arguing. As usual. Almost the first sound she could remember was the sound of her brothers arguing. The first sound that she could remember was a voice singing. Sometimes she could actually remember the words. The singing made her feel the same way as the light dancing above her now.

Nobody had sung to her after she and her brothers had been deposited at the orphanage. So, probably, the song was her mother's. She liked to think that.

Chess was three years old when she had been left at the Elms Orphanage. When they had found her at the door she was clutching a chess piece and so they had called her Chess. That was how they named children at the Elms. Box, who was carrying a wooden box, was called Box and Splinter, who was crying because his finger had been pierced by a splinter from the rough edge of the box was called Splinter. And because they had been left at the doorstep on a Tuesday, they were all called Tuesday.

Chess was eleven now and her brothers were both fourteen. The brothers were twins although they looked very different from one another. Even though they were older her brothers had no memories of life before the orphanage. They had tried to think of things that had happened to them before they were six but they couldn't remember anything. Their memories seemed to start at the Elms. Nobody had told them why they had been taken there and nobody had cared about what was done to them whilst they lived there. Splinter had said it was a bad place for children; that was why they had run away. Afterwards, nobody had tried to find them. So they had come to this place at the bottom of the city.

'A newspaper,' said Splinter with derision, pulling a newspaper from the plastic bag. 'What do you want with this, Chess? You can't even read.'

'I can,' she said defensively. 'A bit.'

He tossed the paper into the air and the pages fluttered apart like birds before drifting absently down to the water. One page floated back to the ledge and Splinter clutched it, casting his eyes over the headline. He read aloud, 'MORE CHILDREN VANISH.' Then he scrunched the sheet of paper into a ball which he threw into the air. 'Nice children, I suppose.'

'Bad things can happen to nice children,' said Chess.

'Bad things happen to bad children,' said Splinter, 'but nobody speaks about that. Nobody cares.' He coughed sharply and spat, pausing to watch the fleck of phlegm trace the same arc as the ball of newspaper before hitting the water below, silently.

'Nice shot, Splinter,' said Box with a thoughtful nod.

'Anything can happen to us and it doesn't matter,' continued Splinter, still looking down at the water, 'but the moment anything bad happens to a jack, it's big news. It matters.'

Splinter never said anything good about the jacks but Chess wasn't so sure. She thought it must be hard to go to school, to always follow rules, to have to get a job, to look after money. But, then again, people like that couldn't slip through crowds like oil, couldn't spirit up walls as silent as fog, didn't know how to claw their way out of corners or how to use drains to vanish when danger came near. They were soft; if they were hurt, they cried. And they hated street rats.

Splinter turned round, quickly. 'Were you followed?'

Chess shrugged her thin shoulders. 'Don't think so,' she said.

'She's just paranoid,' said Box.

'I'm not,' protested Chess. 'Someone's been watching me for days and I've seen hunters and they've seen me and they haven't tried to catch me.'

'Well that doesn't make sense,' said Box, starting to eat the second apple. 'Hunters hunt us and catch us. That's what they're there for.' He crunched apple flesh noisily.

'Unless,' considered Splinter, 'they have been following

her so they can find us.' He turned on Box. 'You shouldn't have burnt that police station down, Box.'

'You shouldn't have robbed that post office, Splinter,' retorted Box through a mouth full of apple.

'Perhaps it's me they're after,' said Chess softly.

'Why would they want *you*?' sneered Splinter.

Chess shrugged again. 'Someone has been watching me. Or something.' She was definite about that.

Box crunched the apple and Splinter put the ring inside one of his pockets before disappearing into the shadows at the back of the ledge. Chess looked at the grey crescents of dirt beneath her toenails and wished that Splinter would believe her. She knew that someone or something had been watching her for weeks. There had been signs; footfalls close behind, a strange reflection in a shop window, a figure slipping into a doorway as she approached. She hadn't always been able to see who or what it was but she could tell that she was being watched in the same way that a wild animal can.

But this morning had been different. It was different because no one had been watching her. What had happened outside the shop didn't count. It wasn't very nice but it was what happened to street rats. What unsettled Chess was that the watching had stopped.

It has stopped, thought Chess, because enough has been seen. Which meant that something was going to happen.

It was midday; a busy time in the city but the quietest time at the wharf. Street rats were sleeping or talking quietly, repairing clothes, cleaning tools. Somebody had lit a fire and put a tyre on it to burn. It smelt better than the river stink.

Box had stretched out on the ledge and was snoring. Even the look-outs positioned just inside the mouth of the tunnel were nodding sleepily in the heavy calm of the afternoon.

It had been hot for days and mists had been steaming over the river, draping the wharf in humid clouds until the brick walls had been dripping wet. Autumn had been sweltering. But today the sky was the colour of soot and the morning air had been sweet with the smell of approaching rain. Chess lay on her back and watched the light patterns fade and glow overhead. She felt drowsy but she could not relax enough to sleep.

She had noticed before how you can become aware of a sound without ever noticing when it started. Now she realized that she could hear a thumping, whirring noise. It was deep and shrill at the same time and it was constant although it had been faint at first. Chess sat up and turned her head to try to hear better. It seemed to come out of the air rather than from any place in particular and it seemed to be coming nearer because it was getting louder.

Warning cries from the look-outs pierced the slumbering gloom of the wharf. Children, some no older than five or six appeared from the shadows of the tunnel to find out what was happening. They slid down ropes, jumped from mounds of old boxes and slithered out of cracks in the walls. In seconds the tunnel was full of them. They were quiet at first, listening to the noise that was coming closer.

Nothing could be seen through the mist.

'Box!' hissed Chess. 'Box, wake up,' and she gave his ankles a kick.

He woke at once, eyes squinting. 'Helicopters!' he said

and beneath the approaching screech and hum there was another sound, distant at first but also coming closer. Dogs.

Splinter appeared back at the lip of the ledge. 'Hunters,' he shouted and there was an explosion of activity as a hundred or more street rats started stuffing their belongings into bags and sacks and then scrambling to the tunnel opening to try to get out before the hunters could trap them. There were cries and yells mixing with the screaming of the helicopters, and a splash when one of the rats lost his footing in the panic and fell into the water.

'We'll never get out,' Box shouted.

The whine of engines and thump of rotor blades made Chess's ribs vibrate. She couldn't see the helicopters yet but from the roar of noise and the way that the water was churning and swelling, they must have been hovering just out beyond the tunnel openings.

It was chaos below the ledge. There were more street rats than there was space on the slippery stones of the quays and with so many of them jammed tightly together and pushing nobody was able to move forwards. There was a lot of shouting. Two small boys were sitting on the floor at the back of the crowd and Chess could see that they were crying although it was too noisy to hear them. Nobody noticed them except Chess. She looked for Gemma but couldn't see her amongst the jostling bodies.

As Chess and Box watched, the rats surged backwards. Some stumbled to the floor and some were barged into the river as they swarmed over one another. Then they saw what had made them retreat. Charging out of the mist came a troop of hunters, batons raining down, breaking bones and spilling blood. Their black uniforms and helmets drove into the tunnel in a wedge and at their sides came dogs, unchained and savage.

'There are loads of them,' said Box. 'They must have blocked the docks and walks.' He puffed out his cheeks. 'This is massive.'

Chess said nothing because there was nothing to say. She stood above the mayhem lamely and watched as forty or fifty hunters ploughed into the children and deeper into the tunnel. At their rear came a commander, flanked by two lieutenants. He wore a throat-mike and was talking into this. The black lenses of his glasses tilted up at intervals as he scanned the walkways and alcoves on the tunnel walls.

The tunnel was filling with hunters and the rats were being forced back. Children screamed, dogs snarled. When all the hunters were inside a thick net dropped down the mouth of the tunnel like a portcullis, preventing any escape.

Had Chess been on the opposite bank of the river, and had there been no mist, she would have seen the same thing happening at each of the tunnels along the wharf. She would have seen a legion of hunters, some armed with rifles, packing the quaysides and pouring into the arches and she would have seen the nets unfurling from the helicopters that hovered over the wharf like a swarm of locusts. Every entrance to every tunnel was sealed by the nets. Every rat was trapped.

'We've had it,' said Box to Chess. Chess was silent.

A black gloved hand was pointing up at her. It was the commander and he was looking straight at her. His two lieutenants also turned their impenetrably darkened glasses towards her. The commander spoke into his throat-mike. Five hunters turned back from those pushing into the tunnel and halted in front of him. He spoke to them sharply, giving orders. Three of them ran to the foot of the ladder that would take them up to the ledge where Chess was standing. The other two unslung their rifles.

All the time that Box and Chess had been watching the rout, Splinter had been busy in the shadows behind them.

'Follow me,' he shouted.

'Where?' shouted Box, watching the hunters.

'You'll see.'

Box hesitated and then hurried to where the gantry joined the side of the ledge. The platform was chained to a pair of iron posts that were firm in the stone. He looked for a way to loosen it so that the platform would collapse and the hunters would not be able to reach them. Already there were two of them climbing up the ladder.

Box gave the chain a yank. The platform swung sideways but was secure.

Chess saw one of the hunters who had stayed by the commander raise his rifle to his shoulder and drop his head to the stock, taking aim. The barrel was trained on Box. She ran to Box, shouting his name. As she grabbed his shoulders she saw the commander place his hand on top of the rifle muzzle and push it towards the floor.

'Let's follow Splinter,' she urged Box.

'Where to?' he asked.

'I don't know. Come on.'

They ran to the back of the ledge to find boxes strewn about the floor and barrels upended. Where they had been stacked there was a low portal in the wall and Splinter was on his haunches on the other side, beckoning them on.

'I never knew about this,' yelled Box.

'Why do you think I wanted the ledge?' came the reply. 'We were always going to need an escape. We always will. Now come on.'

Stooping, Box and Chess ran through the opening and found themselves at the foot of an iron stairwell with a corridor that sloped down to the left of them.

'We have to get up the stairs, across the roof and down the fire escape on the far side.' Splinter was able to talk without shouting although the whirr of helicopter engines still filled the air. 'If we get to the bottom on the other side we're OK.'

'And if we don't?' asked Box.

Splinter didn't reply. He turned and charged up the stairs, two at a time and Box followed at his heels. Chess ran as fast as she could but there was flight upon flight to the warehouse roof. She gulped air and her lungs were tight as if they were being crushed. Her thighs were screaming hot and her feet were hard to lift. She heard Box yelling at her, encouraging her to go faster, but it was the ringing of boots on the iron steps below that made her forget about the pain and run harder.

'Get the girl,' snarled a voice behind her. 'Kill the others if you have to but get the girl. Alive.'

When she staggered to the top of the stairs, Box and Splinter were flinging themselves at a wooden door that led outside. It was dark in the stairwell but Chess could see light outlining the door. As she reached her brothers the door smashed open and all of them tumbled out into daylight and driving rain.

'What did they shout?' grunted Splinter, splashing to his feet.

'I didn't hear,' gasped Chess, even though she had. There was no time for questions; no time for blame. The hunters were coming for her and she didn't know why.

The roof was wide and flat. The air was fresh and cold. They ran for the far side where an iron ladder vanished over the parapet.

They might have reached the ladder. They might have made it to the bottom. But before they had run halfway across the roof a helicopter swooped in low and three hunters dropped from it, blocking their way, rifles ready.

Splinter halted. Chess and Box stopped beside him. 'They really want us,' said Box as the helicopter hovered overhead and the hunters closed in.

Splinter considered his options. He had none.

Box slipped a hand into his trouser pocket and grasped the lock knife that he always kept there. It wasn't easy to work the blade open but he did so slowly, without cutting his fingers. The hunters from the helicopter faced them, rifles at their shoulders, barrels steady and levelled at the children. Rain dripped from the black rifle muzzles.

Marching from the door behind came the commander and his two lieutenants. They walked round to face the children. The commander was not much taller then Chess. He had a lean and hungry face which he thrust so close that his hatchet of a nose was almost touching hers. His lips were pulled tightly against his teeth which she couldn't see but which she sensed might have been longer then normal and very sharp. She didn't blink and she barely breathed. Rain spotted the black lenses of his glasses.

He is smelling me, Chess thought, and at the same time caught a sour stink of dog, although there were no dogs on the roof.

Then the commander stepped back. 'This is the girl,' he said. 'Now take them.'

As one of the lieutenants stepped forwards, Box lunged towards him, knife at throat height. This was unexpected and it was only because the hunter turned his shoulder at the last moment that the knife slashed air and not flesh. But the hunters were fast and well drilled. Before Box could regain his footing the other lieutenant had extended his stun stick and cracked it across Box's back.

There was a brilliant flash as the electricity discharged and then Box was on the floor, body wracked with pain. Even as he writhed at their feet, the lieutenant rammed his stun stick into Box's belly and sent another bolt of electricity into him. Chess shut her eyes and Splinter stared hard at the iron ladder that they hadn't been fast enough to reach. All the time the commander kept his hidden eyes on Chess.

The helicopter descended to the roof, rocking slightly and making web patterns on the rain-lashed concrete. Chess and Splinter's thin arms were manacled and they were frogmarched into it. Then two hunters seized Box's arms and legs and they carried him to the open door through which they slung him. He landed with a thud on the floor beside the others and lay there, whimpering.

The commander and the lieutenant who had used the

stun stick climbed into the cockpit beside the pilot. Three hunters sat in the cargo hold with Chess, Box and Splinter, stun sticks drawn and faces rigid.

'Enjoy the daylight, rats,' the commander shouted to them. 'You won't see much more of it.' Then he spoke to the pilot.

The helicopter rose, tipped forwards and plunged into the driving rain.

CHAPTER 2

Chess, Box and Splinter sat in silence in a corridor inside the detention unit. On arrival they had been marched here, chained together and ordered to sit on iron chairs that were lined against the hard white wall. Then they had been manacled to the chairs. They were left waiting. And waiting. Water had dripped from their clothes onto the floor where it had collected in little pools around their bare feet.

It was very quiet. Sometimes, Chess thought she could hear echoes of shouting or screaming or laughter coming from rooms far away. Sometimes there was the clang of iron bars and the boom of a door slamming. And there was the sound of clicking.

The clicking came from the far end of the corridor where a scruffy little lady sat on a chair beside a steel door. She was wrapped in a patchwork shawl and tatty plastic bags bulging with whatever they held were crammed under her chair. She wore spectacles and her short grey hair hung loose and scraggy over her face as she worked with a pair of long knitting needles and a ball of green wool, paying no attention to anything else.

'She's still knitting,' whispered Box. They hadn't spoken for over an hour and all the time the old lady had been knitting. 'She's one of the bag ladies.'

'I wonder what she's in here for?' said Splinter.

'Something weird, like murdering children,' suggested Box.

'No way,' said Splinter. 'They'd give her a medal for that.'

Silence again, apart from the clicking.

Box sniffed hard and screwed up his face. 'This place smells like a swimming pool.'

'It's the bleach they use to clean blood off the walls,' said Splinter. Nobody laughed.

The minutes passed and still nobody spoke.

'What do you think they'll do to us, Splinter?' asked Box after he could bear the silence no longer.

Splinter's head was hanging down almost between his knees and he ran his manacled hands through his spiky white hair before looking sideways and up at his brother. 'We've had it, Box. They're going to do us. They've been after us for ages. They hate us.'

'The labs?' said Box, his voice hoarse.

Splinter was silent but he sat up, chains clinking, and leant back against the cold wall of the corridor.

'Not the labs, Splinter. No way. They can't do that. We're only . . .'

'Children?' said Splinter. 'Street children. Remember, Box, we're vermin. Rats. They hate us; us in particular.

'Because we burnt down the police station?' Box said incredulously. 'They deserved it.'

'Well you just tell them that,' said Splinter, closing his

pale blue eyes. He was thinking about what he had heard of the labs. They were places where street rats were sent so that they could be used for experiments that were forbidden on any other creature; injections, electric shocks, chemicals, dissections, amputations, genetic interference. Nobody ever returned from the labs. Not looking like a normal human being anyway.

Chess's huge brown eyes closed tight and she squeezed them tighter still to stop the wet burning of her tears.

'You're crying,' said Box. 'That won't help.'

'Shut up, fly head,' said Splinter. 'Someone's coming.'

Chess looked and her throat tightened. Two officers clad in the black uniforms and bearing the silver skull and cross-bone insignia of the hunters were walking towards them, boots thudding on the concrete floor. Their dark glasses reflected the bright strip lighting. Chess recognized the shorter of the two as the commander who had caught them. The other hunter was the one who had used the stun stick on Box and when he came to Chess he unfastened the irons that locked her to the chair. Then he did the same to her brothers.

'Follow.' The commander spat the word at them and marched on, not turning to look whether they did as he said.

Chess, Box and Splinter stood up and shuffled after the officers. It was difficult to walk with so much metal hanging from their wrists and ankles. They followed the hunters to where the scruffy little lady was still engrossed in her knitting. She didn't raise her head until the officers were standing right in front of her, their prisoners clattering to a halt behind them. Then she looked up, smiling gently.

'Inspector,' she said, as if presented with an unexpected but delightful surprise.

Standing close to the shorter officer, the Inspector, for the second time that day, Chess noticed again his hard, sharp features. His skin was pale and his hair was fuzzy and short and black and his nose arched, broad and flat like half a shark's fin. It had long thin nostrils. She did not breathe in because she did not like the smell of him. It wasn't the usual sort of bad smell but it wasn't the sort of smell she was used to in a person. His black gloved fingers were twitching by his side.

'All right, Ethel,' he said. 'They're yours. For five minutes. Just five minutes.'

The other officer said nothing. He just looked at the children through the black lenses of his glasses and the corners of his mouth tightened.

The old lady dumped her knitting under the chair where the plastic bags were and stood up quickly, brushing her hands over her skirt. Chess thought she was surprisingly business-like.

'Thank you, Inspector,' said the lady. She stuck her head forwards and tilted it up so that it stopped about an inch from the Inspector's. Her lank grey hair flopped all over her broad and wrinkled forehead. 'Do we have a room?' She smiled politely.

The taller officer took a key from a pouch in his black tunic jacket which he used to open the steel door. He pushed the door and it swung open noiselessly.

'Chains?' She smiled again, pointing at the shackles binding Chess, Box and Splinter.

The officer began to unfasten the bolts that secured the chains around Splinter's wrists. At the same time the Inspector grasped Chess's thin wrists and twisted her arms. She winced because her skin snagged sharply in the hunter's grip. He undid the handcuffs and wrenched away the heavy chain that bound her hands and forearms.

By the time that all the chains had been removed from Chess, Box and Splinter there was a small heap of ironmongery on the floor. Now that the blood could flow freely through her wrists, Chess realized how sore they were.

The old lady looked from Chess's raw skin to the Inspector's impassive face.

'You're too kind, Inspector,' she said.

'We'll be waiting out here,' he growled.

'Very thoughtful, Inspector. I'll know where to find you if I need you.' She turned on the heel of her decrepit sandal and stomped into the room beyond the steel door.

The Inspector turned to face the children. 'Go on, filth,' he said. 'I don't know what she wants with you but you're getting away with nothing.' Then his sharp white face split with a grin revealing teeth that looked normal. Barely moving his lips he whispered, 'You're dead. Dead,' and he kept grinning as the children walked past him and through the doorway.

When they were all in the room, the bag lady pushed the thick door and it closed with a muffled thud. She walked to a steel table that was standing in the centre of the room and sat on it. Her feet did not quite touch the floor. Chess, Box and Splinter stood in front of her. Apart from the table and the bright strip lighting the room was bare.

'Now, we don't have long,' she said. 'You must know that the Inspector out there wants your guts for garters. If he has his way it will be very bad for you.' Her spectacles had slipped down to the tip of her small pink nose and her eyes peered over the top of them. They were grey and a little bloodshot. 'I can help you. Possibly.'

'Are you just another one of them?' interrupted Box, nodding towards the door.

'Box Tuesday,' said the lady. 'You have no idea of who I am or what I am,' and as she said that, Chess felt the air turn chilly.

'You're a bag lady,' said Box. 'A smelly old bag lady.'

Chess felt the hairs on the back of her neck prickle. She could see the air about the lady shimmer, like when heat rises from a fire.

Box continued. 'You are old and smelly and either you are one of them or a weirdo.'

Chess never forgot what happened next.

They were in the room no longer. She and Box and Splinter were clinging to one another on a narrow pinnacle of black rock. Far below them boiled a sea of clouds, yellow and white and blue. Above them towered a woman whose swirling ebony hair filled the sky and was spangled with the stars. Her long fingers, bone white and tipped by blood red nails, were pointing at them and her almond eyes were deep and dark and keen as a tiger's.

When she spoke it was as if the world was filled with the boom of her voice. 'I am the Baroness Mevrad Styx, Grand Mistress of the Outer Crescent and you may look on me and live.'

And then they were back in the room in the detention unit, shivering and holding onto one another and Ethel was smiling kindly. 'I'm sorry, my loves. I don't like to do that sort of thing but time is short. Would you listen to me now?'

Chess, Box and Splinter nodded, dumbstruck. Box was trembling.

'I will make this as simple as I can so let me start by telling you three things.' She held up one stubby finger for them to look at. 'First, there are many different worlds in the universe.' Another finger was raised. 'Second, it is possible for people or things to move between these worlds. And third,' displaying three fingers now, all with rough, bitten nails, 'children are not welcome in any of these worlds. But they have their uses.' Ethel leant forwards, lowering her voice. 'They are valuable.'

Box was silent. So were Chess and Splinter.

Ethel nodded and smiled. 'That's got you, my loves, hasn't it? This is the truth: nobody really likes children. Apart from their parents. Sometimes.'

'Nobody likes us at all,' said Box.

'Well, you don't know about your parents, do you?' Ethel pointed out.

There was a banging on the door and a voice shouted, 'One minute, Ethel.' She frowned to herself and swept her grey and greasy fringe away from her spectacles.

'Time is such a relative thing. Such a nuisance.'

'She's talking to herself,' whispered Box to Chess.

'Never enough when you need it. Too much of it when you don't.' She chewed her lip and then she waved her left hand in front of her face in an anti-clockwise direction and it seemed to Chess that she was rotated as if she was attached to Ethel's hand. Her feet swept up to where her head had been and her head was somewhere near to the floor and then she was standing still and upright again but feeling very dizzy.

'I feel sick,' said Splinter, rubbing his stomach.

'I'm sorry, dear,' said Ethel. 'I'm breaking too many rules this afternoon but we needed the time. I've put us back five minutes. If you feel funny it's just the after-effect of reverse time.'

Splinter began to heave and cough.

'Disgusting,' said Box. 'He's puking.'

Ethel reached up into her sleeve and pulled out a grubby handkerchief. 'Wipe your mouth with this.'

'You said you can help us,' said Chess, thinking of the Inspector with his sharp face and hatchet nose.

Ethel nodded at her. 'Like I said, children are valuable. They have their uses. That's why something is stealing them; stealing them from your world and taking them to another place.'

'Children can't be stolen,' Splinter muttered through the handkerchief as he wiped his mouth. 'Not like that.'

'Can't they?' replied Ethel. 'Can't they disappear? Think about street children you have known, Splinter. Children who have vanished.'

'Yeah, OK,' said Splinter. 'They do disappear. But that's just the hunters and sometimes other people, weird people.' Ethel took the handkerchief back from him, smiling patiently as he spoke. 'And, well, you know, things like that.' Then he stopped talking because he knew that Ethel was right; children did disappear.

Ethel was still smiling at him kindly, 'Exactly, dear. Now as I was saying, there is a link from your world to this other place.'

'You didn't say anything about a link,' interrupted Splinter. 'What do you mean "a link"?'

'You remember I said there are many different worlds in the universe? A link is like a path or a road, from one world to another. This link is a suck worm; we call it the Fat Gobster. The Fat Gobster is being used to swallow children here and take them to another world.'

'What's a suck worm, what's the Fat Gobster and who is "we"?' Splinter spat something lumpy and bitter from his mouth.

Ethel sighed. 'You know, I'm trying to keep this as simple as possible, Splinter. Listen carefully. There is an organization. We call it the Twisted Symmetry. It is everywhere and it does many things, bad things, and that includes stealing children. Stealing children is only one small part of what the Twisted Symmetry is all about. But that is the part we are concerned with right now.'

'This is mad,' said Box.

'It is mad,' agreed Ethel. 'But it is real and it is happening. I work for another organization. We call ourselves the Committee.'

'The Committee,' sneered Splinter. 'Do you organize tea parties?'

'No, Splinter. We fight the Twisted Symmetry. Listen to me. The Symmetry is all around us and it has many servants. They come in different forms: warps, spooks, troopers, traders, and there are worse. Far worse. Things that crawl through the dark spaces in the universe, things that have been grown from pain. Things that have no names because they should not exist. And at the heart of it the Symmetry, ever brooding, ever calculating, ever manipulating, are the Inquisitors.'

'The Inquisitors,' echoed Splinter, lingering over the word, enjoying its sound.

Ethel frowned. 'The Inquisitors are lies and death. Be very careful; they use promises and fear and torment to control the most treacherous tools of all.'

'Which are?' enquired Splinter.

'People, Splinter. People.' Her voice trailed off and she closed her eyes. When they flashed open, Chess jumped. 'Trust no one,' she hissed.

'Do we trust you?' asked Splinter.

'You have to trust me.' Ethel pointed to the door behind which the hunters were waiting. 'They have orders to let you come with me if you choose to. If you don't come with me you will be theirs. It won't be nice for you.'

'What are you after?' Splinter's eyes narrowed.

'We need you to help us,' said Ethel. 'We need you to steal something for us.'

'Stealing's bad,' said Splinter, sounding as if he didn't think stealing was bad at all.

'This stealing ain't bad,' said Ethel.

'We're good at stealing,' volunteered Box brightly.

'I know you are, my love,' said Ethel.

'And fighting. We're good at that too.'

'That's very nice, dear. It usually comes in handy.' She removed her spectacles and wiped the lenses with the handkerchief before holding them up to the light to inspect them. Then she put them back on her nose and tucked the grimy rag up her sleeve. She fixed the Tuesdays with a keen gaze. 'The Committee needs you.'

Splinter looked hard at Box who shrugged and scratched his head. Chess looked hard at the floor. When nobody had said anything for several seconds Ethel said, 'The fight against the Twisted Symmetry goes on at all times and in all places. Ordinary people don't know about it because they don't see it. They think the world is what they can see or hear or touch. They're wrong. All the time, all around them there is a desperate battle and the balance is very fine, my loves. The least defeat and the Symmetry breaks through. When the Symmetry does break through we have to fight very hard to drive them back. If the Symmetry were not held at bay, this world would become a painful and frightening place.' She stopped to look at Chess and Box and Splinter with their ragged clothes and bare feet and then said, 'Even more painful and frightening than it already is.' Ethel coughed to clear her throat. 'You know, my loves, sometimes people have to take sides in all of this. I'm asking you to help us and I'm offering you a way out of this place but I'm also asking you to take a side.'

After another long silence, Chess said, 'I'll come with you.'

Ethel smiled kindly at her. 'Such a pretty little girl,' she said softly and she sounded sad. 'You will have to be very brave.' Chess nodded slowly.

'I'll come too,' said Splinter but he added, 'For my sake, not for anyone else's.'

'Well, I'm not staying on my own,' said Box.

Ethel's old grey eyes were still fixed on Chess's big brown ones. Then she flicked her gaze towards the door, propelled herself off the table and marched forwards saying, 'Follow me.'

She pulled open the door and strutted past the hunters saying no more than, 'Thank you, Inspector. They're coming with me.' She was followed by Box and then Splinter. Last out of the room was Chess.

Chess tried to keep her eyes focused on Ethel's back. She could feel the malevolent glare of the hunters' eyes searing into her as she passed them. She could smell their hot and fetid breath as it licked her face. She didn't want to look at them but without meaning to she was slowing down and turning. The others were marching up the corridor and away from her. Her legs moved slowly as if from the waist down she had been sucked into mud.

'Don't look back,' she said to herself, 'never look back.' But sometimes it was hard not to look. Chess stopped.

She turned round and looked at the Inspector who was standing at the same place outside the room. He had taken his glasses off and his eyes were glazed but fixed on her. A funny noise was coming from his throat, like growling. He grinned at her, dropping his lower jaw and letting a long pink dog tongue loll out of his mouth. It fell to below his chin and spittle ran from it. There was a cracking sound from his nose which began to stretch forwards and broaden into a long snout dragging his mouth with it. His lips, now black and wet drew back, revealing a row of white fangs. He snarled at Chess.

Chess began to run.

CHAPTER 3

'What is it, dear?' asked Ethel, who had turned as Chess came running up the corridor. She rested a hand on Chess's shoulder, plastic bags and knitting clenched in the other. When Chess looked back down the corridor, she saw two ordinary, black-booted, black-uniformed, silver-badged hunters. Pale-faced and thin-lipped. No fangs. No dog snouts. But also, she felt cocooned and strengthened by the touch of the old lady's hand on her shoulder and as the Inspector met Ethel's gaze, Chess saw him shuffle uncomfortably and then slip on his dark glasses.

'All right?' said Ethel.

Chess nodded and hoped that she was breathing normally now. 'Yes. Thank you,' she said. 'It's just . . . I thought . . .'

'Yes, I know, dear, but don't worry about what you thought,' said Ethel. 'The time for thinking is coming to an end. That's why you're with me.'

'Well, let's go then,' said Box. When they had started walking again he said to Splinter, 'I can't believe we're just walking out of this place.'

'But where are we going?' questioned Splinter.

'Away from them at least,' and Box spun round and made a gesture towards the officers that would have been worth ten shocks on any normal day. They did not react. With a sense of deep satisfaction he followed Chess and Ethel and Splinter.

'The time for thinking is coming to an end.' Chess repeated Ethel's words to herself as she walked. It was a funny thing to say and she didn't know what it meant.

Ethel led them through the detention unit and although people in uniforms watched them walk by, no one said anything. It seemed to Chess that the place was filled with a thick, dead silence. Even the movements of those around them were soundless as if everyone was moving underwater. When a hunter drew a stun stick from her belt and swung it against her thigh she did so without a noise. All that Chess could hear was the sound of Ethel's sandals and their own bare feet slapping the floor.

Chess kept her eyes down. She didn't like the bright lights and the way that they were reflected in the black glasses of the hunters who were all around them. The black glasses were like bulging wasp eyes that jerked to follow her as she walked past.

Ethel took hold of Chess's hand as they approached the iron stairwell that would take them up and out of the detention unit. Chess gripped the hand hard. There were so many hunters, all of them armed. As far as Chess could tell it would be easy for the hunters to stop them leaving. Supposing the Inspector decided to go back on his agreement with Ethel? Supposing one of the others decided to shoot Ethel anyway? Then they could do what they liked to Chess and her brothers. She was so close to the terror of the black uniforms and silver skulls.

But no one stopped them and Chess wondered how this was possible. The iron rang as their feet stamped up it, announcing their departure. The outside was a few steps and one door away.

Chess snatched a final glance at the wave of darkness where the hunters had gathered below. Then she felt Ethel grip her hand with unexpected vigour, yanking her away from the top of the stairs and into the blast and sting of driving rain. They were outside and the door slammed hard behind them.

'We're going to have to walk to my flat,' said Ethel, directing a critical eye at the naked feet.

'We walk everywhere anyway,' said Splinter.

'Unless we nick a car,' added Box.

'We ain't nicking any cars,' said Ethel, setting off up the street.

Already the rain had plastered their hair flat to their heads. The air had become much cooler than it had been that morning. Their clothes were damp and Chess shivered as a trickle of water ran from her hair, down her neck and between her shoulders.

The sky was low and grim and the rain was ice cold but Chess was glad to be anywhere other than the underground detention unit. They had come out in a side street that led to one of the city's main thoroughfares and they trooped along this, following Ethel in a line with heads down and bare feet splashing.

It was early evening and the city was a smudge of raincoats, umbrellas and cars swishing through oily puddles. The smells of pizza, cigarette smoke, diesel and coffee seemed to compete for attention in Chess's nose until she stopped noticing them altogether.

A bag lady followed by three street rats was soon lost in the jumble and rush of the streets. They passed almost unnoticed although a well-manicured, elderly woman caught Chess's eye. She was standing in the doorway of a smart shop that sold silk scarves and she shook her head and frowned at Chess as she walked by. 'Little savage,' said the lady so that Chess could hear her. 'Put some shoes on and stop fouling the streets.'

They walked for nearly an hour.

By the time that they stopped outside a tall terrace they were soaked to the skin and the rain had stopped. Ethel took them down a short flight of stone steps so that they were below the pavement. Chess guessed that there must have been three or four floors above this basement level.

Arching his back to look up, Splinter noticed the plush red curtains in the windows above and the yellow lamp glow that leaked out into the dusk. But Ethel's flat was in darkness. All that Splinter could tell was that the windows were cracked and caked with grime and behind them were ragged net curtains, streaked with filth and hanging at crazy angles.

Ethel plonked her bags on the floor where they sat in a puddle and then rooted about in a purse. It looked as if it had been made from a thick piece of tartan travel rug and it had a narrow brass clasp on the top.

The sort of purse that old ladies always have, thought Splinter. He knew a lot about purses. And pockets. And wallets and handbags, and briefcases and money belts. He knew how to ease a purse from a trouser pocket as smoothly as taking a letter from an envelope. He knew the way to push past a person with a fat breast pocket, slipping in a hand to whip out a wallet. He knew how to snatch a poorly guarded handbag and the places to run to when he was pursued. He watched Ethel closely as she produced a key from the purse and then realized that she was watching him. She winked at him and put the purse back in a pocket somewhere beneath the shawl that she was wearing.

Unlocking the door to the flat she ushered them in to a hallway that was gloomy and reeking.

'This place stinks,' Box whispered to Splinter, not very quietly.

'Like a cat's toilet,' agreed Splinter.

Ethel did not seem to hear them; at least, she didn't say anything back.

Whilst they stood just inside the doorway with the door still open behind them, Ethel switched on the hall light and then disappeared into a room at the end of the short hallway. From the sound of a tap clunking and then water rushing and the noise of a kettle banging on a hob it was obvious that she had gone into a kitchen.

'Cup of tea?' shouted Ethel. 'Or water? I haven't anything else apart from spirits and I can't give you those. I'm in *loco parentis*, my dears. Not that there's been much by way of *parentis* for a long while.' Her voice trailed off and it sounded as if she was muttering to herself.

Chess looked at her surroundings. The cracked ceiling was meant to be white but it was the colour of ear wax.

There was a low bookcase by one wall. The top was thick with a fur of dust through which were dotted small paw tracks. She couldn't see any books on the shelves. The carpet was dark orange and threadbare and covered with stains.

As she looked about, Chess noticed something move inside the bookcase. Then out of the darkness of the shelves came a slim grey leg followed by whiskers, nose, head and the rest of a cat, large, fluffy and grey. It bounded to the floor, landing in perfect silence and without paying any attention to the human visitors trotted to the kitchen. Moments later it reappeared from round the door accompanied by a leaner, dark-eyed, tortoiseshell cat. They padded side by side to the bookcase and then sprung in unison to the top where they sat like bookends, regarding their visitors with interest and purring gently.

The kettle whistled.

'Why don't we just go?' suggested Box.

Splinter considered this. 'She might come after us. She's not an ordinary wrinkly.'

'So? We can hide, can't we? We can hide better than anyone. And what's she going to do if she finds us?'

'She might turn you into a frog,' said Splinter.

'Big deal,' said Box, bargaining on not being found.

Splinter looked at the open door. It was nearly night. 'OK,' he said. 'We'll go. But let's have a quick snoop first. She might have some stuff, jewellery or something. Chess, you keep her talking in the kitchen.'

'Shouldn't we just wait here and see what she wants?' Chess had liked the way that Ethel had held her shoulder and her hand and had taken them away from the hunters. She didn't want to steal from the old lady.

'Just go in there and keep her busy,' snapped Splinter. 'And stop being pathetic.'

Chess walked towards the kitchen slowly and her brothers slunk though the nearest door. The cats watched, unblinking.

Ethel was bending over a steel sink washing mugs. She had put on an orange, floral house-coat that came down to below her knees. Chess could see the backs of Ethel's calves. The skin was more grey than pink and was mottled and knotted with dark blue veins like a piece of stilton cheese. When Ethel spoke, Chess was startled.

'Have you met my two friends?' she asked without turning round. 'They live here. Their names are Argus and Sekhmet. Argus is the big grey one.' Chess guessed that Ethel was talking about the cats who were sitting on the bookcase. She looked back at them and they were blinking slowly and licking their paws.

'I know you feel uncomfortable,' said Ethel, turning round now and drying a mug with a grubby dish cloth. 'But you mustn't. Don't worry about your brothers, dear. They can't help themselves but they will learn. Eventually.' She walked across the small kitchen. 'Come and sit down. I've made some tea and there's bread and butter.'

Chess saw that bread and butter was piled high on a plate in the middle of a small table that was pushed against the wall of the kitchen. A brown teapot with steam rising from the spout sat beside the bread and butter. Ethel put four mugs by the teapot.

'They won't find anything they can take but I am worried that one of them will get a nasty shock. He might even be hurt.'

Chess's eyes widened with concern and she made to leave the kitchen so that she could tell her brothers to stop whatever they were doing.

'Stay!' commanded Ethel and her voice was hard. Then, more gently she said, 'Sit down, Chess.'

Chess sat down at the table. Ethel sat in the chair next to her. She patted Chess's hand. 'It isn't really their fault, my dear, but as I said, they have to learn.' She began to pour tea into the mugs and then hesitated, head on one side and said, absent-mindedly, 'I think we'll hear some screaming in a moment.' She smiled, sweetly.

Box and Splinter had entered a bedroom. It was cramped and windowless and smelt of cat. Most of the space was occupied by the bed but a wardrobe was squeezed against one wall and a dressing table against another. Light stole in from the hallway.

On the dressing table there was a hand mirror, face down, and near to it a hairbrush and between the two there was a small wooden casket. It was just the sort of thing in which an old lady would keep her jewellery. Box edged round the bed to the table.

'Go on then,' said Splinter. 'Let's see what's in it.'

Box hesitated. Quite suddenly he didn't want to open it. It looked like a little box with simple carving on its sides. It might have something in it, it might have nothing. But Box, who normally could not snoop and sneak and steal quickly enough, hesitated.

'Quickly, Box.' There was only a narrow gap between the bed and the dressing table and Box filled it. Splinter pushed him back.

'I don't think we should do this,' whispered Box.

'Shut up,' muttered Splinter. It was just an ordinary box on an ordinary dressing table in a stinking little flat. He put his hand out but before he opened the lid he sneered at his brother, 'You're not scared, are you?'

Box said nothing.

Splinter lifted the lid.

Light poured out, bathing the room and Splinter's face in a lemon-yellow glow. The inside was filled with mist or smoke and the light seemed to be shining through this. The vapours tumbled over the wooden lip of the box and gathered in small clouds over the top of the dressing table.

Splinter stared into the smoke.

Box backed away from his brother but Splinter put his face right up to the mouth of the box, so close that his face was shining with the glow and his eyes were like silver. He thought he saw something move inside.

He picked it up. It felt light and it was motionless in his hands but there it was again; within the smoke he glimpsed something dark, something solid. Something moving.

'Put it down, Splinter,' pleaded Box, voice shaking.

Splinter said nothing. He was holding the casket in his left hand at chest height. Gingerly, he dipped the forefinger of his right hand into the swirling smoke within.

'It's cold, Box, really cold,' said Splinter, feeling his arm go numb to the elbow at once. But he didn't pull his hand away. He moved his finger about to find out what was inside.

He felt only cold air so he put his whole hand in. Still he touched nothing and so he reached further. He heard his brother gasp.

'Your arm, Splinter. Where's your arm?'

Splinter realized that he had put the whole of his right arm into the box. Yet his left hand was holding the same little box in front of his chest. Even though it looked like his right arm had vanished, he could move it about as he wished and wiggle his fingers.

'Put it down, Splinter, take your arm out.'

'I can feel something, Box,' whispered Splinter. It was rough, like metal and it moved against his fingertips.

'Get your hand out. Please, Splinter. Stop it.'

'It's gone,' said Splinter. Just cold air on his groping hand now.

'Good. Now stop it. This is mad.'

'All right, fly head,' said Splinter. 'But we're taking this.' He began to pull his arm out of wherever it had gone.

And then it happened.

Splinter's right wrist was gripped as if by a clamp. He shrieked as his arm was jerked back inside, so hard it felt as if either his hand would be torn off or his shoulder ripped from its socket. His right arm was swallowed up to his armpit and whatever had hold of his hand kept pulling it downwards. His body slammed onto the dressing table, hard against the box.

Box was screaming and Splinter was screaming. Every joint and sinew in his arm felt as if it was on fire. The grip on his wrist tightened and the pain ripped through his body.

He could imagine how the rough metal would be tearing skin and grinding into the bone.

'Help. Please, help,' he screamed. 'Get it away from me,' and he thrashed against the table, legs drumming the floor, but he was held fast. He could feel his shoulder stretching. 'My arm,' shrieked Splinter. 'It's going to pull my arm off.' He sucked lung-fulls of air as waves of pain made him dizzy.

Through eyes screwed tight in agony he saw the old lady standing beside him. She placed her hand across his forehead and bent forwards to whisper into the box.

Immediately, the thing that had gripped Splinter's hand released its hold. Splinter fell backwards and landed on the bed amongst the cushions. The old lady snapped shut the wooden lid. The last wisps of smoke curled over the top of the dressing table and then were gone.

CHAPTER 4

Splinter flinched as Ethel dabbed his wrist with a cloth. She had taken a large glass bottle from the top shelf of the kitchen cupboard and poured a little of the liquid from it onto the cloth. The liquid smelt of alcohol and felt like fire when pressed against his wound. She wiped the blood away and a pink bracelet of flesh glistened.

All of them were sitting at the kitchen table. Chess was nibbling at a piece of bread and butter. Box was eating relentlessly. The only person who had been talking was Ethel.

'A regular little thief, ain't you?' she said to Splinter. Her spectacles were perched on the tip of her nose as she inspected the laceration. 'That needs a nice bandage. You should always make sure you know exactly what you're stealing.'

She pushed her glasses up to her eyes and put her nose close to Splinter's wrist and sniffed where she had been dabbing. She started talking to herself, 'Hmm. It will heal ... given time. Could have lost the whole hand. Maybe the arm.' Then, talking to Splinter again, 'Can you move your fingers yet, dear?'

Splinter tried to wiggle the fingers of his right hand. Nothing happened. 'They might as well be lumps of wood,' he mumbled. 'Useless. I can't even feel them.'

'Well, that's to be expected,' observed Ethel. 'Still numb, you see. It'll pass.'

She got up from the table and went to the cupboard. Jars and tins rattled as she rooted about within it. She returned with a cobwebbed duster. 'I use this for cleaning, but my little home will have to go without until I've saved up to buy another.' She shook it and a cloud of dust specks rose into the air and vanished. 'Your need is greater than mine,' and she tied it above his hand.

'Can't you just do some sort of magic on him,' blurted Box.

'Why should I be doing magic, dear?'

'Well, you are a witch or something aren't you?' he suggested.

'Box Tuesday,' said Ethel, fixing him with one steely eye whilst she kept the other on the bandage she was making. 'You can't go around accusing every old lady you meet of being a witch.'

'Well, you're not normal,' said Box, scratching his curly-haired head.

'What do you know about normal, dear?' observed Ethel. 'Look at the three of you!'

Chess stopped chewing and stared at the floor.

'Anyway,' continued Ethel. 'Normal is all right in its own way but I think being different is better.'

When she was satisfied with the makeshift bandage she poured tea into the mugs. Argus had entered the kitchen silently. Now he was sitting on the floor in front of the oven, blinking at Splinter.

'Your cat's got funny fur,' said Splinter. Chess noticed how the cat's grey coat was dappled with dozens of dark spots, fuzzy-edged in the cat hair.

'It helps him to see,' said Ethel.

'To be seen, you mean,' Splinter corrected her.

'No, dear, to see.'

Splinter sniffed to show that he thought Ethel was wrong but that he wasn't going to waste any more time discussing Argus. His wrist was stinging although he didn't want to admit how much it hurt.

'What was it?' asked Splinter. 'What was in the box?'

'First of all,' said Ethel, 'it isn't a box.'

'It looked like a box,' said Box.

'Not everything that looks like a box *is* a box,' said Ethel, chuckling to Box's annoyance. She took a slurp of her tea, dunked a piece of bread and butter in it and after she had chomped and swallowed, she continued to talk. 'This "box" is a portable vortex.'

'A what?' asked Box.

'A portable vortex. It's like a door. But instead of going from one room to another or in and out of a building, it goes from one place to another.'

'From one world to another?' asked Chess.

'Yes, that sort of thing, dear.' Another chunk of bread was plunged into the mug and munched heartily by the old lady. Crumbs and an oily ring of butter floated on her milky tea.

'There's a lot more space in the world than you can see,' said Ethel when she had stopped chewing. 'A lot more "dimensions" the experts would say.' She licked her pale, thin lips. 'You live in one part of space, in one universe, but there is much more space tucked all around you and there are different times, all happening at once. You only know about the bit of time and space you're in.'

'How can there be more space than we can see?' asked Splinter.

'Think of a box with lots of other boxes inside it,' said Ethel. 'You can only see the outside box but all the ones inside have space inside them as well. It's a bit like that.'

Box stopped eating for a moment and poked the air in front of him with a thick index finger. 'Seems normal space to me,' he said. 'No hidden boxes.'

'It was only an illustration,' explained Ethel. 'There are no invisible boxes in my kitchen.'

'Just one stupid one,' observed Splinter.

'How can it be a door when it's so small?' asked Box, ignoring his brother.

'And how can it be so big inside?' added Splinter.

'None of this is simple.' Ethel sighed and then cleared her throat. 'The moment anything passes the wooden edge of that box it is in the vortex. The vortex is the swirling, bubbling, yawning space in between everywhere else in the universe. It goes forwards and backwards in time and space all at once. If you try to imagine all the places at all the times that have ever been or ever will be, the vortex is what you would find in-between them.'

Box tried hard to imagine it, frowning and screwing up

his face with effort. Chess giggled. 'You look like you need the toilet,' she said to her brother.

There was a long gurgle that rose into a squeal of trapped air and ended with a stream of flatulent pops. 'You sound like you need the toilet,' said Splinter.

'It's not me,' protested Box vigorously, and he pointed to a pair of thick metal pipes that ran down the wall next to him from ceiling to floor. 'It came from there.'

'It's the central heating, dear. It doesn't work but it makes shameful noises. Now listen, I said the vortex was hard to imagine. Try thinking of a fruit cake. If the bits of fruit are actual places in the universe then the vortex is the rest of the cake. Except that this is a fruit cake that fills the whole of time as well as space.'

Box's face relaxed. 'You look more comfortable,' said Chess.

'Does that help explain it?' asked Ethel.

'Not really,' said Box. 'I just like thinking of fruit cake,' and he smacked his lips.

'Fly head, pig boy,' muttered Splinter.

Ethel snorted, drank some more tea and continued. 'When you put your hand inside the box, Splinter, it would have been like putting your hand through a wooden frame and into the rest of the universe. The box doesn't actually have an inside at all. It's just a door or gateway.

'You could actually get the whole of your body inside if you tried. Once you do that you are in the vortex. You could go to any place, in any world, at any time that you wanted. But be careful. You have to know exactly where you are going and how to get there. The vortex is not somewhere to get lost. It is lonely and endless. Anyone or anything that is lost in the vortex is lost forever. Remember that.'

Everyone took a drink of tea, gulping together as Ethel's words sank in.

'But what did this?' asked Splinter, sticking his arm in front of Ethel.

'A mortice-gate,' she said.

'A mortice-gate?' queried Box, through a mouth crammed so full of bread and butter that it sounded as if he was speaking through a blanket.

'Your manners aren't up to much, are they?' said Ethel, frowning at the shower of bread crumbs that sprayed from Box's mouth to the kitchen table.

'What's a mortice-gate?' asked Chess.

'Very big, dear. Massive. A grid made of rare metal that extends in a web across time and space from the very point where the entrance to the portable vortex is located. It makes sure that nothing goes into the portable vortex that shouldn't go into it. More importantly, it makes sure that nothing comes out of it that shouldn't come out.'

'There was no need for it to attack me,' grumbled Splinter.

'There was no need for you to go poking about in the vortex, my love. Anyway, it wasn't attacking you. It was merely preventing you from entering.'

'What? By practically ripping my arm off?' Splinter stared at his arm which lay outstretched on the table in front of him.

Ethel leant forwards to examine his arm. 'Hardly ripped off,' she announced. 'Scratched, I'd say.' Splinter opened his mouth to say something but before he could, Ethel continued. 'You see, at the centre of the mortice-gate there's a small hole. It's right over the entrance to the portable vortex and the gate rotates about it, like an endless wheel. This hole is programmed to open wide if you speak the password. But if it hasn't been deactivated and if anything is foolish enough to enter the hole …' She clicked her fingers. 'It snaps shut, barring the way and trapping whatever was trespassing.' She looked at Splinter. 'You were trespassing.'

'Trespassers should be prosecuted,' snapped Splinter. 'Not have their wrists crushed in a mortice-gate.'

'Don't come all legal with me, dear. This is the vortex, not the *palais de justice.*'

'Do you know the password?' asked Chess.

'Of course I do. How else did I get it to release your brother?'

'What is it, then?' asked Splinter

It was what he had asked or his tone of voice when he asked it that made Ethel fix him with a cold, hard glare. 'A password like that is a secret not to be shared. To know such a thing would allow you to enter any time and any place.'

'You wouldn't trust us with the password?' asked Box, eyebrows raised.

'I wouldn't trust you with very much at all, my loves,' said Ethel, still looking at Splinter. He avoided her gaze by inspecting the bandage on his wrist.

'Why have you got a portable vortex?' asked Chess.

'So I can get about the universe, dear,' said Ethel. 'Although there are other ways of travelling; natural vortices, sink holes and the like. And there are suck worms.'

Splinter looked up. 'You were talking about suck worms at the unit.' He spoke slowly. Warily. 'What on earth is a suck worm?'

'Nothing on earth is a suck worm. Suck worms are found between places, not on them or in them. They connect one place to another, one world to another. They suck things in at one end and they come out at the other.'

'They must be very long,' said Chess.

'Not really dear. It's more a matter of being in two places at once. There is a mouth at one end, the tip of a tail at the other and as for the bit in the middle, well, no one can see that.'

'Sounds a bit dodgy,' muttered Box, dabbing the remaining crumbs from the plate with the tip of his finger.

'Not at all, dear. Normally there are no problems.' She poured herself another cup of tea, sipped and smacked her lips. 'But there is a problem with the Fat Gobster. The Fat Gobster is a rogue suck worm.'

'A rogue suck worm?' asked Box, wondering at how every answer Ethel gave created more questions.

'A suck worm that won't stay in one place,' explained Ethel. 'Most suck worms stay at the same time and place. A bit like most roads. You know where they are when you want to use them. But a rogue suck worm moves about. So it pops up at different times and places. It's very troublesome, dear. Like somebody opening up an invisible manhole cover and then moving it around the place so you never know where it will be next or where you might fall into it. This rogue worm, the Fat Gobster, is being used by the Twisted Symmetry. They use it to transport the children they steal from this world to another place. Where they go to and what happens afterwards,' she shrugged, 'we don't know.'

Then Ethel leant forwards and spoke quietly. 'But the thing is this, my loves,' and she held up a short, wrinkled finger. 'If the Fat Gobster is a rogue suck worm, how do the Symmetry know where to find it?'

'They've tamed it?' suggested Box.

'Brilliant, fly head,' said Splinter. 'The Fat Gobster is really the Twisted Symmetry's pet suck worm.'

Ethel's eyes loomed behind her spectacle lenses. 'The Symmetry have built a computer. A very unusual computer, my dears. A computer that can calculate exactly where and when the Fat Gobster will strike.'

'And you want us to steal this computer?' asked Splinter, yawning.

'No, my love, we want you to steal a piece of this computer.'

'You can't steal a piece of computer,' stated Splinter.

'You can steal a piece of *this* computer,' replied Ethel. 'You can steal a small slice of it.'

'A computer made of cake!' exclaimed Box.

'No, Box. Not cake. Brain. A computer made from the same stuff that's in your head.'

'Don't count on it,' muttered Splinter. 'That would be a computer made of nothing.'

'With a small piece of the Symmetry's computer we can grow our own,' explained Ethel. 'That is important for the next part of the plan. But the Symmetry mustn't know what you have done. That is crucial, my loves. You will be in amongst the enemy but you must do this without their knowing what has happened.'

'I'm not doing it,' said Splinter.

'I'm not,' agreed Box. 'Far too lively.'

'Lively?' repeated Ethel.

'He means dangerous,' said Chess, with a glance at the window. It was bright in Ethel's kitchen. Chess could see all of them reflected in the glass. Night pressed against the other side of the panes. She wondered if Splinter felt as uneasy as she did. The kitchen seemed to be floating in an ocean of darkness.

'You agreed to help me,' Ethel said firmly. 'However "lively" this looks, the alternative is whatever the hunters have planned for you. Nothing very nice, I imagine.' She peered into her cup, as if expecting to find something interesting inside it and said, 'People say that in the labs the hunters pull the toenails off street rats just for fun. But I'm not sure about that. I think they do it so they can break the toe bones more easily, to stop them running away.'

Nobody spoke whilst the implications of this sunk in.

'The Committee needs you.' Ethel looked at each of them in turn but her bloodshot eyes rested on Chess the longest. 'This is the start of something very important, my loves. It is the first move.'

'The Committee could do this without our help,' insisted Splinter. 'If they're any good.'

'We have considered the business very carefully, Splinter,' stated Ethel. 'We need to use people who are devious and cunning and brave.' She rapped the table top with her knuckles, which made Chess jump. 'So you lot fit the bill, if you don't mind me saying so.' Box smiled smugly. 'And there are other reasons. Very complicated ones.'

Chess thought of what the Inspector had shouted that morning: 'Kill the others if you have to but get the girl. Alive.' She remembered what had happened to his face in the corridor. She looked at Ethel. You haven't said anything about why the hunters wanted me, she thought. But she said nothing.

Splinter frowned at the table top. 'So the Committee use children as well?'

'We use whatever we can to fight the Symmetry and in turn we are used. We have agents and they are everywhere. The battle is all around you but you don't see it. Not yet.'

A gust of wind clattered rain against the kitchen window like a fistful of pebbles.

'It's just stealing, Splinter,' said Box. 'Same as usual.'

Splinter regarded his brother coldly. 'You really are very stupid, Box,' he said.

It didn't take long to settle down for the night. There was one sofa in the lounge and an armchair. There were cushions on the sofa. Box and Chess lay head to toe on the sofa under one blanket and used the cushions as pillows. Splinter lay on the floor under another blanket. Ethel sat in the armchair, knitting by the pale orange glow of an electric heater, Argus and Sekhmet curled around her ankles.

Chess listened to the clicking of Ethel's knitting needles and the monotonous purring of the cats. Not so long ago the same needles had been clicking in the detention unit. Before that, she and Box and Splinter had been at the wharf. That was just this morning. Until then the world had been the wharf, the city and the hunters. Now it was bigger and more complicated: a jumble of ideas about the Fat Gobster and the Twisted Symmetry and the Committee and Ethel. The names of these things and the masked faces of the hunters and the sound of clicking needles went round in Chess's mind until she began to slip under her thoughts and into sleep.

She woke once, deep in the night. She thought that she had been crying and she shivered. Through eyes dim with sleep she saw Ethel kneeling by the sofa, silhouetted by the orange light of the electric heater. Ethel's hand was resting on her forehead.

'All of this has happened before,' whispered Ethel. 'It is all the same and yet it is so different. And you are so different, my love. Not at all what I had expected.'

Chess couldn't tell whether Ethel was talking to herself. Maybe she was still asleep and dreaming Ethel's words. But she was too tired to think more than that. She stopped shivering and sank back into the forgetfulness of sleep.

CHAPTER 5

Chess was woken by a smell; a fine, rich, smoky-sweet smell. The smell of bacon frying. Her mouth was watering even before her eyes were open. When she did open them she saw that she was the only person in the lounge. Argus and Sekhmet watched her from where they lay on the armchair, enjoying the warmth that Ethel had left behind. Through the dirt-streaked window, Chess could see that the morning was grey and wet but after years of waking in the dank wharf above the stinking river water, this felt like luxury.

Then she started to think about the other street rats, the other members of their gang, and her belly began to ache with an emptiness that wasn't hunger. She wondered what had happened to them. Probably not lying on sofas. Probably not relishing the aroma of bacon frying. Probably taken by the hunters. Probably injured, definitely frightened. Maybe some were dead.

Dog snarls echoed in tunnels and over water, children screamed, boots thumped on stone cobbles.

Chess opened her eyes again and now heard only the

rasping purrs of the cats and the clattering of pans from the kitchen.

'Time to get up, sleepy head,' she said out loud.

Sekhmet yawned, jaws stretching wide to display pin sharp teeth; so wide that Chess could see the pink-ribbed roof of the cat's mouth and the black gullet. The mouth closed and a shudder of pleasure rippled under her short tortoiseshell fur. Then she licked her front paws with her neat tongue. When she had finished she winked at Chess.

Chess rolled off the sofa and brushed her thick brown hair with her fingers. In the kitchen she found Ethel at the stove and Box and Splinter at the table helping to prepare breakfast. Box was buttering a slice of bread and Splinter was peering inside the tea pot.

'I've got to leave you,' Ethel said as soon as Chess sat at the table. The weight lurched in Chess's belly. 'Not for long,' she added. She turned round, fork in hand. 'Just for ten minutes. We're out of bread. You did eat a lot last night.'

'*He* did,' said Splinter.

'It doesn't matter who did,' intervened Ethel. 'There's plenty more in the shop.' She cocked her head on one side and pouted at Chess. 'Don't look so worried, my love. I won't be long and Argus and Sekhmet will look after you.'

'Stupid names for cats,' muttered Splinter.

'Not when you know who they are,' Ethel muttered back. She approached the table, frying pan in hand and proceeded to fork rashers of bacon dripping with grease onto the thickly buttered piece of bread in front of Box. Hot and tasty food wasn't something that Chess, Box or Splinter usually got but Chess had stopped feeling hungry now.

Ethel set the frying pan down on the table and frowned out of her kitchen window. She wrinkled her nose at the black-bellied clouds hanging low in the sky.

'Don't you want to wait until it's stopped raining?' suggested Chess. 'I don't mind waiting.'

'It hasn't started raining yet,' observed Splinter. 'And if it's all the same to you, I'm hungry. Watching pig boy stuff his mash is torture.'

'I buttered the bread,' Box protested through a mouthful of bacon sandwich.

'That's because you grabbed the only slice that was left you greedy ...'

'Ten minutes,' said Ethel in a stony voice, cutting Splinter short. She patted Chess's hand. 'The enemy don't know you're here, my love. This is a safe-house; its whereabouts are known only to the Committee. Nothing bad will come here.' She smiled. 'You're safe.'

Chess nodded but started as the kettle shrilled suddenly on the hob. Ethel didn't move. She looked at Chess until Splinter had got up and turned the gas off. Then she said, 'Make the tea please, Splinter. It'll have brewed nicely by the time I get back.'

'Ten minutes?' asked Chess.

'No more,' promised Ethel.

'And you think *she's* capable of stealing a slice of computer from the Twisted Symmetry?' snorted Splinter.

'If you work together you're capable of a great deal, dear,' replied Ethel. 'Now, where's my mac?' She took a blue plastic raincoat from a hook on the outside of the kitchen door and then opened a cupboard and lifted down a marmalade jar that rattled with loose coins. As she picked some out she cast a wry glance at Splinter.

'Don't worry,' he said, carrying the kettle to the table, 'I've already looked. Nothing worth having.'

'I've never mastered the trick of getting rich,' muttered Ethel.

'You can probably magic up gold coins if you need them,' volunteered Box.

'I don't magic up anything,' Ethel said sternly. 'Otherwise I'd be magicking up a loaf of bread, dear.' Then she put away the jar of coins, pulled on the raincoat and with a bang of the front door she left the flat.

'Ten minutes,' whined Splinter, girning at Chess. 'You're pathetic.'

Chess couldn't think of anything to say back. Splinter was much better at arguing than she was. He tipped the contents of the kettle into the teapot clumsily and hot water splashed onto the table.

'The old witch leaves the house for a loaf of bread and you're practically sobbing.' He banged the empty kettle back on the hob and stuck his hands into the pockets of his trousers. Then he stared out of the window.

'She's not an old witch, Splinter,' protested Chess.

'She's not an old witch, Splinter,' mimicked Splinter. 'You'll be wanting her to adopt you next.'

'Shut up, Splinter,' said Box, who was stirring the tea.

Argus and Sekhmet padded into the kitchen.

'Oh good, we're safe,' said Splinter. 'The cavalry have arrived.'

Argus, fat and grey, sprang silently onto the kitchen table

and lapped at the spilt water. Sekhmet leapt up to the stainless steel sink and from there onto the window sill where she lay down and looked through the window, ears twitching.

'What do you think has happened to the others?' asked Chess.

Splinter remained with his back to her but shrugged.

'Been captured by the hunters, I suppose,' said Box.

'Do the hunters work for the Twisted Symmetry?' asked Chess.

This time it was Box who shrugged. 'Maybe. I just thought they were a special part of the crashers.'

'It would make sense,' pondered Splinter. 'If the Twisted Symmetry want children, the hunters could provide them with plenty of street rats.' He chuckled. 'Very efficient.'

'Will they have caught Gemma?' asked Chess hesitantly.

This time Splinter did turn round. 'Unless they have made an exception for your one and only friend, yes.'

Chess concentrated on pulling one of the strands of wool that hung loose from her pullover so that Splinter wouldn't see her eyes which were stinging.

Splinter stuck his hands into his trouser pockets, the tails of his morning coat dangling over his forearms. He squinted at his feet before saying in a soft, calculating voice, 'Of course, we don't know what the Twisted Symmetry are *really* like. We don't know who's right and who's wrong. We only have her word for it.'

'Why would she lie to us?' ventured Chess.

'Trust no one, remember? That's what she says.' Splinter's words were laced with sarcasm. Then he looked up and half smiled at Chess. 'Come on, Chess. How can we know what's really going on?' When he saw that his brother and sister were watching him, listening, waiting for his wisdom he began to pace up and down the kitchen, talking knowledgeably.

'All we know for sure is that she wants to use us. She wants to use us for something she hasn't the guts to do herself. Maybe she's just trying to frighten us into cooperating with her.'

Argus and Sekhmet were both watching Splinter as he walked back and forth. They purred, patiently.

Chess heard the cats and listened to Splinter but felt the heavy stillness around them all gnaw at her guts. 'What about me?' she asked.

'What about you?' snapped Splinter, annoyed that his sister should interrupt his cleverness.

'If she's making this up, why would the hunters be after me?'

Splinter approached the chair where Chess was sitting and leant towards her, so close that the hairs on the back of her neck prickled as if chilled. 'What makes you think the Symmetry are after *you?*' He spoke deliberately, twisting each word into her. 'Why would anyone be after you?'

'I'm frightened, Splinter.' Chess's voice was very quiet.

'You're always frightened,' Splinter whispered. Then he ruffled her thick brown hair. 'Relax, Chess. Don't be spooked by a weird old lady,' and he began to hobble around the kitchen on bow legs. Chess laughed because her brother looked funny and because it was a relief that Splinter had released her from his closeness.

Box didn't laugh. He had stopped studying his plate for

crumbs and was looking into the space about him with his nose screwed up. He smelt the air.

'You get frightened too much,' Splinter said to Chess, standing up straight. 'Nothing's coming to get you.'

There was a bang at the door and a metallic rattle. Chess looked round, mouth open. Splinter craned his head to look down the gloomy hallway. Then he grinned. 'The post.'

Chess laughed with relief. 'Calm down,' said Splinter. 'You're so jumpy. Nothing's even happened yet.'

'There's a funny smell, though,' complained Box.

'It'll be one of yours,' said Splinter. 'It usually is.'

'No seriously,' insisted Box. 'Sniff the air.'

Cautiously, Splinter and Chess sniffed the air. There was the smell of fried bacon and tea and the damp smell that hung everywhere in Ethel's flat. But there was something else. Chess could taste it at the back of her throat; a sweet, sharp, numbing smell, like alcohol.

'Has the old witch been at the gin?' enquired Splinter.

'It's not drink,' said Box. 'It's lighter. Sort of finer.'

All three of them turned their faces towards the ceiling, sniffing tentatively. Splinter walked to the centre of the kitchen and then back to the stove.

'It's coming from up there, I think,' and he pointed to where the wall behind the stove met the ceiling.

Chess looked where he pointed and saw nothing.

'It's getting stronger,' said Box.

'Like something's coming closer.' Splinter spoke quietly, backing away from the stove and closer to the table where Chess and Box were sitting.

'Up there,' said Chess. She spoke softly because she wasn't

sure what she had seen. 'In the corner, above the door.' She pointed at the space between the cupboard top and the ceiling.

Splinter screwed up his face and tried to see what she was pointing at. Nothing at first and then he did see something; a narrow black line in the air, six inches below the ceiling. The line lengthened until it stretched nearly three feet, from just below the ceiling into the kitchen. Then it contracted. Then it extended again and this time it grew thicker so that the blackness looked like a slit in the air.

A chair clattered to the floor as Splinter backed away. The air at the bottom edge of the slit shimmered as if it was being pulled into the darkness. The movement became more violent. Where the kitchen fringed the slit it buckled and disappeared and in its place the darkness spread. The smell had become much stronger.

'Something's making a hole in the air,' said Splinter, slowly. 'Something's trying to come into the kitchen.'

Silently, the kitchen ripped open from the ceiling to just a couple of feet above the floor, vanishing into the darkness like a canvas flap. With a screech of chairs, Chess and Box shot to their feet and scrambled away from the table until their backs were against the rear wall with Chess in-between Box and Splinter.

A metallic leg, thin as an iron bar, came out of the darkness, stepping over the rent in the air where the kitchen ended and feeling its way down to the kitchen floor. A ring of iron spikes bristled round the narrow ankle. A hand appeared on either side of the darkness, metal rod fingers clutching at the edges where the kitchen began. Long, sharp, iron spikes clustered round each wrist. Above the hands and out of the void came a head. Gaunt and metal and ringed with iron spikes like a crown of thorns, it tilted on an angle as if taking stock of the kitchen through its skull-socket eyes.

'What ... is ... that?' gasped Box.

'I ... don't ... know,' Splinter gasped back.

'Argus!' choked Chess. 'Look at Argus!'

Argus was lying on the table, back hunched as it had been since he had first jumped up but his fur was twitching and bulging as if something was bubbling inside it. The movement stopped and now, where there had been dark spots on the cat's coat, there were lumps like small boils. Instantly, the skin of every lump slid open to reveal bulbous eyes which rotated in their sockets, looking about the kitchen; at Chess, Box and Splinter, at the doorway, at the radiator pipes. Then, as one, they turned in the cat's fur to focus on the slash of darkness that tore the centre of the room.

From out of this darkness the metal creature vaulted into the kitchen. It was man-high with a smooth dull-metal body no thicker than scaffolding. It moved its limbs like whip cord and at the end of every limb clustered spikes that were long and sharp: spikes which could smash bone and pierce flesh. It turned its head from Box to Chess to Splinter.

Chess gulped for air but found none. Her knees felt so weak that she had to push the palms of her hands against the wall to stop her legs from buckling. She looked at the creature's pitch black eye sockets and then at the long iron spines thrusting from its wrists.

The creature looked at Box and then at Splinter and then

back at Box before it sprang towards them, arms raised high.

Argus wheeled from the table; that was how it looked to Chess. His body corkscrewed and as it did so it grew explosively with a flap and crack of swirling cloak. Spinning from the table, an arm reached from the cloak and tore a length of iron radiator pipe from the kitchen wall. A jet of water sprayed across the room, soaking Chess and her brothers. Now, between her and the iron-spined creature there was a man in a cloak of grey fur that teemed with eyes. His face was hidden beneath shaggy black hair and a beard and in his hands he gripped the iron piping like a staff. He swung the piping up, smashing it into the creature's wrists and blocking them, inches from Box and Splinter's wide-eyed faces.

The creature swung forwards, pivoting on the pipe and kicking its feet towards the wall. Chess saw the cloak twitch as a clutch of eyes jerked to look down at the ankle spikes that were hurtling towards Box and Splinter. Argus spun left so that the creature's legs whipped through the air before smashing into the kitchen table. Wood splintered and the teapot shattered against the wall whilst the frying pan clattered across the floor.

'Move,' yelled Splinter.

'Where to?' yelled Box.

Argus lost his balance and stumbled over the broken table. His spine-crowned opponent flipped backwards to land in front of Chess. It leant towards her, the spines on its head almost touching her face, vacant eye sockets boring into her. Chess held her breath and closed her eyes.

Something nudged her shoulder hard. Box had pushed

her away and she was toppling to the floor. Landing on her elbow, she saw the creature jerk its head to look at Box before drawing back its fist to strike him.

As it punched a nest of spikes at his face, Box slid down the wall, hearing it crack and feeling the plaster shower down. Now he was on the floor, crawling through a shallow puddle. Above him, the creature raised a foot and stamped. Box rolled fast and the back of his hand struck the frying pan. He gripped the handle. As a spike-crusted wrist drove down, he swung the base of the pan up to meet it. There was a hollow clang and his shoulder felt like it had been jolted out of its socket but he succeeded in batting the spikes away from his face.

'Box,' screamed Chess, as the other arm hammered down. Box blocked the deadly points with a reverse swing of the frying pan. But he wasn't quick enough to stop the creature from thrusting its head towards his chest.

Now, Sekhmet sprang from the window. She leapt swift and smooth with her body outstretched, and as she leapt, she changed. Her haunches thickened with taut strands of muscle, her chest barrelled, her forepaws extended wide with black talons, her fur hardened to a dark sand pelt and her muzzle snarled back with a roar that tore Chess's ears. The full weight of the lioness rammed into the body of the creature, knocking it aside so that its head raked across the kitchen floor rather than Box's chest.

By the time it had got to its feet, so had Argus. He whirled the iron piping with both hands directly at the creature's midriff. The creature blocked the blow with its wrists but the strike was so powerful it was belted backwards. With a ringing clang of metal it cannoned into the cupboards so hard that two of them smashed open and lurched from the wall to the floor, spilling tins.

'We have to get out,' shouted Splinter. He was edging along the kitchen wall, picking his way across the remains of the table. Box scrambled back to Chess who remained on her hands and knees in a pool of water by the rear wall. Opposite them, the fighting was frenzied; a chaos of driving spikes, swinging pipe, gouging claws and disintegrating kitchen.

'This place is total madness,' shouted Box.

However, Argus and Sekhmet were working together. Whilst the lioness used her forepaws and hind legs to grapple the spine-crested limbs, Chess could see Argus trying to swing the piping into the creature's middle. But Sekhmet's body was in the way.

'I'm bleeding,' gasped Box, gawping at a splash of red across the front of his T-shirt.

Chess shook her head. 'It's not blood, it's beans,' she said.

'Beans?'

'Yes. From that,' and she pointed.

Box looked and saw that a tin of baked beans was speared on the creature's left wrist. As it fought, tomato sauce spurted out and into the air. Box began to laugh, hysterically.

'It's not funny,' shouted Chess.

'We're being attacked by a can opener,' choked Box.

Sekhmet yowled and reared away as the creature tore her soft belly with its ankle spurs. Then it swung an arm at Argus's head. The crowd of eyes saw what was coming and Argus blocked the swing with the pipe. The creature's wrist was stopped abruptly but the tin of beans rocketed from its wrist like a sling shot and only stopped when it hit Splinter's head.

Splinter had stealthily negotiated the smashed table and was inches from the kitchen doorway when he saw a burst of light and felt a hammer-blow to his forehead. He fell like a post, bursting a bag of pasta with a bang as he landed unconscious on the floor.

The sudden movement and noise distracted the creature. It looked to see what Splinter was doing and in that moment, Argus swung the piping square into its narrow middle. Instantly there was the sound of glass shattering and the creature detonated into a shower of fragments that twinkled briefly before fading into dust.

Argus dropped the length of pipe. It landed in a pool of water with a splash. He slumped forwards. The eyelids in his cloak all closed and as his back arched, he shrank back to cat; fat, grey, smooth-furred, and licking the pads of his front paws which Chess could see were pink and sore.

Sekhmet, small and sleek again, sat beside Argus before bending her head to her white belly and licking the dark gash from which blood was seeping.

Splinter groaned and began to push himself up. A china saucer rolled from one of the lopsided cupboard shelves, glanced off the draining board and smashed with a dainty clink on the floor. Water dripped from the broken radiator pipe.

The black rip in the centre of the kitchen had vanished.

Ethel was standing in the kitchen doorway with a bag of bread dangling from her hand. 'The enemy are coming, my loves,' she said. 'You have to run.'

CHAPTER 6

'You must go to the nearest blockhouse. From there we have to get you to HQ.' Ethel ushered them out of the kitchen and into the gloomy hallway.

'HQ?' asked Box.

'Headquarters,' explained Ethel. 'Committee Head-quarters,' and then she muttered to herself, 'How did the Symmetry know you were here? They shouldn't have known. Somebody's talked.'

'And what was that?' continued Box, rubbing at the tomato sauce stain on the front of his T-shirt and then licking his fingers.

'What was what, dear?' Ethel was distracted, pushing Splinter towards the front door and looking to see what Chess was doing.

Chess had wandered back to the kitchen door. 'Is Sekhmet all right?' she asked, watching the cat who was still cleaning the wound on her belly.

'Never mind the cat, what about me?' complained Splinter, whose left temple bulged and was purple with bruise.

'She has a flesh wound,' said Ethel, ignoring Splinter. 'Nothing too serious. It will heal.'

'Your cats are weird,' grumbled Splinter.

'They're none too impressed with you, dear,' observed Ethel.

'What was it?' asked Box, who was waiting by the front door.

'What was what?' repeated Ethel, getting flustered.

'That thing. That spiky thing.'

'And what's a blockhouse?' asked Splinter. Ethel turned from Box to look at Splinter who added in a quiet voice, 'And where is it?'

'Are we going to carry on playing twenty questions or do you want to live?' demanded Ethel.

After a pause, Box said, 'Live. Definitely.'

'Good. Then listen. That thing was a spindle ripper. Dangerous. Very dangerous, my loves, but very brittle when struck in the right place as you saw.' Ethel sniffed the air. 'That smell is mist. It comes from the deep vortex: a passageway has been opened.'

'We saw it,' said Chess. 'A black hole in the kitchen. It's gone now.'

'They don't stay open for long,' explained Ethel. 'Spindle rippers attack in packs. That was just a scout: more are coming. They will be here; very soon.'

'It didn't attack me,' Chess said hesitantly.

'No dear. That was because they have been sent to fetch you.'

'To fetch *her*?' quizzed Splinter and he cast a frown at Chess. Chess looked away from his narrow blue eyes. Splinter stared at her until he heard Box whispering, 'The mighty Splinter, defeated by a tin of beans.'

'Shut it, fly head,' hissed Splinter.

'Careful, Splinter,' taunted Box, 'or I'll hit you with a lettuce.'

'A blockhouse,' Ethel was saying, 'is a place where you can be protected. The Committee has blockhouses in many different places, manned by our agents. The nearest one to here is the Citizens Information Centre. It isn't far.'

'I saw it on the way,' said Box. 'Left out of your door and about three streets up on the right.'

'Very good, dear. That's the place.'

'A Citizens Information Centre?' ridiculed Splinter. 'I thought we needed protection, not tourist maps and museum opening times.'

'They'll know what to do when you get there,' Ethel answered him. 'I won't be away for long but there is something I must see to first. You will be brought to me as soon as possible.' She sniffed the air again. 'The rippers are close, my loves. You won't see them until they break out but they will be right behind you, moving quickly through the hidden spaces. When you get to the Citizens Information Centre, say that I sent you. And you must tell them that the rippers are coming.'

The she wrenched open the front door. 'Now go. Run.'

Chess, Box and Splinter sprinted down the oil-smeared, dropping-spattered pavement beneath a sky that hung low and dark. They were enclosed by the charcoal grey walls of office blocks, dashed yellow where electric lights lit rows of windows. The slap of their bare feet reverberated from the walls so that it sounded as if more than just the three of them were sprinting through the streets. But Chess knew that whatever was pursuing them was coming silently.

'Back here,' shouted Box. Splinter had run ahead, his long legs carrying him swiftly over the pavement, the tails of his black morning coat flapping behind him. Box had stopped and was pointing down a side street. Chess caught up with him and saw the large plate windows plastered with flyers advertising city entertainments and the blue letters 'CIC' on a white sign over a doorway.

Box and Chess were at the front door of the Citizens Information Centre by the time that Splinter had doubled back to them. He bent forwards with both palms resting against the window, panting hard.

'I'm just too fast for you two,' he gasped.

'This place doesn't look up to much,' observed Box as he pushed open the door. A brass bell tinkled lamely on the door jamb and they entered.

The Citizens Information Centre was small and stuffy. Opposite them was a wooden counter that spanned the room. On it were strewn leaflets and guidebooks and over it slouched a fat lady with a cigarette hanging loose from the corner of her mouth and a mug of tea in her thick hand.

Mounted on the walls behind the counter were wire racks stuffed with more leaflets. There were orange plastic chairs down either side of the room and posters on the mock-wood panelled walls. Splinter noticed that the posters were years out of date.

In one of the chairs on the right hand side of the room, next to the large front window, sat a scrawny man with a dirty green cravat and a flat cap on his head. He held a faded leaflet that advertised the botanical gardens and he looked up from this and nodded at Chess, Box and Splinter when they entered.

The woman behind the counter pulled the cigarette from her mouth, snorted thickly, took a mouthful of tea which she swallowed with satisfaction, put the cigarette back in her mouth, inhaled, exhaled slowly and then, inspecting the street rats through a rising screen of smoke, said, 'Yeah?'

Chess looked at Box and Box looked at Splinter. Still catching his breath, Splinter said, a little uncertainly, 'Ethel sent us. The rippers are coming.'

'Get behind the counter. Now!' yelled the man in the flat cap, springing from his chair and sprinting across the room. He jumped up to the counter, sliding over it on his bottom to land on the other side. As he was doing this, the fat lady shoved the wire leaflet rack that was on the wall immediately to her right. Chess saw it depress and then the section of wooden panelling to which it was attached dropped open, revealing a rack of weapons mounted on the wall behind. There were rifles, silver-barrelled machine guns, steel-blue pistols and pump-action shotguns. She snatched a shotgun and a box of cartridges and threw them to the man. Then she pulled down two more shotguns and placed them on the counter in front of her. Tearing open a cardboard box of cartridges she began to load the shotguns. The cigarette still jutted from the corner of her mouth.

'Move!' shouted the man.

Chess could smell mist. Box and Splinter had already hurdled the counter. She stooped to pick up the leaflet which the man had dropped and saw a slash of black rent the air inches from her face.

'Chess,' shouted Box.

Another gap tore open above her and a thin metal arm reached through, fingers opening and closing, long spines glinting beneath the electric light. More arms thrust through the same gap and the darkness widened down the room.

'There's loads of them. Come on,' urged Box.

Chess ran and clambered over the counter, slipping on leaflets. The woman stopped stuffing cartridges into the shotguns and elbowed a green button the size of a mushroom that was behind the counter top. With a crash, a solid steel shutter slammed down creating a barrier from ceiling to floor right across the room. By the time the bottom of the shutter had hit the floor, the woman had returned to the work of loading the shotguns, fingers swiftly filling their chambers with cartridges.

The steel shutter shook as something slammed into it on the other side. The woman didn't flinch. 'Almost done,' she muttered under her breath.

Another crash against the shutter and this time the metal dimpled inwards. Crash followed crash more and more rapidly as the length and breadth of the steel shutter dented and creased. Chess backed away from the counter as the first spine broke through the steel.

'Ready for business,' announced the lady, taking one of the pump-action shotguns in her hands, leaving the other on the counter in front of her.

The man was squatting down, speaking into a radio that was housed under the counter, headphones over his flat cap, shotgun across his thighs. When he stood up he had to shout to be heard above the din of clashing, tearing metal.

'On my signal we go through there,' he shouted, jerking his head at a door behind them. 'Through the kitchen and out. Then you'll be picked up. OK?'

'OK,' shouted Box and Splinter.

Chess was staring at the shutter. It gaped open in jagged slits that were being tugged apart by thin, spine-fringed hands. Through the widening gaps she could see the press of hard, metal bodies.

'Here they come,' bellowed the lady.

When the first spindle ripper thrust its head through the demolished screen, she didn't fire. She waited until it had crawled out and was leaping through the air, arms and legs bent and ready to strike. Then, with an ear-ringing bang she blasted the ripper in its middle. It exploded into fragments and as they drifted to the ground, she pumped another cartridge into the breach and took aim.

The screen had been torn open in three places and through each gap there came more spindle rippers. They flung themselves towards the counter. The air was thick with the tang of gunpowder and spent cartridges rolled across the floor. With each shot the lady's shoulder jolted back, the shotgun kicked and another ripper was obliterated. But the attack was incessant and Chess noticed that already the lady was using the second shotgun.

The man with the flat cap was kneeling down, reloading the woman's empty shotgun. When it was full he slid it across the floor where it came to rest by her feet. Then he grabbed his own weapon and stood up.

'Now,' he shouted, and stopping only to shoot down a ripper that had landed on the counter, he turned and barged his way through the door at the back of the room.

Box looked over to Splinter. 'Madness,' he mouthed.

Splinter shook his head as if in disgust. Then they darted after the man and into the kitchen. It was long and narrow and the surfaces were cluttered with stained mugs, teaspoons and dried old teabags. Chess tried not to breathe through her nose because the stink of sour milk stung her throat. Even in here, the blast of the shotgun and the crashing of the steel shutter were so loud that the man had to shout to be heard.

'Your transport's out there,' he bawled, voice hoarse, and he pointed to a door at the other end of the kitchen. 'Get in it and get off.' He looked towards the door they had just come through. 'We can't keep this up for much longer.'

'What'll you do?' asked Chess.

'Never you mind,' replied the man and he winked at her. 'You lot just get out. Now.'

'We're going,' shouted Splinter and he headed for the far door.

The door to the front room opened and the fat lady burst through, kicking a box of cartridges across the floor. She slammed the door shut behind her and immediately a cluster of spikes smashed through the wood. The man in the flat cap raised his shotgun and took aim whilst the lady knelt on the floor and began to reload.

'Get out,' she roared at Chess, who was watching her. Chess spun round and ran for the exit. Behind her wood splintered and a shotgun blasted.

She emerged into a narrow back street. She looked for Splinter and Box but she could see them nowhere. A milk float was trundling slowly away from her, bottles jarring in their crates. She looked down the street and then back and to her surprise, saw Splinter's spiky-haired head pop out from the side of the driver's cab of the milk float. He beckoned her to hurry up and she chased after the float. It wasn't far away and it moved so slowly that it was easy to catch up with.

As she did so, she noticed the muzzle of a machine gun poking out from under a grey tarpaulin that was spread over the roof of the float. The muzzle rested on a bipod and lying next to it was a man. Chess could only just see his face in the gap between the tarpaulin and the roof. He wiggled the fingers of the hand that was resting on the gun barrel to wave at her and he rocked from side to side as the milk float jolted along the street.

'Keep yer 'eads down,' growled the driver of the milk float once Chess had jumped into the cab and squeezed between Box and Splinter. 'Cover yerselves with this,' and without taking his eyes from the street ahead he tossed a brown blanket to them from the footwell.

Their breath was hot under the blanket. They huddled together, absolutely still. They could hear the bang of the shotguns some way behind now. At the same time another sound grew louder; the rumble of motor bike engines, coming towards them.

'Hunters,' the driver warned. 'Six of 'em.'

'A milk float's no use,' complained Splinter from under the blanket.

'Shuddup,' croaked the driver. 'A milk float's perfect.'

'But no one would ever use a milk float to escape,' protested Splinter.

'Exactly,' grunted the man. 'Now shut it.'

The roar of motor bike engines filled the street as the bikes sped by on either side of the milk float. As soon as they had passed, Box, Chess and Splinter wormed their way from under the blanket so that they could see out of the rear cab window and look back the way that they had come.

The motor bikes growled to a halt at the rear door of the Citizens Information Centre. Their black and chrome bodies slumped on their stands as the hunters dismounted, jackboots crunching over the tarmac of the street. The uniforms and dark glasses and black crash helmets meant that all the hunters looked the same. Even from the end of the street, Chess could see the silver skull and crossbones insignia on the shoulders of their leather jackets.

The shotguns were still blasting from the other side of the back door.

One of the hunters pulled a fist-sized object from his utility belt.

'A grenade,' whispered Box.

Two other hunters drew machine guns from holsters on their motor bikes and waited behind the first. A fourth hunter kicked the back door wide open with the flat of his boot.

The grenade was thrown into the kitchen. The hunters stepped back from the doorway. There was a moment's delay during which Chess thought that maybe the grenade wouldn't detonate. Then she heard the crump of the explosion. The noses of the machine guns were thrust through the doorway and the hunters opened fire, stopping only when their magazines were empty and the street was strewn with spent cartridges.

Then there was silence from the Citizens Information Centre. The milk float turned out of the side street and into the main road along which it clattered slowly.

Mouths open, eyes agog, Chess, Box and Splinter continued staring out of the rear window of the cab until Box said, 'This is too lively. Far too lively.'

They all turned round, slumping on the bench seat of the cab, not bothering to hide under the blanket. Chess looked at her hands and saw that she was still holding the faded leaflet advertising the botanical gardens. It had been shredded as her fingers had ground into it and print had rubbed off on her palm. She bit her lip.

'That wasn't fair,' was all she could think of saying. She couldn't find the words for what she really felt.

'Nothing's fair,' stated Splinter.

'Dangerous business, working for the Committee,' said the driver, voice gentler than it had been a minute ago. 'No one can expect to last very long.'

'Why do they do it then?' fired Splinter.

'Can you imagine what would happen if we didn't?' replied the driver.

Splinter shrugged. 'The strongest side wins,' he announced. 'Same as usual.'

They all lurched forwards as the driver stopped the float. 'You lot get out here,' he said. 'Wait by that fountain. Ethel will meet you there.'

'Thanks,' said Box, and he and Chess slid out of the cab.

The driver grabbed Splinter's elbow before he climbed down. 'This isn't about the strongest side,' he growled. 'It's about the *right* side.'

Splinter didn't move but he looked at the driver with ice-blue eyes unblinking until the driver let go of his arm. 'Thanks for the advice,' he said and he jumped out of the float without giving the driver another look.

'What did he want?' asked Box when Splinter had sauntered across from the milk float.

'His head examining,' said Splinter, slumping to the floor with his back against the low stone parapet of the fountain. Then he stretched his legs in front of him, white ankles and grubby feet protruding starkly from the black trouser bottoms.

The fountain was built of orange stone. It was low and broad and in its centre was a bronze-green catfish that spurted water into the air. The water splashed down, spattering the stone with droplets. It sat in a small square that was lined with hat shops, clothes shops, shoe shops, book shops, toy shops and cafés.

It was nearly lunchtime and the square was busy. Parents pursued their children over the concrete paving stones, shrieks of delight piercing the drone of traffic. The benches were shoulder-tight with people reading newspapers. Outside the cafés, customers sat at small tables and nibbled pastries. Conversation and the roasted savour of coffee drifted across the square.

'Stupid jacks, chasing their stupid jack sprogs and stuffing their stupid jack faces,' said Splinter, not very quietly.

'I'm hungry,' groaned Chess, dropping down beside him.

Splinter slipped a hand into one of the pockets inside his morning coat. He pulled out some chocolate wrapped in silver foil. 'Here,' he said, breaking off a strip and handing it to Chess. 'From yesterday.'

'What about me?' complained Box.

'What about you?' asked Splinter, popping a square of chocolate into his own mouth.

'I'm starving.'

'You had all the bread this morning, remember?'

'There was only one slice.'

'And all the bacon,' continued Splinter.

'Who had all the beans?' retorted Box.

'Why don't you shut up about beans,' spluttered Splinter, feeling for a stone to throw at Box.

Box picked up a small lump of concrete to throw back and shouted, 'Come on, then,' half joking, half not joking. He raised his arm, ready to throw.

The bustle of people in the square swirled away from them, leaving hard glances behind. Street rats. Filth.

'Don't draw attention, Splinter,' pleaded Chess. 'Everyone's looking.'

Splinter threw the pebble at a pigeon that was hopping close to his feet.

'You live,' decreed Box magnanimously, and dropping the piece of concrete, he turned his attention to a rubbish bin that spewed a fountain of refuse beside him.

'We shouldn't wait,' said Splinter. 'We should do one.'

'What, run off?' asked Box, poking the surface of the rubbish.

'Why not? Unless you want the old witch to introduce you to more homicidal garden forks.'

'We said we'd help her,' protested Chess.

'That was before we found out what helping her means,' insisted Splinter.

'I don't think getting away from her would be easy,' ventured Box.

'Scared, fly head?' jeered Splinter.

'No, just not as good at sneaking off as you are.'

'Just not as fast. And also,' Splinter added, kicking his foot towards the pigeon that had landed beside it again, 'what about the enemy spy?'

'What enemy spy?' asked Box.

'You heard her. It was meant to be a secret that we were at her house. But somebody tipped off the other side. Somebody told the Twisted Symmetry where we were. The Committee have got a squealer, fly head. How safe does that make us?'

'Well, it's Chess they're after,' said Box thoughtfully.

'Which shows how stupid this is, because there's nothing special about her,' said Splinter, as if that settled any disagreement.

Chess didn't hear Splinter. She was looking at the shops that enclosed the square. 'It must be weird, just buying things,' she said.

Splinter looked at her as if she had gone mad.

'I mean just going into a shop and getting trainers, saying, "I'll have those, please." And then being given them.' She brushed a coil of thick brown hair behind her ear.

'You need to have grease to do that,' said Splinter with

contempt. 'Money. They don't just give stuff away. No grease, no goods. Not without nicking.'

'I know that,' said Chess, 'I'm just thinking what it would be like.'

'Enjoy thinking about it,' he stated. 'That's as close as you'll get.'

They had the square to themselves now. A blast of wind gusted over it. Splinter stood up decisively. 'Ethel or whoever she is wants us to go to the Twisted Symmetry and steal from them, right? Well tell me this: what happened to the man and woman at the Citizens Information Centre?'

'Slabbed,' said Box.

Splinter nodded. 'As dead as we'd have been if the spindle rippers had got us. Now, that was the hunters working with the rippers and all looking for us.'

'For her,' Box corrected him with a jerk of his head towards Chess.

'For *us*,' insisted Splinter, his face cold and bruised and pale, and his body narrow in its black cloth, like a needle in the centre of the square. 'Now, where's she going to send us?' The others were silent. 'And what do you think will happen to us when we get there?'

'She helped us get away from the hunters,' Chess argued but Box said nothing. 'We're meant to be trying to help,' and then, as if it might sway Splinter, she added, 'We're meant to be doing something good.'

'You're pathetic,' Splinter spat back. 'This lot are all as bad as each other, except that the Committee or whoever they are seem a lot more useless than the Symmetry. Why can't they have a pack of their own spindle rippers? Why can't they be in charge of the hunters? Why can't they do their own stealing? They can't even trust their own people.'

The wind blew hard across the square. The paving slabs started to spot with drops of rain. People were leaving the tables and retreating to the sweet smells and warmth and glow of the cafés. The rain fell harder now, sweeping across the square in a curtain.

'I'm off,' announced Splinter. 'I'm not stealing the Symmetry's computer. I'm not going to end up slabbed for the old crone.' He jammed his fists into his trouser pockets and leaning into the wind, stalked away from them.

'Come on, Chess,' said Box, wiry hair impervious to the downpour, 'Splinter's right. Let's go.' He didn't wait for her but set off straight after Splinter.

It felt like cold marbles of rain were spattering Chess's ears. The dirt began to run off the tops of her feet in corkscrew rivulets and the ground felt rough under her soles as it always did when it was wet. She turned on the spot, trying to see up every street that led away from the square. She thought that she saw a figure in one alleyway staring back at her; tall, with wild, dark hair, and wrapped in a long grey coat. Beside the figure sat a lean, black dog. But she couldn't see Ethel anywhere and when she looked back at the alleyway, nobody was there. She shivered and the crumpled leaflet fell from her hand. It blew across the square and into a side street.

Chess knew where Splinter would go; the only place where any of them could go. She started to walk in the direction that he had taken, moving quickly beneath stone buildings that leant over her and through rain that drowned the footfalls which followed her.

CHAPTER 7

Box whistled slowly and then swore under his breath. 'What a mess,' he said quietly.

'They've wrecked it,' said Splinter.

They were standing on a road which crested the high ridge above the river. A light drizzle was falling and the sheets of leaden cloud were tearing apart to reveal drifting plumes shot pink and pale blue. Now that the wind had dropped, soot-grey columns of smoke spiralled skyward, rising gently from the charcoal timbers and scattered rubble of the wharf.

Behind them, the city was a jagged sweep of geometric concrete and blank glass that cloud-punched its way to the far edge of the sky. Ahead of them and tumbling down the ridge, was the Pit; a shanty town of corrugated iron sheets, canvas and old pallets that clung to the sheer banks along the course of the river. The rickety hovels were crammed together without streets or sewers until they burst open at the edge of the river, where putrid waste festered in long, gurgling cesspools. It was a foul, naked, hidden place. Nobody chose to live in the Pit but it was always full.

The wharf had been built on the mudflats at the foot of

the Pit. Beside it swirled the river in a slow, wide, filthy drift. On the far bank, factories shunted and steamed without ever sleeping.

Looking down onto the charred remains of the old brick docks, the Tuesdays could see the harbours exposed, no longer dank and dark beneath the tunnel roofs. Only at the far end of the wharf had any of the warehouses survived the destruction and even there, the walls were breached by scorched cavities and the rooftops had been blasted open.

'Where's everybody gone?' asked Box, squinting at the ruins

'Where do you think, fly head?' came the reply.

'Come on,' said Box. 'Let's have a look anyway.'

They began to walk down the hill, following the one road that led through the Pit. Chess stopped to look back before she joined her brothers.

'What's up with her?' asked Splinter.

'She thinks someone's following us,' explained Box.

'Not all that again.'

'You can't blame her, Splinter.'

'Nothing,' said Chess, running back to join her brothers. 'No one's there.'

'Of course no one's there,' huffed Splinter.

The smell of the Pit grew stronger as they walked. It was an oily, salty, musty smell that swelled with the stench of open drains. The dwellings pressed up to the margin of the road as thick as forest and as dark. It was impossible to see more than a few metres into the narrow alleys that threaded between the hovels.

Chess heard dogs bark, pots clatter, children shout and

the bray chords of a mouth organ played badly. A scream drifted from the crowded murk but who screamed or why, she couldn't tell. The children playing at the edge of the Pit and the old men smoking watched Chess and her brothers pass by as they watched everything pass by and then thought of them no more.

'In here first,' said Splinter, turning suddenly off the road and onto a path that was more like a tunnel than an alleyway. Box and Chess followed him, Chess wondering what he was doing since this wouldn't be the quickest way to the wharf.

Chess ducked to avoid hanging washing that was strung between shacks. She tried not to step in the pools of liquid that puddled the rough ground. Up ahead, Splinter stopped by a blue van that was nestled between wooden lean-tos. Although they hadn't gone far into the Pit, the road was out of sight.

Food was frying inside the van and the smell wafted out of the open shutter in its side. Chess felt her mouth water. She nudged up to Splinter who was at the shutter where there was a counter with plastic forks and salt, soy sauce and vinegar.

Inside the van was a short, globular man in a white apron that was smeared with fat. He wore spectacles with thick black rims and small round lenses. His lank, black hair was scraped over the top of his head and between the oily strands the skin of his scalp sweated as greasy as his apron. Iron pots filled with gravy and curry sauce bubbled on a hotplate behind him.

'Nice to see you, Mr Splinter,' said the man.

'Hello, Spoons,' said Splinter. He dipped a hand into one

of his coat pockets and then slapped it down on the counter. When he drew back his long white fingers, Chess saw the ring that Box had given to him yesterday. Chess stared. So much had happened since yesterday.

The man called Spoons wiped his fat fingers on the front of his apron, took off his spectacles and from under the counter produced another pair with long lenses like little telescopes. He put them on and inspected the ring, leaning over the counter to do so.

'I'll give you twenty,' said Spoons when he looked up.

'Twenty-five,' replied Splinter, impassive.

'Twenty-two. That's final.'

'Twenty-two and three bags of chips,' said Splinter.

'You drive a hard bargain, Mr Splinter.'

'You're the one who gets fat on our bargains, Spoons.'

Spoons replaced his spectacles. 'OK, OK,' he said, sweeping the ring off the counter and into a wide pocket on the front of his apron.

'Big bags,' added Splinter.

Spoons pulled two bank notes from his trouser pocket and then two coins which he handed to Splinter. Then he shovelled chips into three paper bags. Splinter handed one bag to Box and another to Chess.

'There,' he said, smiling. 'No need to be hungry.'

'Thanks, Splinter,' said Chess, helping herself to salt and vinegar, her stomach aching.

'Brilliant,' said Box, helping himself to salt, vinegar and soy sauce.

As they walked away, Spoons leant out of his wagon and shouted after them, 'Watch out for the big men.'

'Sure,' shouted Splinter in reply without looking back.

'What's he talking about?' asked Box.

'The hunters, I suppose,' said Splinter.

Chess was not so sure. She thought of the tall figure in the long grey coat that she had seen in the alley off the square. But she said nothing because she knew that Splinter would tell her to stop being stupid.

They followed the path back to the road and walked down to the wharf, cramming hot chips into their mouths, eating noisily in silence. As they came closer to the ruined warehouses and docks, the stink of the Pit was blotted out by acrid smoke which drifted over the charred wreckage in misty veils or snaked out of vents in the rubble. Isolated walls were still standing although they were blackened with soot but apart from the warehouses at its far end, the wharf was as low and shattered as a deserted building site.

'It's strange,' said Chess, 'being able to stand here and look over it all at the river.' The river seemed much higher and much closer without all the walls and sheds and tunnels that had lined it yesterday. 'Strange with everybody gone,' she added quietly.

'Let's have a look,' Splinter suggested, dropping his empty chip bag and setting off across the scorched rubble.

Chess still had chips left so she folded the bag shut to make it easier to carry. But as she started to follow Splinter, a shadow came through the smoke that rolled between the wharf and the Pit. The shadow darkened as it came closer and then a black dog, slim, muscular, snout narrow like a Doberman and ears pricked up loped over the bricks and snuffled at the empty chip bag Splinter had dropped. It was close to Chess and as it licked the bag it looked at her sidelong.

I know your smell, thought Chess, but she couldn't tell why she knew it.

'Come on, Chess,' called Box. 'It's just a dog.' When his sister didn't move he picked up a piece of brick and threw it. 'Get off,' he shouted.

The black dog scrambled away from the brick, hard muscles ribbing its shoulders. Box picked up a bigger brick. The dog looked back at him and then, head low to the ground, it looked up at Chess. One black lip pulled back revealing a row of fangs.

Chess closed her eyes. She didn't like being stared at and she knew the dog was looking at her, sizing her up like humans did. Then she heard claws scraping over stone and when she opened her eyes, the dog was running away, back into the smoke.

'It's gone now, Chess,' Box reassured her. 'We'd better catch up with Splinter.'

Chess looked over to the long ridge above the river, crowded with slum shacks. She looked up the strip of road they had come down but saw nothing to explain the feeling that gnawed inside her chest. There was no time to tell Box what she was thinking because he was already halfway between her and Splinter. She began to pick her way over the mounds of bricks, taking care not to tread on smoking timbers, arms outstretched for balance with the half-eaten bag of chips in one hand.

The sky streaked low above and the river flowed wide beside them. They worked their way across the wide expanse of debris slowly, watching for broken glass and smouldering coals and for stacks of bricks that collapsed when trodden on, revealing sharply rutted hollows that could rub skin from flesh or catch an ankle and break it.

At the far end of the wharf where some of the warehouses still stood, battered and burnt, Splinter squatted behind a slab of wall that lurched out of the rubble as if someone had thrown it there. Its face was caked in yellow plaster. Chess and Box squatted next to him.

Ahead of them was a series of low brick walls. When Chess had last seen them they had stood crooked but tall as part of a row of ancient harbour offices next to one of the warehouses. Now they were half-collapsed with edges rough, bricks jutting out like broken teeth. Their roofs had vanished but thick rafters lay propped against the remaining walls, notched and black.

Immediately beyond the low walls was a taller one that formed a side of the remaining warehouses. Even now Chess could decipher bits of letters once painted in white, high on the wall, announcing the proprietors. Chess couldn't see the bays within the buildings but a stream of creamy smoke curled into the air from the front of the nearest of them.

'Someone's lit a fire,' whispered Splinter.

'The wall's blocking our view,' said Box. 'Could it be hunters?'

'How should I know, fly head? These aren't X-ray eyes.'

'Throw a stone,' suggested Box.

'And wait for them to throw a grenade back?' responded Splinter.

Box took the lock knife out of his pocket and opened the

blade. He held the knife in his right hand and picked up a lump of stone in his left. 'Ready for action,' he whispered, crouching.

'Wait,' hissed Splinter, gripping the sleeve of his T-shirt. 'Listen.'

They listened.

'Stone, scraping,' said Splinter. 'Over there,' and he pointed towards the remains of the harbour office walls that stood between them and the warehouse from where the smoke was coming.

'Now you're the one who's imagining things,' said Box.

Then they all heard the clink of rubble slipping from somewhere to their left.

'It's circling us,' breathed Box, turning, trying to track the sound.

Splinter whipped out his knife and scanned the broken ground for movement.

'It's very close,' whispered Box and then there was silence.

'Hello, Chess.' The voice came from the mound of rubble nearest to them, without warning. Out of the smoke walked a girl who looked the same age as Chess but was much smaller. She wore a tattered blue dress and had fine blonde hair that hung short and unkempt around her pale face. Her eyes were the same sky-blue as her dress and she wore spectacles with brass yellow rims but no lenses.

'Gemma!' said Chess, her voice hoarse with relief. She wanted to hug Gemma but her arms felt lame and awkward so she just smiled. Gemma grinned back, creasing up her eyes, wrinkling her nose and displaying her uneven, stubby teeth.

'I knew you'd come today,' she said and she held out her right hand and opened it. 'Green leaves, see. I always find green leaves when I'm going to see you, Chess.'

Box and Splinter both slumped back against the piece of wall, knife arms lowered.

'Well, not everyone's gone,' said Box.

'No. *She's* hanging around. As usual,' growled Splinter. Then he spun round the edge of the bricks to see what was crunching over the rubble towards them.

Two boys were approaching from the warehouse where the fire was burning. One was very tall and broad and dressed in jeans that were too short for him, and a jumper. He had a hare lip and was carrying a short plank of wood with nails protruding from one end. The other boy was dark-skinned and his hair was short, almost shaved. He wore trousers and a black combat jacket.

Box and Splinter put away their knives.

'So we're not the only ones!' shouted the dark-skinned boy.

'You nearly are, from the look of it,' replied Splinter.

'All three of you survived?' said the boy.

'With me in charge, of course they did,' boasted Splinter.

'Chess doesn't need you to look after her, Splinter,' laughed the boy. 'How's it going, Chess?' he shouted.

'OK, Pacer,' replied Chess, smiling back at him but not sounding convinced.

'See, Splinter,' said Pacer. 'Chess is cool.'

'Yo, Hex!' said Box to the tall boy.

'Yo, Box,' replied the tall boy whose name was Hex.

'We've built a fire,' said Pacer with a grin.

'I know,' said Splinter. 'It's easy to see.'

'Well, it's not like it stands out,' laughed Pacer and he swept his arm out. 'I mean, look.'

'What happened?' asked Box.

'Hunters,' said Pacer. 'Took everyone.'

'What about Lynch?' Box kicked a piece of brick with his toe and frowned. 'Jerky?'

'They took everyone. Everyone.' Pacer repeated the word as if Box might not have understood it the first time. 'Rounded them up and put them on boats.' He nodded at the river. 'Gone.'

Pacer began to walk back to the fire but carried on talking as the others followed him. 'Then they smashed the place up. Bulldozers, explosives, everything. And they torched the lot. You should have seen it.'

'We were hiding,' volunteered Hex, who wore a pair of unlaced boots and did not have to walk over the debris with as much caution as everybody else.

'We got out at the back where the sewers run into the cesspools at the bottom of the Pit,' explained Pacer.

'I thought you smelt worse than usual,' grunted Splinter.

'Thanks,' replied Pacer with a big grin. 'Smelly, but still here.'

'I see little Miss Weird escaped the hunters.' Splinter looked at Gemma with a mixture of irritation and disgust. 'Obviously they didn't want her; same as everybody else.'

'She just walked away and kept on walking and no one stopped her.' Pacer shook his head. 'So we're stuck with her.'

'Unlucky,' said Splinter.

'We're the lucky ones, Splinter,' said Pacer. 'I don't know

what's happening to all the others now, but …' He stared out at the swell of the river without saying more.

'You need a new name,' Splinter said to Hex. 'You were lucky when it mattered.'

'Very lucky, Splinter,' agreed Hex, throwing his plank down by the fire and sitting on an oil drum. 'Must have been saving it all up for the right time.'

The front of the warehouse gaped high as a barn. Chess could see that all the remaining warehouses had been smashed open like this and the partition walls had been demolished so that what had been a row of warehouses was now one cavernous shell. The backs still had walls intact or were blocked with piles of masonry through which spots of daylight glimmered. Inside, they were tall and gloomy as forgotten chapels. Water dripped from the high, broken roofs onto the rubble-strewn floors.

Just inside the first warehouse a rough shelter had been built. A sheet of polythene had been slung over a low, narrow girder that jutted from the wall. Where it reached the ground its edges had been wedged under bricks and roof slates so that it formed a tent. Inside the tent the floor had been scraped clear leaving the old cobbles bare. A small wood fire was burning not far from the shelter, in the mouth of the warehouse. A stone's throw from the fire flowed the river.

Chess followed Gemma who crawled into the shelter, holding the half-eaten bag of chips that Chess had given her. Box and Splinter sat down on stones around the fire. Pacer joined them, kicking some glass away before he knelt down. Everybody looked into the flames.

Box found a short length of rope on the floor and began

to knot it and then unknot it. He made a loop, tested it, undid it and then made it again using his other hand. 'Bowline,' he announced to no one in particular and then he blurted, 'You wouldn't believe what happened to us.'

Splinter silenced him with an icy glare and asked, 'Have you seen anybody else?'

'A couple of regulars have been down here,' said Hex.

'What do grown-up crooks want with this place?' asked Splinter. 'Thought they'd have stayed away. Particularly now.'

Pacer shrugged and threw a handful of sticks on the small fire. 'Only half an hour before you came, actually,' and he cast a quizzical glance at Splinter.

'Don't look at me like that,' objected Splinter. 'Who came?'

'Klinky Mallows,' said Hex.

'That old hag!' scorned Splinter.

'She's not that old,' protested Box. 'She just wears too much make-up.'

'Do you fancy her or something?' sniggered Hex.

"Course not,' said Box.

'And the Night Porter,' added Pacer, watching Splinter's face closely.

'Well, I don't know what he was doing here. He's hired to kill people and there aren't many of us left down here to kill.'

'They came here together, Splinter,' said Hex. 'They wanted to know if we'd seen you lot.'

'They wanted to know where Chess was,' Pacer added, looking over at the shelter where Chess and Gemma were talking to each other in low voices. Then he looked back at Splinter, accusingly.

'Everybody wants to know where Chess is,' announced Box helpfully.

'Just shut up, fly head,' hissed Splinter.

'What's the big secret, Splinter?' asked Pacer, standing up, stony faced.

'There isn't a big secret,' insisted Splinter, scowling at the little flames that licked along the burning sticks. 'She must have done something wrong, that's all.' He hunched forwards, staring into the fire.

Box worked the rope absent-mindedly, tying and then untying a series of knots, alternating the hands that he was using and muttering to himself, 'Reef, figure-of-eight, sheet bend,' as he did so.

'Help us with the den,' said Hex, getting up.

'Yeah,' agreed Pacer, changing the subject. 'We need more plastic for the roof and we need more wood for the fire. More rope too if you can find any.'

'What about those two?' asked Box, dropping the rope on the floor and indicating Chess and Gemma.

'Leave them,' said Pacer.

'They can be weird together,' agreed Splinter.

'Shouldn't one of us stay here?' suggested Box. 'To keep an eye on them: an eye on Chess?'

'What do we need to keep an eye on Chess for?' asked Pacer, genuinely confused.

'Yes, Box,' Splinter said severely. 'What do we need to keep an eye on Chess for?'

Box wasn't sure how to reply. He wasn't sure what he was

meant to say and what he was not meant to say. So he shrugged and settled for, 'I don't know. Just thought it would be a good idea.'

'She's fine,' Pacer reassured him. 'Come on, let's get looking. It'll be dark in a few hours.' But Box was the last to leave the warehouse and he kept looking back until Chess and Gemma had been hidden by smoke and broken walls.

'They don't want me with them but they are letting me stay,' Gemma was saying. She spoke slowly and very particularly.

'They don't mind you being here,' Chess reassured her. She was kneeling in the tent with her back to the fire and the river.

'They won't mind now that you and Box and Splinter are back.'

'You're OK here.' Chess held Gemma's hand. It was the only hand she ever held and it made her feel safe and strong at the same time.

'I thought of going to the Pit.'

'No, Gemma. Not the Pit.'

'I'd be all right, Chess. I think that the people here aren't used to me,' explained Gemma.

'People should know better,' replied Chess angrily. Then, quietly, 'There aren't many people here now, anyway.'

'And also,' added Gemma, moving effortlessly to a different subject, 'I might be able to have my glasses fixed in the Pit. I'm glad you're back, Chess.'

'So am I,' said Chess, although she wasn't sure how she felt.

'And anyway,' continued Gemma, looking over Chess's shoulder, 'I can see perfectly well.'

'I think so,' agreed Chess.

'I get headaches,' Gemma reminded her, staring at Chess through the empty rims of her spectacles, blue eyes solemn, before she looked back over Chess's shoulder. 'But my eyes are good. They're good enough to see *him*.'

Chess wondered what Gemma was talking about and she frowned quizzically.

'That man,' explained Gemma, pointing over Chess's shoulder. She spoke slowly and clearly. 'I can see that man without any difficulty.'

Chess turned her head to see where Gemma was pointing and saw a man standing in front of the far end of the warehouses. He was tall, at least seven feet, but Chess could tell that his body was bulbous and small; all his height was in his legs and in his arms which were very long. He wore a grey greatcoat with a broad black belt buckled round his waist and heavy boots. Coarse black hair tangled to his shoulders. His eyes glowered beneath a ridge of bone that bossed his steeply sloping forehead. His nose was wide and flat with flared nostrils and jutting below it was a slab of chin. The gnarled head looked too big for his hunched body and it was jammed on his shoulders with almost no neck. In his right hand he held a coiled whip.

'Oh no,' breathed Chess.

With great strides the man came towards them, boots thumping the ground, squat body jerking like a magpie's. When he moved, the bottom of his greatcoat flapped open revealing legs so long they were like stilts.

Chess grabbed Gemma's wrist and began to pull her out of the tent. 'We have to hide. Now. Right?'

Gemma nodded. They had crawled out from under the lean-to but already the man was half way across the warehouse frontage. He flicked out the whip and it uncoiled silently like a long brown rat's tail.

Still gripping Gemma's wrist, Chess pulled her round the side of the warehouse. She shouted Box and Splinter's names once, her voice echoing lamely through smoke, over rubble. Then she pushed Gemma back against the warehouse wall.

'Hide. Hide until the boys get here. They won't be long. OK?'

Gemma nodded.

Then Chess ran. She headed for the end wall of what had been the harbour offices. At the foot of the wall she found a deep cavity between mounds of collapsed brick and, scraping her shoulders, she squeezed into it. Unless the man looked exactly where she was hiding, he wouldn't see her, but she could see back the way she had come through gaps in the bricks.

The rubble was packed close to her face. She was breathing loudly, her breath rasping against the bricks. She could smell the brick dust and taste the grit on her lips. She tried to breathe more quietly by breathing slowly but that just made her chest ache and the blood pump more loudly in her ears.

The man's head emerged from the side of the warehouse wall where, seconds before, she and Gemma had been standing. He stepped out, whip in hand and sniffed the air with his head tilted back. Chess's wide eyes stared through the bricks looking for where Gemma might be hiding. She did not have to look far. She forgot about her breathing.

'No, Gemma. No,' she whispered.

Gemma was crouching on the floor at the foot of the warehouse wall not more than ten feet from where the man was standing. She had her back to the corner and her head down as if that might shield her from view but it was plain to Chess that the moment the man looked back along the wall he would see the blue dress. Even now he was swinging his big, bony head one way and then the other, scanning the wharf, whip twitching in his shovel of a hand.

Come on, Box, come on, Splinter, yelled Chess inside her head.

No one came.

The man stepped clear of the wall, boots scuffing stone. He cleared his throat and spat. He looked left over the river. He looked ahead, towards where Chess was hiding but he didn't see her. Then he began to turn his head right, towards Gemma. He couldn't miss Gemma.

Grazing her forehead against a saw-edged blade of concrete, Chess scrambled out of the hole. Then she stood up.

'Here,' she shouted. 'I'm here.'

CHAPTER 8

Gemma was safe because the man was looking at Chess.

And now he was coming for her.

Chess's feet were as heavy as stone, as if they didn't realize they had to move. Then they were pounding over rough brick, hot wood and glass. She tried to watch where they landed but it was more important to get away. She could feel the rutted ground score the soles of her feet but for now there was no pain. She ducked and veered left and right to keep her balance and to find the safest route across the remains of the wharf. Behind her came the crunching boots of the man.

Not far ahead lay the ditch where the wharf ended and the hill began. Chess could smell it already and the stench made her eyes water. This was the place where the waste from the Pit drained; where the sewage stewed in long, deep, stinking cesspools whose treacle surfaces swirled with mucus-green sludge. The smell was so foul that it didn't just sting her eyes; she could taste it, burning the back of her throat.

The air snapped at the nape of her neck. Nothing touched her skin but Chess knew that the tip of the whip must have missed her by inches. She ran faster, not caring now what the ground did to her feet.

She reached the low embankment by the ditch with the man only metres behind. The ditch was too wide to jump but to her left she saw a long, narrow joist that spanned the filthy sludge and which must have been thrown there to make a bridge. The joist was barely wider than the ditch, its ends jammed precariously into the damp earth. If she tried to cross, it might slip free and into the cesspool: or she might slip. But if she made it, she could hide in the Pit.

She had to be quick. Without looking back, Chess slid a foot onto the iron bar and tested it. It rocked from side to side. She stepped on to the bar, arms wide apart like a tightrope walker. Shuffling her feet over the rust-rough surface, she began to cross the cesspool.

Sliding over the cool metal, the soles of her feet began to throb. Chess looked down for a moment. A metre below, a chain of bubbles broke the surface of the sewage with little spatters and puffs of ammoniac gas. Above that she saw her feet balancing on the joist, their edges etched by a dark tracery of blood.

Halfway across and the man was at the ditch. One crack of the whip would snare her neck or ankle. Chess went faster even though it felt as if the cuts on her soles were catching on the flakes of rust. Then she was over, her feet hitting the soft mud of the embankment at the bottom of the Pit.

The man was crossing. He couldn't use the whip because he needed his arms for balance as Chess did. She could see his face clearly now; the savage eyes, the thick, leathery skin, the heavy jowls and the wild hair. Like a cave man, or a troll, she thought. But what long legs and what a weird, hunched-up body.

She looked down and saw what she wanted. Picking up the lump of concrete with both hands she squatted at the place where the joist nestled on the lip of the embankment. The man wasn't more than two steps away and he shouted at her angrily but she didn't understand the words he used.

Swinging the concrete as hard as she could, Chess drove it down and into the side of the joist. The effect was immediate. The end of the joist jolted free of the earth and straight down to the cesspool whilst its far end also sprung loose.

Running hard, Chess heard the splash as the man plunged into the sewage, followed by the slosh and gloop of the sludge as he hauled himself out and up the bank. He roared at her.

Chess headed for the place where the ditch disappeared under the road that came down the ridge. It was easier to run here and she darted along the strip of open ground between the long pools of sewage and the lowest hovels of the Pit, a clutch of hens shrieking in protest as she sent them flapping. She hazarded a look behind but could not see the man. Chess guessed that he must have gone into the Pit. Not far ahead now was the road and she saw a big white van with rusty wheel arches parked up where the wharf ended and the road began.

Her legs were tiring and with the man out of sight, Chess slowed until she was half jogging, half walking. When she came to the road she stopped to catch her breath and then she began to walk up the hill. She wasn't sure where she would go but heading for the top of the ridge where she could look back to the wharf seemed a good start.

Behind her, the big white van with the rusty wheel arches shuddered into life. Chess didn't think anything of this at first, she barely noticed it, but when it started to follow her at no more than walking pace, she wondered why it went so slowly. She looked back. It was difficult to see through the wide windscreen but as the van rumbled over the tarmac towards her she picked out details of the driver: a heavy head with coarse, black hair that straggled over the shoulders of his grey coat; big, walnut-knuckled hands gripping the steering wheel, legs so long that the knees were jammed up to his shoulders as he hunched forwards in the cab of the van and a long black beard that was twisted in a plait from his thrusting chin. The white van coughed and speeded up.

Her feet were hurting now but that didn't stop Chess from pelting up the hill. She knew that there was no way to outrun the van but she also knew that the other man was already in the Pit, probably waiting for her. She wanted to cross the road and run into the other side of the slum but the white van had drawn level with her so she broke right, into the nearest alley.

The van crunched to a halt and a door slammed shut. Heavy footfalls and the man with the beard was closing on her already. Not caring which filthy puddles she splashed through, Chess recognized this alley. These were the same strings of washing and not far ahead between the lean-tos was the van where Spoons sold hot food and bought stolen goods. Chess sprinted to the van.

Spoons smiled when he saw her. 'Still hungry?' he asked.

'Is the curry hot?' gasped Chess.

'Very hot,' replied Spoons. 'Be careful you don't burn yourself.'

'Please,' begged Chess. 'Please, Spoons, give me a cup.'

'I don't get rich by giving food away,' explained Spoons.

'Please,' Chess implored.

The heavy tread of boots behind her and the grip of a hand on the back of her neck. The man with the beard had her now.

'You come with me,' growled a voice that mangled the words as if it was unused to using them.

Spoons looked from Chess to the man who was standing behind her. He had to lean forwards and look up to see the man's head. Then he looked back to Chess, frowned at the graze on her forehead and nodded.

'OK,' he said. 'You're a very pretty girl. Much better looking than your brother,' and he turned to his bubbling pots. Ladling a stream of steaming, dark-ginger sauce into a polystyrene cup, he placed it on the counter.

The man shook Chess's shoulder so hard her head jerked like a doll's. 'We go. Now,' he barked in the same contorted voice.

'Thank you,' Chess mouthed at Spoons and she snatched the cup of boiling curry from the counter before spinning round and dashing it up and into the face of the man behind her.

He howled and clutched his scalded skin which was dripping with the boiling hot sauce. Chess broke free and ran. She was going to keep running until she couldn't run any more. Feet slapping on earth, she careered over cardboard boxes that littered the alley and through laundry and ran headlong into the first man, standing statue-still in front of her, greatcoat dripping filth and stinking.

She backed away. There was a narrow passage on her left. Stumbling into it, she started to sprint. Beard and Stink charged after her.

She didn't hear the whip but she felt it loop her ankle tight and she spun and slammed down to the floor, landing so hard that the breath burst from her lungs. She looked at the ring of brown leather round her ankle and followed the line of the whip until it stopped in Beard's fist. Standing at his shoulder was Stink. They walked towards her.

Chess pushed herself up on her elbows. Stink knelt down and shoved the palm of his hand into her chest, pushing her flat again.

'Girl,' he said roughly, and for the first time his face cracked in a grin which revealed pegs of yellow teeth in his huge mouth. His broad, heavy hand slid up her chest until it rested on her white throat.

'*The* girl,' growled Beard.

She was aware of Stink reaching into his sodden greatcoat with his free hand and pulling out an object that flashed silver at the edge of her vision. There was a click and then she felt the cold steel of an extendable cosh against the side of her face.

'You come with us now,' grunted Beard, standing over them. 'He make you sleep.'

The cosh was raised to strike her head. Chess squeezed her eyes shut but before the metal cracked her skull, she heard another, crisper, click. The click of a gun being cocked. She opened her eyes and looked upwards.

Directly above her face was a long, black cylinder. One end of the cylinder rested on the front of Stink's head. The other end was attached to the muzzle of a pistol. The pistol was held by a gloved fist, extended by a man in a black donkey jacket. Chess couldn't see his face as he loomed over her but from her position on the floor she could see his jeans which were spattered with paint and a pair of steel toecapped work boots that were mottled with dry concrete.

Stink was staring up at the cylinder, his eyes wide and crossing slightly as they focused on where the silencer was pressed to his forehead. His mouth hung open.

Chess rolled away from the cosh. Now she could see that the man with the pistol wore a black woolly hat pulled close to his head and that he had a thin face with bright blue eyes and a shadow of stubble. His thumb rested on the hammer of the pistol which he had just cocked and his finger was curled on the trigger. The gun didn't move a millimetre.

By the man's side stood a woman in a short red skirt, stockings and high-heeled shoes. She had a red handbag slung over the shoulder of her black leather jacket and a fizz of orange hair. Her face which must once have been very beautiful was creased with experience and hung tired at its edges. The cupid's bow carmine lips parted and she said, in a voice that rasped like gravel in a barrel, 'Shouldn't you be picking on someone your own size, boys?'

Stink dropped the extendable cosh, stood up and backed away from the gun which remained trained on him, unwavering. He bumped into Beard and they started to retreat together, glowering from under their gnarled brows, whips in hands. When they came to the end of the alley they hesitated long enough for the woman in the red skirt to wave her bejewelled fingers and drawl, 'So long, boys.' At that, Beard spat in the dirt. Then they stalked into the gloom and out of sight.

Now Chess could see that behind the man with the gun and the woman stood Ethel and behind her were clustered Box, Splinter, Pacer and Hex. Chess noticed how Splinter was glaring at her. Box pushed past Ethel and hurried over.

'Sorry, Chess,' he said, dropping down beside her.

'Where's Gemma?' asked Chess.

'Still at the wharf. She's OK. As much as she ever is.' Box laughed bleakly. He looked at the graze on her forehead and then at her bleeding feet. 'Sorry.'

'It's OK. It wasn't your fault.'

'I shouldn't of left you,' insisted Box.

'It doesn't matter. Anyway, you found me.'

'It was Klinky Mallows and the Night Porter who found you,' explained Box, nodding his head at the woman and the man who were standing with Ethel.

'Thank you, Mr Fazakerley,' said Ethel to the Night Porter.

The Night Porter lowered his pistol and unscrewed the silencer. Holding both in the same hand he tugged something from the inside of his donkey jacket. It was the head of a spade, its crescent edge glinting. He screwed the long silencer onto the spade head. Then he took a T-shaped handle from where it had been tucked down the back of his jeans, opened it, clipped the pistol inside, closed it and then screwed the handle into the top of the silencer. Now it looked as if he was holding nothing more sinister than a spade. He rested it over his shoulder.

'You all right?' asked Klinky Mallows, stepping over the puddles to stand by Chess and pulling her to her feet.

Chess nodded, catching the pungent scent of sweet perfume and enjoying it. 'What were they?' she asked.

'Traders,' said Klinky Mallows. 'They work for the Twisted Symmetry. Big, ugly, stupid. Good at catching children. Usually.' Then she grinned at Chess and licked the tips of her slightly yellow teeth. 'But not on this occasion.' She spat on her long-nailed fingertips and rubbed the graze on Chess's head. 'They do that to you?' she asked. Chess shook her head.

Now that she wasn't running, wasn't gasping for breath, wasn't sweating with fright, Chess felt the cool air, clammy on her skin and she shivered. She looked down the alley, the way that the tall men had gone. 'Are they . . . people?' she asked. 'Humans?'

'You've seen some weird people if you think those might be human,' commented Klinky Mallows.

'They're not human, dear,' said Ethel, who had come to stand by Chess. 'Although they are humanoid. Humanoid is a successful model; you find it across the universes in many different varieties. The trader variety comes from a place where the force of gravity is much stronger than here so their bodies are all scrunched up, whilst their limbs are long and powerful for leverage.'

'And their faces!' observed Box. 'Puke ugly.'

'It's true that they are not greatly admired for their physical beauty, my love, but that's not gravity; that's just bad luck.'

Ethel took Chess's hand. 'I'm ever so sorry, dear. I'm sorry I left you and I'm sorry I didn't meet you on time. Although,' she added pointedly, 'it would have been better if you'd waited.'

'Splinter thought we should go,' explained Chess without thinking, immediately regretting what she had said as Splinter flashed an angry glare. 'Where were you?'

'I had to nip into the vortex, to deal with the ripper outbreak from the inside. It took a bit longer than I expected.'

Chess noticed the wrapping of a bandage under the cuff of Ethel's orange blouse, just above her scrawny wrist. 'There were more of them than usual,' she explained.

'It's OK,' said Chess, more worried now about what Splinter was going to do to her than anything else.

'You did very well,' Ethel assured her, patting Chess's hand. 'Gave all of us quite a run for our money.'

It was late in the afternoon and although it was not yet falling dark, the dull light had the expectancy of dusk about it. And in the tunnelling alleyways of the Pit, night was always waiting to happen.

'Why did they want me?' asked Chess.

'Traders work for the Twisted Symmetry, like Miss Mallows said,' explained Ethel, not actually answering Chess's question. 'They catch human children for the Symmetry.'

'I thought the hunters did that?' interrupted Box.

'They do. They both do. The Symmetry has many servants, dear. But the traders also run the amarantium mines.'

'What's ama ... aman ... what's that?' asked Box.

'Crystal, my love. Amarantium is its proper name but

everyone calls it crystal. Crystal is very precious to the Twisted Symmetry.'

'Why?' asked Splinter, leaving the rotten hoarding against which he had been lounging with Hex and Pacer, and sauntering across to Ethel. 'Why is crystal so precious to the Twisted Symmetry?'

'You know, dear, you have a rare talent for asking questions about dangerous things.'

'I'm only asking,' protested Splinter.

'Of course you're *only* asking; but that's how it starts,' and then Ethel pushed her wrinkled face right up to Splinter's pale one. 'Let me tell you, my love, there's no such thing as *only* asking. Asking makes things happen. You need to be careful what questions you ask because the answers you get might be bad for you.'

'I'll ask what I want,' stated Splinter.

Whilst he and Ethel stared at one another, the Night Porter's boots scraped on the floor and he said, 'Got to go, Ethel. I've got a job on the other side of the city.'

'You work too much, Mr Fazakerley,' said Ethel.

'Watch how you go,' he said to Chess and for a moment his bright blue eyes smiled at her although his mouth was motionless. 'I'll look out for you. Easy does it, Klinky,' he added, and then he started to whistle. He marched into the shadows with the spade over his shoulder. The whistling could be heard long after he had disappeared from view.

'Crystal?' persisted Splinter. 'You're the one who brought it up.'

Ethel spoke briskly. 'Crystal is impervious to change; it always stays the same. Every piece of pure crystal exists in every dimension throughout time. Think about that. If you hold a piece of pure crystal in your hand, you are holding something that is everywhere at once. Of course, you only experience it in the time and place where you're holding it but that same piece of crystal will be touching other parts of other universes and other times, simultaneously. This property is valued by the Twisted Symmetry. They need it. That is why they mine it. That is why great battles are fought over it.'

'Do the Committee fight over it?' questioned Splinter.

'No,' snapped Ethel. 'The Crystal Wars are of no interest to the Committee.'

Box was inspecting the cosh that the trader had left behind. He picked it up and tossed it in his hand before swinging it one way and then the other. It was two feet long but when he depressed the button in the bottom of its handle it collapsed to a six inch cylinder. When he pressed the button again it telescoped out instantly.

'Nice slipjack,' was his verdict and after spinning it into the air and catching it, he dropped it into the trouser pocket that didn't contain his lock-knife.

'You OK?' Klinky Mallows asked Chess, who had been watching Box. Chess nodded. 'Here,' she said, after rooting in her handbag. 'Keep this. Every girl should have one,' and she handed Chess a long nail file. 'Keep it in your pocket but be careful when you sit down.'

'Why don't you give her some lipstick too?' suggested Splinter. 'Then she can look like a real clown.'

Klinky Mallows sidled up to Splinter who yelped as one of her high heels found the top of his bare foot. 'Your mouth is very clumsy, Splinter,' she murmured in his ear. 'And clumsy hurts.' She leant on her heel a little harder before removing it. When she did so, Splinter sat down gasping and rubbed the top of his foot.

'Baked beans *and* shoes,' whispered Box to his brother. 'Only the most deadly weapons can harm the mighty Splinter.'

Splinter was too occupied with his throbbing foot to reply.

'I don't have nails to do,' Chess was saying to Klinky Mallows.

Mallows pinched her cheek and managed a weary smile that cracked her make-up like it was grouting. 'In this life you've got to use what you've got.' She smoothed down her skirt although it was neither dirty nor long enough to need smoothing down. 'Remember what the old girl says,' she whispered in Chess's ear. 'Trust no one.' Then, bag swinging over her shoulder and heels gouging the earth, Klinky Mallows strolled away.

'Nice friends,' muttered Splinter, still cradling his sore foot. Chess had sat down and was inspecting her feet also. They weren't as badly cut as she had expected but there was a deep gash along the outside edge of her right foot.

Ethel knelt down and rubbed Splinter's foot. 'They're not what might be called respectable personages,' she said. 'But their talents have assisted the Committee on many occasions.'

'I didn't know Klinky Mallows and the Night Porter worked for the Committee,' said Box.

'Why should you, my love? You didn't know about the Committee until yesterday. There's a lot going on that people don't know. Which is probably just as well.' She hummed to herself as she switched her attention from Splinter's foot to Chess's.

'Great,' grumbled Splinter. 'The Twisted Symmetry have got spindle rippers and traders and every other deadly thing you've been telling us about and you've got Klinky Mallows and the Night Porter working part-time.'

'Ouch!' exclaimed Ethel. She tore a strip of material from the tatty hem of her long dress and bound it round Chess's foot. 'We can tidy it up when we get to HQ.' She patted Chess's foot and then turned to Splinter. 'The Committee has many agents and forces at its disposal. It isn't all one way. But the Twisted Symmetry are very powerful. You are right about that. Truth to tell, dear, they are far more powerful than you can imagine.'

She gave Splinter a knowing smile that made him feel silly and irritated him greatly. 'You haven't seen nothing yet, my love. This has been a gesture. It is only the start.' She pushed her spectacles up to the top of her nose and brushed steel grey strands of hair away from her creased forehead. 'You just have to make sure the Twisted Symmetry don't break you before the end.'

'Nothing breaks me,' stated Splinter, standing up.

'How's your foot?' sniggered Box.

Splinter started for Box but Ethel gripped his bony shoulder with sufficient force to stop him dead. 'The Symmetry are very clever, my love. Let them get close and they will find a way to possess you; a way to use you.'

'Can we go now?' asked Hex. He and Pacer had been hanging back from the others.

'Frightened?' wheedled Splinter, his back towards them. 'The Twisted Symmetry spooked you, has it?'

'I don't know what you're all going on about,' replied Pacer with a shrug. 'Don't care really. Just don't want to bump into any hunters. They like to patrol when it's getting dark. It's safer for us at the wharf.'

'Nowhere's safe,' growled Splinter.

'You have very good friends,' Ethel said to Chess. 'Without knowing what risks they might be running, these two young men came looking for you straight away. Very loyal, dear. Very brave.'

'Yeah, well, you know where to find us if you need us,' said Pacer.

'Will you look after Gemma?' asked Chess.

'Can we avoid it?' Then Pacer grinned at Chess which made her smile before she looked down, as if fascinated by the bandage on her foot. When she looked up they had gone.

'Well, it's just us again,' announced Ethel cheerily. 'Now, it will be dark before very long and we have to get to HQ. You'll be safe there, for the time being.'

'Is this a war that we're in?' asked Box enthusiastically.

'It is definitely a war,' replied Ethel.

'Yeah, the enemy have had to hide all the food now they know you're coming, fly head.'

'Actually,' admitted Box. 'I am quite hungry. Have you got food at HQ?'

'Plenty,' said Ethel.

'Great,' said Box.

Ethel led them out of the alley but before they left the Pit, Splinter grabbed Chess's wrist and pulled her back.

'Sorry, Splinter,' she said because she knew what was coming.

He punched her hard in her upper arm where the muscle was closest to the bone, still holding her wrist. 'That's for dropping me in it with the old crone.' Then he punched her harder in exactly the same place and she gasped, eyes hot. 'And that's for being an idiot and nearly getting caught.'

'But it nearly got Gemma,' protested Chess.

Splinter raised his hand again, this time levelled at her face. Chess didn't try to pull away but she turned her face so that the blow would only fall across the side of her head.

'You're pathetic,' spat Splinter, arm still raised. But he didn't hit her. He let go of her arm and walked off after Ethel and Box, and Chess followed him, rubbing her arm which was numb with pain.

CHAPTER 9

Chess walked with her head down. The pain in her arm had faded but her foot really hurt, particularly when she put her weight on it. She concentrated on where she was stepping. It took her mind off the pain and by looking down, she hoped that less attention would be paid to her by the jacks who loured at her as they passed. She did not observe where they were going so when she stopped to pick a small piece of grit out of the sole of her foot she was surprised to see that they had come to a different part of the city.

Old brick warehouses were slumped beneath weed-encrusted smokestacks. Metal sheds streaked orange with rust leant against one another and static cranes stooped crookedly over sidings where clumps of yellow-headed ragwort grew thick and tall. The streets were barren. Dogs loped in alleyways, their ribs like iron rails. A chill wind was blowing.

'We're heading for the old bus depot,' said Splinter.

'What's she taking us there for?' asked Box. 'It's full of drunks and tramps.'

Splinter didn't answer. He was looking up at the brick

walls that flanked them, blue eyes narrowing. Set high in the walls were rows of windows with glass smashed like daggers. Beyond the sharp edges of the glass was darkness. He could sense what his eyes couldn't see.

'We're being watched,' he said to Box.

They stopped at the front of the bus depot. It sat square at the end of the road which swept through the entrance gates and into the empty parking bays. Above the entrance there was a clock tower. The clock hands showed the time as three o'clock.

'Clock's stopped,' said Box.

'Has it?' said Ethel and she headed for the parking bays and the deeper gloom of the platforms beyond.

They crossed the platforms and passed through a set of doors that swung shut behind them. From the noise that her footsteps made, Chess could tell that they had entered a large hall. A pale light seeped through a glass dome in the ceiling but this only lit the patch of concrete floor immediately beneath it. Specks of dust swirled up the shafts of light. The rest of the hall was in darkness.

Chess stayed close to Ethel now and so did Box and Splinter. She thought that she could hear footsteps in the shadows; maybe it was just their footsteps echoing off the hard walls. There was the tinny clatter of a glass bottle rolling on the ground. A gust of wind sent a sheet of newspaper flapping in her face and she clawed it away as if it had been a bat. She didn't notice the body on the floor until she had tripped over it. She fell with a shriek that echoed round the hall. There was a moment's silence and then a low murmuring.

'Mind yer feet,' growled a voice from the floor. In the half-light Chess could pick out a thickly bearded face, a greasy raincoat and hairy hands clutching a bottle.

'Have we got visitors, Harry?' came a shout close by.

'Four of 'em,' replied the bearded man. He staggered to his feet and swayed towards Chess.

A shuffling came from the darkness around her. The shadows coalesced into shapes and twenty or maybe thirty tramps groped their way out of the murk. They were dressed in long coats or thick jackets and they carried bottles and sticks. One of them was moaning gibberish to himself and another was singing heartily, keeping time by bashing the pickaxe handle he held against the floor. The stink of sweat and alcohol was rank.

They surrounded Ethel, Chess, Box and Splinter.

Harry thrust his bearded jowls towards Chess and, eyes rolling, said, 'What's a tasty little thing like you doing here?' He followed the question with a loud, rasping belch that was so acrid, Chess felt sick as well as frightened.

'Harry!' snapped Ethel, cutting the gloom.

'Ethel?' said Harry, drawing back.

'Yes, you twit. How many times have you been told to stay sharp?'

'Sorry, Ethel, I can't 'elp it, you know me.'

'Yes, I know you and the rest of your gut-wobbling, bug-eyed, booze-swilling crew.'

There was an affronted muttering from the tramps.

'We was just doin' our best, Ethel. Keeping watch and all that.'

'Keeping watch of the inside of your eyelids,' said Ethel.

'What use is it having sentries on the warehouse approach if you lot are away with the fairies? Just remember, dear, not everything that wants to get in here will be kind enough to trip over you first.'

'OK, Ethel. Sorry.'

'Don't be dozing, Harry. It could be your head on a stick if you're caught napping.'

Harry scratched his chin through the beard and appeared to be about to say something but then decided against it and withdrew into the gloom.

'Were those guards?' asked Box as they crossed to a door in the far wall.

'Yes,' said Ethel. 'Pathetic, isn't it? Geese would be better. There are other guards around the place. This is a maximum security zone, would you believe? But you see, in this part of Committee HQ, where strangers are most likely to wander, we can't have anything too outlandish. Harry and his men manage to keep most humans away and they fit in with the style of the place. If you could possibly call it style, dear. The last thing we want is to draw attention to ourselves.'

'Is that why you go around looking like an old bag lady?' asked Box. Even in the shadows he could see Ethel frown. 'I mean, when you're actually a witch or something.'

'I'm not a witch, Box. But you could call this a disguise. You could say I'm operating "undercover."'

At the door Ethel said, 'You wait here. I have to speak with a couple of people through there. No offence, my loves. As soon as I can, I'll take you to your quarters and you can have some food.' She patted Chess's arm. 'We'll get that foot looked at too.'

She hurried through the door, pulling it closed behind her. She couldn't have pulled it very firmly because it swung open a couple of inches as soon as she had gone. Chess, Box and Splinter didn't need to say anything to one another. In seconds their faces were at the opening, Chess's at the bottom and above her, Box and above him, Splinter.

The gap revealed part of a room. The floor was concrete and the ceiling was low. Iron mesh caged the grime-streaked windows in the wall opposite. Pigeons were roosting on the top of one of the mesh grilles. They shifted from pink foot to pink foot, wrapping and unwrapping their clawed toes round the wire, bobbing their heads and blinking into space vacantly.

Under a solitary, low-hanging light was a tired wooden desk with uneven drawers, some of which jutted open. At one end of the desk was a tower of nine in-trays that were stuffed with papers and which leant precariously, spilling the uppermost layer of documents towards the floor. The top of the desk was littered with a snow of paperwork.

In front of the desk a man was sitting in a wheelchair. He wore a long coat made out of patches of different colours. He was bald but he had a thick, ginger moustache that drooped either side of his mouth and fell to just below his jaw. A black patch covered his left eye and from the way that his coat stretched over his tummy it looked as if he was very fat.

Chess could see a profusion of tendrils that sprouted between the man and his wheelchair. As her eyes adjusted to the light she realized that these tendrils were cables and tubes. They connected the man to his chair by his arms and shoulders, his chest and back and the back of his head.

From the grey metal shade of the hanging lamp a yellow cone divided the murk and bathed the desk and the man in light, making the top of his bald head shine but leaving the rest of the room in shadow. He turned from his desk as Ethel entered, still clutching the dictaphone into which he'd been speaking. It was tiny inside his fist which, thought Chess, had a look of boiled ham about it.

Ethel and the man were talking together for several minutes before he raised his voice loud enough to be heard by the Tuesdays. His voice was deep and phlegmy as if he needed to clear his throat. He spoke with a heavy accent.

'Are you sure about this?' he demanded. 'Are you sure this is the girl?'

'Yes, Joachim,' Ethel replied. 'I'm sure. As sure as I can be.'

'As sure as you can be?' the man in the wheelchair said. 'How sure is that?'

'I have been searching for her for years. Even then I nearly lost her. The others were very close, Joachim, very close. That should be proof enough.'

'Even then, they can be wrong.' The man sighed and his voice lowered but he still spoke urgently enough to be audible at the door. 'We must be right, Mevrad. This cycle is drawing to a close; the fifth node is approaching. The Symmetry must not find the girl; they must not be able to use the Eternal. We cannot afford to be wrong.'

'I am not wrong,' said Ethel.

Then someone else spoke, someone who was hidden from

Chess's view. His voice was smooth and sonorous. 'You have been wrong before, Mevrad.'

Ethel turned to face the voice from the shadows. 'Yes, Julius, I have been wrong before. Once. Just once.'

'She's really angry,' whispered Box.

Ethel was pacing back and forth in front of the man in the wheelchair as she spoke. 'I have searched endlessly. I have done all that I can. I have consulted everybody; the astrologers, the sibyls, numerologists, the necromancers, clairvoyants, metaphysicians, priests. I have discussed the matter with the sages who spend their lives studying the Histories. I have been to the furthest libraries to learn from those whose days are spent poring over the time charts, deciphering every last node of the cycles. I have interrogated every agent who has or may have information. I have travelled up and down and across every universe and have gathered every clue and considered every piece of information. I have thought long and hard and deep and I am sure this is the girl.'

The fat man in the coat grunted. 'And she knows nothing. You have not told her?'

Ethel paused. 'I have not spoken to her about this,' she said.

'It's you they're going on about, Chess,' whispered Box.

'Shut up,' hissed Splinter. The voices in the room had dropped and he struggled to hear what was being said until the person they couldn't see spoke loudly and abruptly.

'We are sure this is the right thing to do? She will be in very real danger.'

'The children are our best hope, Julius,' replied Ethel.

'The boys are sneaky and determined. They are two of the most cunning rogues you could find. As for the girl, well, the girl is the girl.'

'If the Symmetry take her she will never withstand the pain,' said Julius. 'What happens then?'

'We have to start this way,' insisted Ethel. 'And the Symmetry will never expect this. It is the last place they would expect to find the girl.'

Joachim tossed the dictaphone behind him. It landed on the desk amidst the papers. 'Unless they are thinking ahead of us,' he said.

'And who's to say I'm not thinking ahead of them,' said Ethel. 'I think I see what happens at the end of all of this. This is just the beginning.'

After a pause, Julius asked, 'You have the children here? Now?'

'Yes,' said Ethel. 'They are waiting, just outside.'

'Bring them in,' he demanded.

'Yes,' agreed Ethel. 'Why not?' and she started for the door.

Chess, Box and Splinter recoiled from the gap, as if they had just been electrocuted. Box moved so quickly that he knocked Splinter's legs from under him. Then he fell over Splinter and Chess fell backwards over him. But they scrambled to their feet before Ethel opened the door and when she did, she was presented with the three of them leaning against the wall, hands in pockets as if they hadn't the least interest in what had been going on behind the door.

Ethel peered at them sternly. 'Don't tell me you weren't listening,' she whispered. 'I know you were. I left the door open for you. They want to see you. Come in.'

She led them into the centre of the room so that they were standing in front of Joachim. Close up, Chess could see where the cables from the body of the wheel chair burrowed into the skin of his wrists, below the cuffs of his coat and into the side of his neck. In these places the skin was a grey-purple colour as if it was bruised or as if there was an object beneath the surface into which the ends of the cables had been screwed.

Joachim leant forwards with a jolting of cables and said, 'Hello.' His ginger walrus moustache spread softly over his big smile.

Chess, Box and Splinter stared back at him with faces like stone. They said nothing.

'Well,' said Joachim. 'This must be a surprise,' and he waved his right hand around the room. 'You probably wonder what it is all about, no?'

The Tuesdays nodded.

'Naturally,' Joachim reassured them. 'But for now we just meet.'

'Let me see you.' The voice came from behind them, smooth but firm. All three turned at once. At the far end of the room, the shadows stirred and took shape and a man came out of them, boots treading slow.

He was tall and he wore a black leather coat that reached almost to his ankles. His yellow hair hung loose from the back of his head to below his shoulders. The left side of his face was deathly pale, the right looked as smooth as skin but seemed to be constructed of a bright metal like silver. The two sides joined perfectly down the centre of his face and, as far as Chess could see, over the hairless crown of his head.

His left eye was ice-blue, the right was blood-red. His hands were the same colour as the right side of his head and looked as if they were made of the same metal. A pair of broad and heavy machine pistols were slung from his belt like chunks of iron.

The man's eyes were fixed on Chess's face. Not once did he look at Splinter or Box who were standing on either side of her. Chess stared back at him and wondered why he stood so close to her. She flinched when his silver hands held her face: not because they were cold, they weren't, they were warm like normal hands. She flinched because she did not like being touched and because she hadn't expected the way in which his palms and his fingers seemed to reach into her.

He lowered his left hand but continued to push the silver fingers of his right hand against her cheek, the arch of her eyebrow, her forehead, her lower jaw, rubbing her skin, digging down to feel her bone. Chess wanted to move her head away but all the time his eyes searched hers and she found that she could not look away from the blue ice and the red fire.

'Chess.' Julius said her name slowly, breathing it out so that it sounded like surf breaking. He raised his left hand to the left side of his own face and felt it, just like his right hand had been feeling hers.

When he stopped touching her, she felt a sudden coldness, a distance. This was a weird feeling and it made her step back from Julius although she realized, with surprise, that what she really wanted was to stay close to him. He turned away.

'This is the girl,' he stated.

Joachim coughed. 'Still, a test will be necessary.'

'I must go,' said Julius. 'It has not been easy to join you here.'

'I know,' said Ethel.

'The Symmetry want her, Mevrad,' said Julius, slow and soft. 'If they get her, it is over.'

Then where Julius had been standing there was an empty space.

'Nice one,' whispered Box.

'Ridiculous,' muttered Splinter.

Joachim cleared his throat, a tube that hung under his chin bobbing as he did so. 'Mevrad, there is something I must talk to you about. But not right now.' Splinter noticed how Joachim's good eye flicked to where he was standing with Box and Chess before flicking back to Ethel.

Something you don't want us to hear, guessed Splinter.

'And there is something I have to talk to you about, Joachim. But first I must see to our guests.'

'Prisoners, more like,' grumbled Splinter.

'Don't grouse, dear. I'm sure you're all hungry?' Box nodded. 'And Chess is injured.'

'So am I,' muttered Splinter whose forehead had swollen into a pale blue egg and whose foot still ached from where Klinky Mallows had trodden on it.

'Fifteen minutes then,' suggested Joachim. 'I have other matters to attend to. We shall meet back here?'

Ethel nodded. The cables sprouting from Joachim's hips and shoulders arched taut and the wheelchair spun abruptly to face the opposite end of the room. 'Don't try to reorganize my paperwork,' he called over his shoulder as he rolled from the room.

Ethel let out a sigh and leant her bottom against the table but did not sit down.

'Who were they?' asked Box once the far door had closed behind Joachim.

'Members of the Committee,' said Ethel. 'Important members. Generals you could say.'

'Are you a general?' asked Splinter.

'As much as they are.'

'Who was the man in the wheelchair?' Box asked.

'His name is Joachim Breslaw.'

'What is he?' Box screwed up his face.

'He's a professor.'

'Of what?' asked Splinter, with a slight sneer in his voice.

'Of everything,' said Ethel.

'And who is Julius?' asked Chess, a little shyly.

'He's a weird-looking man. Pretty ugly,' observed Box.

'He's not a man,' said Ethel.

'I don't think he's ugly, or weird,' said Chess defensively. What *are* you thinking? she asked herself.

Ethel looked at Chess quizzically before saying, 'Julius is many different things, my loves. He is unlike you, which is to say, he isn't human. And he exists in different places in different ways. He is difficult to deal with but we would be lost without him.'

'He looks,' Chess hesitated as she searched for the right word, 'brave.' That was it. He had touched her and she knew that his fire and ice and constant strength were there for her. Then she saw Splinter smirking at her and she felt stupid because she knew that she was nothing. Nothing to Julius. Nothing to anyone.

'He fights the Twisted Symmetry,' said Ethel. 'He fights it with his mind and he fights it with his body. He has fought against the Havoc Legions and the Plague Breed and what you see of him is what is left but he goes on fighting. It isn't that he is brave, my love. It's just that he doesn't know what fear is. He doesn't feel things as you do.' Ethel hesitated now and then shook her head to herself, grey hair flopping, as if she had decided not to say something she wanted to say. 'He does not know about kindness either.'

Of course not, thought Chess. He wouldn't. Not to me, anyway.

'What are Havoc Legions?' asked Box. 'And what's the Plague Breed?' He rubbed his hands against his trouser legs.

Ethel detected the nervous waver in his voice. 'The enemy has armies, my love. Strange armies. These are two of them. But you won't have to face them,' and then she said quietly, 'Not yet.'

'It's just that the Twisted Symmetry have so much,' said Box. 'I don't mind,' he added, as Splinter caught his eye, sneering, 'but there's only three of us.'

'And that's more than enough,' announced Ethel, giving his arm a gentle squeeze. 'The three of you are worth a dozen Havoc Legions.'

'What were you all saying about Chess?' asked Splinter. 'She's nothing special, you know.'

'You don't know her as I do,' said Ethel.

'You don't know her at all,' stated Splinter.

'What's the Eternal?' asked Chess.

'So many questions! And all far too complicated to explain right now,' fussed Ethel. 'I need to sort you out and then I have to speak to Joachim again.'

'About the squealer?' volunteered Splinter.

'The squealer?' asked Ethel.

'Yeah. A squealer is someone who gives away secrets; who talks to the crashers.'

'You mean they "squeal" on you?' confirmed Ethel.

'No,' smiled Splinter. 'I mean that's what they do after we get hold of them.' Box and Splinter sniggered.

'Charming, dear. And whilst we're dealing with your peculiar vocabulary, what are "crashers"?'

'The police.'

Ethel's spectacles slipped to the tip of her small nose and she leant towards Splinter. 'Forgive my ignorance, dear, but I fail to see the connection.'

'Gatecrashers,' explained Splinter, knowledgeably. 'You're having a party . . .'

'We don't have parties,' interjected Box.

'Shut up, fly head, I'm just explaining,' retorted Splinter. 'You're having a party and gatecrashers are the people who turn up uninvited. Usually they wreck it. So crashers is short for gatecrashers. And crashers is the police.'

'I see,' said Ethel. 'Logical, although not entirely accurate.'

'And you've got a squealer, haven't you?' asserted Splinter.

'Like a double agent,' suggested Box helpfully.

'A squealer right here in Committee HQ,' continued Splinter. 'Someone here is telling the Twisted Symmetry what's going on with us. That's why the spindle rippers knew where to find us, and the traders.' Ethel didn't reply. 'I'm right, aren't I?' persisted Splinter. He was standing by the desk now, idly resting a hand on the scattered papers. 'Someone here is helping the Twisted Symmetry.'

'I'm not sure, dear,' said Ethel.

'Oh yes, you are. Trust no one. That's what you said.'

'Well, I'm glad you've learnt something,' said Ethel and then, changing the subject, 'Now, can I interest you in some food and somewhere to sleep?'

Splinter did not reply. He stood with eyes cast down, stooping slightly under the yellow light like a crow.

'Can we have cake?' asked Box.

'What is it with you and cake?' asked Splinter, attention still riveted to the top of the desk.

'It's just ever since Ethel was talking about the vortex and fruit cake. It's been on my mind all the time. I try to stop thinking about it but it keeps coming back.'

'I was thinking of something more in the line of sandwiches,' said Ethel.

'Cake sandwiches?' suggested Box hopefully.

'Probably not, dear. Now,' said Ethel, moving towards the far door, 'shall we go?' and she held the door open. As Box and Chess walked over she asked, 'Have you ever slept in a bulk storage tank before?'

'I've slept in a septic tank before,' said Box.

'Well, you should find this a great improvement,' promised Ethel, leading the way through the door. She held it open and after a short delay, Splinter joined them.

Ethel took them through the old bus depot. The corridors were illuminated by bulbs in wire casings that were screwed at intervals along the walls. The walls were peeling paint from the blotchy damp plaster. There were patches where the plaster had crumbled to the floor in powdery heaps exposing brickwork. Narrow rivulets coursed down the raw brickwork and collected in dirty puddles along the edges of the concrete floor. The air was cool and stale and the plip of dripping water sounded from murky passages down which they didn't go.

Chess noticed that as they walked, Splinter was muttering to himself. 'What are you doing?' she asked.

'Keeping track of where we are,' he replied irritably.

She took no more notice of Splinter but looked more closely at the rooms off the corridor. Some were hidden behind closed doors but she could peer into others through plate glass windows in the corridor walls. There were rooms with desks and cupboards, rooms with maps and charts and boards on the walls which displayed long mathematical equations and astronomical diagrams, rooms filled with rows of chairs and rooms where the glow of data screens bathed the shoulders of the people who were hunched in front of them.

They descended an iron stairwell with a loose handrail and a turn halfway down. Ethel led them through a door at the bottom. Down here the walls were mottled grey with mould. The ceiling was strung thick with cables and in some sections they had fallen loose from their fixings and they hung so low that Chess had to duck to walk beneath them.

She saw rooms with beds and lockers where people were sleeping, rooms crammed with the dormant hulks of machines and monitors, a room better illuminated than the others where workbenches lined the walls, their tops crowded with test tubes, retort flasks, clamp stands, pipettes, generators, meters, electrodes and racks of glass bottles filled with powders and liquids and one room that looked to Chess like an operating theatre. It was in darkness but the meagre light from the corridor glinted on the steel edges of an operating table and the light cluster that hung over it.

There was a tumbling tread of boots. Turning, Chess saw that it came from a group of four men who were coming towards them. They wore grey and brown camouflaged combats under grey body armour and cradled clunking machine guns in their arms. They were big men, tattooed arms bulging like logs as they hoisted their guns. They filled the passage like boulders. They greeted Ethel but said nothing to the street rats crammed close to her.

'One of the night patrols,' explained Ethel when the men had passed. 'There are four or five patrols on duty all the time.' She glanced after them severely. 'I must have a word with the security co-ordinator; there's no need for all that heavy weaponry in one place. Just imagine if there was any trouble. There'd be bullets bouncing round the walls like ping-pong balls.'

'Nice guns, though,' said Box.

'That's the trouble with boys,' observed Ethel. 'They all want the biggest guns.'

'Can I have one?' asked Box. Ethel regarded him over the rim of her spectacles as if he was extraordinary. 'I mean for this mission you're sending us on,' he explained.

'Box Tuesday,' replied Ethel. 'I wouldn't trust you with a pea-shooter,' and she strode down the corridor.

She stopped when they came to an end wall in which

there were set four round doors. The doors were iron and painted white and were fringed with ducts and pipe-work that emerged from the wall and re-entered it like metal worms. Each door was reached by a set of four steps.

Ethel stretched up and rapped on one of them. It sounded hollow. 'These are bulk storage tanks, my loves. They were used to hold fuel. We use them to hold valuables now. They are set in cement, are double skinned and they are very secure. This one is used to keep people safe.'

'It sounds like a prison cell,' said Splinter.

'It looks like a prison cell,' complained Box.

'Have you seen a prison cell with a round door?' asked Ethel.

'Yes,' said Splinter. 'We're standing in front of one.'

'It ain't a prison cell,' insisted Ethel. 'It is a safe place to be. This one has a ten-thousand-litre capacity so there's plenty of room. And there's a flush toilet plumbed in so no slopping out.' She stepped up, pulled the handle and wrenched open the door. 'Go on,' she said. 'Look inside.'

'Promise not to lock us in and cook us in a pie?' asked Splinter as he entered the storage tank.

'It can be opened from the inside and I'm not hungry,' replied Ethel.

'I am,' said Box.

'I know, dear. You always are. Food is on its way so do try to keep going.'

Chess followed Box, stooping to enter. The cylindrical chamber had a wooden, slatted floor and four iron bunks with thin mattresses that pulled down from the curving walls and were held in place by chains. It was about five metres deep and at the far end there was a small portal that swung open to reveal a cramped lavatory. A pile of blankets was stacked on the wooden floor near to the entrance door. It was lit dimly by a strip light in the centre of the roof. The dull light made Chess feel sleepy.

Box dropped onto one of the bottom bunks. 'It's like being on a submarine,' he declared.

'Far more roomy, dear,' Ethel observed.

Splinter sniffed. 'Smells of paint, not fuel.'

'It hasn't held fuel for a very long time, my love. But the Committee have only been using this location for six years.'

'Whilst you've been looking for Chess?' asked Box.

'Yes, dear, that's right,' said Ethel. 'But we have lots of other headquarter locations and outposts.'

'All around the universe?' ridiculed Splinter.

'No, dear,' Ethel corrected him. 'All around the universes.'

Splinter looked around the storage tank and snorted. 'Are they all . . . like this?'

'Splinter,' said Ethel. 'You are going to have to stop being fooled by appearances. There is more to the Committee than you realize.'

'Really,' replied Splinter. 'Then tell me this; who is stronger? The Committee or the Twisted Symmetry?'

'We don't know the answer to that yet, my love.'

'I do,' said Splinter.

Their eyes locked.

'There are mysteries you do not understand,' said Ethel slowly.

'Because you keep them secret from us,' replied Splinter, cool as frost.

Ethel shook her head. 'I've got to go. The food is coming and someone will be down to look at your foot, dear. I'll see you all in the morning.' Then she left them.

'She's useless,' spat Splinter, slumping down next to Box.

'Don't say that, Splinter,' said Chess, sitting on the bunk opposite.

'Don't say that, Splinter,' mimicked Splinter in a falsetto whine. 'Just look at it. There's a war going on and the weakest side has taken us prisoner and wants us to steal something that they can't even get themselves. And they're going to send us to the people that want to catch us.' He shook his head in disgust. 'Great plan.'

'They want to catch Chess,' Box corrected him.

'Same difference,' said Splinter. 'And there's a squealer. The old lady won't admit it but there is. It's obvious. So what's going to happen when this lot send us to the Twisted Symmetry?'

Box rubbed both his hands through his curly hair, stuck out the tip of his tongue whilst sucking his lips and then said, 'The Twisted Symmetry will know we're coming.'

'Correct. They'll be waiting for us.'

Box huffed and leant back. 'This isn't very good, Splinter.'

'Well done, genius. This is what comes of being on the losing side.'

'But nothing's been lost yet,' protested Chess. 'I wish you'd stop going on about winning sides and losing sides.' She felt her cheeks burning hot. 'At least we're on a side for once. At least it's the right side.'

'Says who? The old lady?'

'Yes,' shouted Chess. 'And I wish you'd stop calling her the old lady. She's got a name you know.'

'Yeah, she's got at least two,' replied Splinter. 'Stop squawking like a stupid teacher's pet.'

'I'm not a teacher's pet.' Chess tried not to shout because she could see that Splinter was enjoying this.

'I wish we knew what they're talking about,' interrupted Box.

'Who?' asked Chess, trying to distract herself from Splinter's grin.

'The old . . . Ethel and the Professor,' he said. 'It must be something important.'

'Don't worry,' said Splinter. 'We're going to find out what it is.' His grin adjusted itself into a knowing smile.

'How?' asked Box. 'What are you looking so clever about?'

'I've taken steps to make sure there are no secrets between us,' announced Splinter.

'How?' Box was baffled.

'You'll see,' said Splinter. 'After we've had our food and she's had her foot looked at, I'm going out. Back upstairs. To steal something. Then we can hear what they didn't want us to hear.'

CHAPTER 10

Splinter moved through the night. His thin feet made no noise. He sought corners, alcoves, sunken doors; hugged the damp brick of the walls, hoisted himself into nests of cables to hang like a fly when voices approached; slunk through the places where darkness was deepest. He saw everything and was unseen. He heard everything but was never heard. He was still as stone, quick as thought and strongest where the light was weak.

Splinter did not see as others saw. His acid eyes stripped colour and comfort and living from the world to reveal a place where crowds were clothes, smiles were knives, alleyways were possibilities and trust meant death. Trust no one. Ethel had not taught this to Splinter; he had always known it.

Slinking through the corridors of Committee HQ, Splinter didn't see doors or walls or lights; he saw escape routes and hand holds and danger. He saw what mattered. He saw what was useful to him and he rejected unnecessary data. He assumed nothing. He planned everything. His eyes were always ahead of his body and his calculations were always ahead of his eyes.

He was in the stairwell now. He looked up. Nothing. He began to climb the iron stairs, making no more noise than falling mist. He came to the turn in the stairs but already his mind was through the door at the top and plotting its way along the corridor on the other side to another door that would take him left.

Footsteps. Voices. Three people. Maybe four.

Thinking his way ahead of his body, Splinter heard what was coming seconds before the door above him opened and a four-man patrol clattered onto the top of the staircase, filling the stairwell with the stamp of boots, the rattle of magazines in machine guns, someone grumbling, someone laughing.

Splinter was standing in the middle of the stairs, halfway up the stairwell. There was nowhere to hide.

But there was always somewhere for Splinter to hide.

Dark and quick as an eel, he slipped over the side of the stairs. His fingers gripped the back of the nearest step and he let his body fall into the space below. It hung there like a black icicle. As the patrol began to walk down the stairs, Splinter reached up and gripped the next step. His sinewy wrists were strong. His fingers clamped the back of the metal steps. Creeping under the boots of the patrol, cloaked in the shadow that was thick beneath the stairs, Splinter pulled up his feet and spidered his way under the stairs until he reached the top. The patrol reached the bottom step, satisfied that all was in order. Splinter slithered onto the top step, flat on his belly and waited. The bottom door closed behind the patrol. Splinter entered the upper corridor.

He came to the door that would give him what he wanted.

He listened. He heard nothing. He pushed the door open and retreated to another doorway and waited. If anyone was in the room they would come to the door now. That's what people did when a door opened. He had learnt this. That is why he didn't wait near to the door but a short distance away, where he could see what happened.

No one came.

He went to the open door, listened again and then looked inside the room. It was in darkness now but he saw the silhouette of the hanging light and the desk in the centre of the room. Splinter entered.

The pigeons stirred where they were roosting by the windows. A patch of shadow glided through the night until it was standing by the desk. A long, pale hand reached from the darkness and closed on an object that lay amongst the papers that were strewn across the desk top. The object was slipped inside Splinter's morning coat and then he was gone, the door closing softly behind him, the pigeons blinking at the dark.

Chess was lying on one of the top bunks. She propped herself up on an elbow, rubbed her eyes and yawned. 'You've been gone for ages.' Her mouth tasted horrible. Her foot throbbed beneath the bandage that had been applied to it a couple of hours ago by a man in a white lab coat who had told her he was a medic but made no further conversation.

'Felt like minutes,' said Splinter, pulling the round door of the bulk storage tank shut behind him. He was suddenly very thirsty and he poured a glass of water from a jug that had been standing on the wooden floor beside a metal tray. The tray had been delivered to them stacked with cheese sandwiches but was now scattered with crumbs.

'Thirsty work,' he explained between gulping down one glass and then most of another. The bit that was left he poured over Box's head. 'Wake up, fly head.'

Box woke up immediately, shaking his head and swearing. He grabbed the jug of water but before he could launch the contents at Splinter, Splinter had pulled a slim, grey, plastic item from the inside of his morning coat and held it out, between himself and the jug.

'Don't,' Splinter warned Box. 'Or you won't find out what's going on.'

'What's that?' asked Box, still holding the jug but lowering it.

'Professor Wheelchair's dictaphone,' announced Splinter.

'That's not very nice,' said Chess.

'That's not very nice,' squeaked Splinter. 'What is it with you and weak people?'

Chess was too weary to think of what to say. She slumped onto her back.

'Anyway,' continued Splinter, weighing the dictaphone in his hand, 'now we can find out what the old lady and the Professor were going to talk about once they got us out of the way.'

'How?' asked Box.

'See this little button?' Splinter held the dictaphone so that Box could see. 'That's the record button. I switched it on when we left the room last night. So whilst those two were having their secret conversation, this was recording it all.'

Box grinned. 'That's really clever, Splinter.'

'I know,' agreed Splinter, grinning back. 'That's what I'm here for.'

'Well, let's have a listen then,' Chess said thickly, eyes closed.

'Oh, we're interested now, are we?' asked Splinter.

'Never said I wasn't.' She stifled a yawn.

Box and Splinter sat on the bottom bunk opposite. Splinter pushed the rewind button and the tape inside the dictaphone spun backwards with a stream of shrill babbling. Splinter pressed PLAY and Ethel began to talk. He held down the rewind button again and waited until the unintelligible babbling had stopped. Then he pressed PLAY again. There was silence for nearly a minute and then there was a noise like someone talking inside a paper bag that was being scrunched up.

'I can't hear anything,' complained Box. 'Just mumbling voices.'

'It must have been covered by something,' said Splinter, annoyed. 'Some of those papers must have been knocked onto it.'

There was a sound like a loudspeaker crackling and then Joachim's voice came clearly from Splinter's hand. '*It is folly, Mevrad. It is hopeless.*'

Splinter looked sidelong at Box. 'See,' he said.

'*More children are being taken than ever before, Joachim. The Twisted Symmetry want the energy; they need it.*' There was a pause and then Ethel continued, more quietly than before. '*The end of this cycle is coming and the Symmetry are preparing for it. This is what they have been waiting for. We cannot waste any more time. The time for thinking . . .'*

'Yes, yes, I know. The time for thinking is over.'

'We need to know what the Symmetry are doing. So, first of all, we need to know how the computer works.'

'Which is where we come in,' said Box, proudly. Splinter elbowed him in the ribs to shut him up.

'But the computer is no ordinary construction,' insisted Joachim. *'The cerebral torus is a universal quantum computer: that is why it can calculate the cross-universal probabilities for the Fat Gobster's strikes. But to be able to do that it has an amarantium core and amarantium in that concentration cannot be handled.'*

'What was that amaretto stuff?' interrupted Box.

'Crystal, remember? That's what the old lady said people call it.' Splinter paused the tape. 'The Twisted Symmetry need it because every piece exists everywhere at once or something. It's so important to them that they fight battles over it.'

'Oh yeah,' said Box, digging his fingers into the thick black curls on the top of his head and scratching vigorously. 'The Crystal Wars.'

'Shall we carry on?' suggested Splinter. He started the tape again.

'To touch the cerebral torus and live,' said Joachim, *'that is impossible.'*

'Which shows how hopeless this is,' said Splinter.

Ethel was talking now. *'Not for her it isn't. She can touch it.'*

'If you are right about her.'

'Julius knows I'm right.'

Joachim snorted. '*There will have to be a blood test. To make sure it is her.*'

'They're going to stick a needle in you,' Box warned Chess.

'I don't care,' mumbled Chess, half-asleep, too tired to listen.

'*And the atmosphere surrounding the cerebral torus is highly toxic,*' continued Joachim. '*The gases which nourish it are lethal to humans. So you see, the children have no chance, even if the Twisted Symmetry do not get their claws into them first.*'

'I was wrong,' announced Splinter gloomily. 'It's not just hopeless; it's a suicide mission.'

'*Two weeks of praetorisone injections will raise their immunity to the gas,*' said Ethel.

'Oh no,' groaned Box.

'Needles every day for two weeks, fly head,' whispered Splinter.

'*Two weeks will not be long enough,*' stated Joachim.

'*Two weeks is all we have,*' replied Ethel.

Splinter stopped the tape. 'I said this was mad.'

'Just let's listen to the rest of it,' insisted Box.

'There isn't much left,' said Splinter, looking at the tape through the clear lid.

'Chess is asleep,' said Box, noticing the slow, gentle breathing from the top bunk opposite.

'Then she'll miss the happy ending.' Splinter pressed PLAY.

'*There was something you wanted to tell me,*' Joachim said.

'*There is a traitor here. We have an informant,*' Ethel said bluntly. 'Somebody has been telling the Symmetry what is happening with the children.'

'See!' burst Splinter, triumphant. 'I knew it. I was right. And she wouldn't admit it. She doesn't want us to know. She wants to keep us in the dark.'

'I guessed as much,' Joachim was saying.

'Who Joachim? Who?'

There was a long pause before Joachim sighed loudly and said, 'There has always been this danger, Mevrad. Ever since Sprazkin joined us.'

'We must not jump to conclusions.'

'Come, come, Mevrad. Who else?'

'Lemuel has been with us for over two hundred years.'

'Two hundred years,' said Joachim. 'And the risk has never been greater than now. Lemuel Sprazkin was the Symmetry's primary warp for eight hundred years. To have these children here, now; to have the girl so close. I fear it will be too much for him. Maybe his old appetite has been stirred.'

'You have never liked Lemuel,' said Ethel.

'Lemuel Sprazkin cannot be trusted with the children, Mevrad. The temptation will be too great.'

'He has found a way to control himself, Joachim. You know that.'

'What? By sticking that drill in his brain? That is precisely the kind of deranged science that makes my skin crawl, Mevrad. It is unnatural.'

'It is what the warps do. It is one of the reasons why the Twisted Symmetry are so strong. If Lemuel had not come to us we would never have survived.'

Joachim sounded as if he was spitting in disgust. 'That all

counts for nothing if he betrays us to his former masters now.'

'We cannot be sure it is Lemuel.'

'I can be sure.'

There was another long pause during which the only sound was the monotonous hiss made by the tape turning inside the dictaphone. Then Ethel said in measured tones, 'You are very quick to accuse Lemuel.'

'And what do you mean by that, Mevrad?'

'You are only human, Joachim. Therefore you are corruptible. That is what makes humans so attractive to the Twisted Symmetry. You are fallible. Have the Symmetry got to you, Joachim? Can I trust you?'

'Of course you can trust me.'

The tape stopped and the play button clicked off automatically. In the silence that followed, Splinter and Box continued to stare at the machine in Splinter's hand as if they expected it to carry on playing. But the only sound was the steady rise and fall of Chess's breathing as she slept. Then Splinter tossed the dictaphone onto the bunk opposite and lay back against the concave wall of the tank with his hands behind his head.

'Want to hear any of that again?' He was very pleased with himself.

Box opened his mouth but said nothing.

'The computer brain is lethal to touch,' Splinter began.

'Not for Chess it isn't,' interrupted Box.

'They're wrong about Chess,' snapped Splinter. 'A case of mistaken identity,' and he scowled at the top bunk opposite.

'I don't know why she would be able to touch it,' conceded Box.

'She can't,' Splinter insisted. 'So, one, the computer is lethal to touch; two, the air around it is lethal to breathe; and three, best of all, the Committee have got some top brass member of the Twisted Symmetry working for them who can't be trusted. Like they couldn't have seen that coming.' Splinter laughed bleakly. 'It's no wonder the world's so rubbish if this lot are in charge of saving it.'

'It might be worse if they weren't,' suggested Box.

'What's up with you?' asked Splinter. 'You're as bad as her,' and he jerked his head towards Chess. 'It's like being with a pair of social workers.'

'What's a warp?' asked Box.

Splinter shrugged his narrow shoulders. 'How should I know?' and then he added, 'A kind of scientist from the sound of it.'

'He must be at least a thousand years old,' Box observed and he whistled in admiration.

'That's ridiculous.' Splinter pulled his knees up to his chin. 'Just like you, fly head.'

'You're the one who's being ridiculous,' replied Box.

Splinter responded by kicking his heel into Box's thigh, so Box elbowed Splinter's chest, so Splinter punched Box's stomach, so Box tried to grab Splinter's neck.

The fighting didn't disturb Chess. She was sleeping deeply now. So much had happened in two days that her mind wanted only to drench itself in sleep. No talk of computers or crystal or even injections could keep her awake. When she had shut her eyes they felt sore but as the darkness welled, the soreness eased, the heavy ache in her foot lightened and her breathing slowed and she found that she was back on the ledge at the wharf, watching the patterns glimmering on the roof above her head. The light spangled in a rippling web and the voices from the tape faded behind a sweeter, stronger voice.

'When I was on horseback, wasn't I pretty?'

She knew this voice and she knew its song. She waited for it in the mindless drift between waking and sleep and it always came with feelings that she couldn't find in any other place or at any other time. It made a space for her; a space into which she fitted perfectly.

This must be what it's always like for some people, she had thought. But she didn't mind that it was only when she slept that she felt like this. She knew that the voice could only come to her when she was alone and her body had fallen away. This was how it had to be.

So Chess slept.

Bored with fighting each other, Box and Splinter also slept. In the dim glow of the storage tank, buried in cement beneath the old bus depot, night thickened. There was absolute silence. The hours passed.

Chess only began to wake when her breathing sounded wrong. The noise when she breathed in seemed to last for a little longer than the actual breath that she drew, and when she exhaled, it sounded as if she continued to breathe out for a few moments after her breath had stopped. At the same time there was a warmth on her face. It felt like a glow that came in tingling surges as she breathed out, as if the heat was fanned by her own breath. But her own breath couldn't do that.

Chess realized that this was not her own breath, nor was

it her brothers'. Her brothers weren't there; she sensed that immediately. But someone was breathing; breathing on her. Someone whose face was very close to hers. Chess opened her eyes. Another pair of eyes loomed right in front of her own and a nose brushed the side of her nose. She shrieked and the face that had been nuzzled against hers receded suddenly and a man drew back from her bunk. He held up his hands as if he meant no harm.

'Hello,' he said, and he smiled a wild smile that was all teeth and white of eye. 'Don't be frightened. My name is Lemuel Sprazkin and I *love* children.'

CHAPTER 11

Chess didn't know what was worse; the way in which the man said "love" as if he was talking about chocolate or the way in which he burst into a shriek of laughter as soon as he had said "children". She reared back against the wall of the storage tank.

Lemuel Sprazkin saw her eyes, wide and searching. 'Your brothers have gone in pursuit of their breakfast,' he said and he laughed shrilly. 'Which means that I have you all to myself.' His cascading peal of delight ended abruptly. 'I am so sorry,' he said. 'I have frightened you, haven't I?' He stepped back, his head at the level of her knees and repeated, 'I am so sorry.' He seemed to mean it.

'All right,' said Chess breathlessly. 'That's all right.' She laughed nervously. 'You gave me a shock. I was asleep.'

'I am very, very sorry.'

'I don't know you, that's all.' Chess took a good look at the man. He was dressed in a long black frock-coat that was fastened at the neck with a slender chain. The coat appeared to be embroidered with narrow lines in silver. Some of the lines ran up the coat and other lines ran across it so that it looked as if the coat had been decorated with an intricate maze. Under the coat, the man wore a white silk shirt and baggy, black pantaloons. On his feet were black slippers.

Despite the unusual coat, it was the man's head that caught Chess's attention most. It reminded her of a crescent moon because it was chalk-white and narrow with a long, tapering chin. It was smooth and hairless and although it was difficult to see it all given where she was kneeling and he was standing, Chess thought that a section on the very top appeared to be made of glass.

When he smiled, which he did a lot, a dark-lipped mouth curled up from under an aquiline nose to thin ears. His eyes were large with pale grey irises and tiny pupils and they tilted up towards the sides of his face like his smile.

'I am *very* pleased to meet you,' said Lemuel Sprazkin, and frock-coat rustling, he gave a courtly bow. As his head dipped, Chess saw that set in its crown there was a square of glass. In the centre of the glass there was a small hole ringed with black rubber. She only glimpsed this briefly but it looked to her as if the grey ridges and furrows of a brain were pressing against the glass and jammed within the brain were metal cogs and windings like those inside a clock.

'I apologize for my stealing in like this.' He spoke through his curved nose and his voice was shrill. 'My introduction should have been more solicitous. But you see,' and with this he came closer, 'I have waited such a long time to see you.' He looked into her eyes and although Chess didn't like it when people stared at her, Lemuel Sprazkin's eyes didn't make her feel uncomfortable.

You have unhappy eyes, she thought.

He smiled, dark lips parting slightly. 'May I touch your skin?' he asked. Chess hesitated. 'I won't hurt you,' Lemuel assured her. 'But this is a very special moment.'

Chess held out her hand. Lemuel reached up and ran his finger tips across the back of it. His fingernails were shaped like almonds and were black. The touch of his fingers on the skin of her hand was as gentle and warm as the touch of his breath had been on her face.

He shut his eyes. 'It is as if every minute in every time is waiting and watching, now.' He sighed deeply.

Chess sneaked a closer look at the top of his head. The cogs and miniscule flywheels were cranking and spinning silently, their teeth and rotating dials housed neatly in the larger mass of brain. She realized that Lemuel had inclined his head and was looking up at her out of the sides of his eyes.

'Your brain,' said Chess. 'I can see it.'

'I know,' he replied. 'That way we can keep an eye on it.' He stood upright. 'Tell me,' he asked, with a polite chuckle, 'what does it remind you of?'

Chess thought for a moment before suggesting, 'A cauliflower?'

'Goodness, how ugly! I rather think a walnut. Or maybe even a pecan; grey and perfectly polished. Don't you agree?'

'A bird?' Chess couldn't see the similarity.

'Pecan, not pelican,' and Lemuel Sprazkin laughed his nervy, jagged titter. When he stopped he cleared his throat and said, 'Your innocence is so refreshing. You are so . . .' and he searched for the right word, '. . . possible.' He didn't laugh then. He stamped his foot and shook his head slightly. Then he stepped back from the bed.

'Come along, come along,' he urged. 'You have to come with me.'

'Shouldn't we wait for the others?' suggested Chess.

'Certainly not,' replied Lemuel. 'No time to lose.'

Chess swung her legs over the edge of the bunk bed but didn't get down. She looked at her feet which were dangling in the space between the bunks.

'You can trust me, Chess,' Lemuel assured her. 'I wouldn't be here if you couldn't, would I?'

'I suppose not.' But still, she remained sitting.

'Come on then.'

Chess pushed herself off the bunk and landed neatly on the wooden floor of the tank. She winced as a twinge of pain seared her bandaged foot and she hopped on her good one before putting her sore foot back down and letting it take her weight.

'Where to?' she asked.

'My rooms. I'm going to take a sample of your blood; to see if you are you.'

'I *am* me,' said Chess, perplexed.

'You can only say that if you know who you are,' Lemuel wagged a long finger at her. 'And I rather suspect that you are the last person to know that.'

I know who I am, thought Chess. She didn't want to be anyone different.

Lemuel opened the round door of the storage tank but before he slipped through it, he inched out his head to take a look. 'All right,' he said in a low voice. 'Follow me.'

They didn't talk on the way to Lemuel's rooms. He wasn't any taller than Splinter but he walked very quickly, so quickly that had she not been in the safety of Committee HQ, Chess would have suspected that he wanted to take her somewhere without anybody seeing them. The throbbing in the sole of her foot came so hot and so hard that it ached up to the top of her thigh. Chess wanted to slow down but she didn't want to complain; keeping pace with Lemuel stopped her from thinking very much about anything else.

He led her to a cage which he slammed open. Inside there was a lift. Its walls and floor were wet from tiny droplets of water that cascaded down the shaft. There was no light so they ascended in darkness with the smell of oil in Chess's nose and the delicate weight of Lemuel's hand on her shoulder, the black tipped fingers stirring slightly against her collarbone.

When the lift shuddered to a standstill, Lemuel wrenched open the cage and took Chess down a passageway to a wooden door. He pushed it open smoothly and smiled, the corners of his tilting eyes curling up with the edges of his dark lips.

'Please,' he said softly. 'Enter,' and he waved his hand towards the doorway.

Chess did as he requested.

It was as if she had forgotten how lovely sunlight was. It rushed at her through a pair of French windows that were framed with ivory drapes, shining the dark wooden floorboards white. Chess could feel the light on her skin, the stream of it over her face, the cool brightness inside her. After all the passageways and dim electric lights, and the storage tank, and the rain, and the gloom of the past two days, the sunlight was like oxygen. She breathed it, walking across to the windows and stretching her arms wide.

Silhouetted in front of the tall windows was a round-topped ebony table. It stood slender on a turned pedestal with three cabriole legs ending in scrolled feet. On either side of the table there was a high-backed chair, ornate and dark. Chess stopped in front of the table and looked through the windows. Although the view was of brick walls, corrugated iron roof tops with cracked skylights, empty loading bays and weed-choked chimneys, the brilliant light flashed on glass and washed the walls and roofs until they surprised her with their freshness.

The room was long, like a gallery. She had entered at one end and there were two more sets of ivory-curtained French windows before her eyes reached the other end where a tall, walnut bookcase was flanked by two doors. The bookcase was filled neatly with leather-bound volumes. The doors were closed.

The wall opposite the windows was brick, patched with bare plaster. At the far end, nearest to the walnut bookcase, a collection of steel cabinets had been pushed against the exposed bricks. Closer to Chess and about halfway along the wall stood a black lacquer table. The top was semi-circular and the flat back ran flush with the wall. Its edges were inlaid with gold marquetry. It was supported by one thick leg at the end of which was carved a lion's foot, broad and taloned.

The table was large; Chess guessed that its top was almost as wide as she was tall and as far from the floor as her chest. There were three items on the table; an iron candelabrum, a silver tray and between these, a glass dome on a brass base-plate. Chess crossed the room to take a closer look.

The candelabrum was veined white with wax. Three candle stubs sat in its crusty sockets. The silver tray carried a decanter almost full of a dark, toffee-coloured liquor, a cut crystal goblet and a dish piled with creamy meringues each the size of a small biscuit and topped with a swirl. Although the smell of the meringues made her tummy ache, Chess studied the glass dome before she tried to take one.

The dome was constructed of flat panes of glass set in frames. The frames were arranged in three tiers. Chess counted twelve panes of glass in each tier. Those at the bottom were rectangular, the ones above these narrowed at their upper edges and the uppermost tier were triangular, the apices meeting at the top where there was a brass sphere a little smaller than Chess's fist.

Chess's eyes were level with the middle tier. The dome was filled by an instrument built of hoops that were supported on the base-plate and mounted at different angles to one another. These hoops were also made of brass and were highly polished. Attached to each was a brass sphere. Chess counted twelve spheres in total and they were suspended at different positions. The hoops were rotating on the base-plate minutely, carrying the spheres through the space inside the dome so slowly that it was only by straining her eyes until they hurt that she could judge they were moving.

The smell of sugar was strong. Chess cast a sideways glance to where Lemuel was occupied behind the open door of one of the steel cabinets at the far end of the room before allowing her hand to reach up to the dish that was loaded with meringues. Swiftly she lifted one and popped it whole into her mouth. There was a moment of dryness as the sugared hardness was crammed against the roof of her mouth and then it dissolved into a sweet goo that cloyed her tongue.

'It's an armillary clock,' said Lemuel, by her left shoulder. Chess grunted but couldn't say anything because her mouth was packed with dissolving meringue. She hadn't heard Lemuel close the cabinet door. He had appeared beside her without a noise. She could sense the big grin that he wore between his ears. Her eyes watered as she swallowed the meringue in one go.

'A pan-dimensional armillary clock,' clarified Lemuel and he laughed in the shrill, abrupt way that punctuated his speech. He had bent down to where Chess was looking, his face close to hers. 'It is the only clock that matters,' he whispered and then he straightened up. 'Tick tock.' He laughed before walking to the ebony table in front of the tall windows.

'Over here. No time to watch time.' He laughed again as if he found what he said extremely witty.

It's a funny-looking clock, thought Chess, swirling her tongue round the inside of her mouth to wash away the remaining, gritty specks of sugar. Then she joined Lemuel Sprazkin at the table. He had taken off his coat and hung it over the back of one of the chairs and was opening the lid of a slim grey plastic box. Chess sat down in the chair opposite and squinted in the sunlight.

'Do you work for the Committee?' she asked.

Without looking up, Lemuel said, 'Yes.' He removed a glass ampoule, no longer than a bullet, from inside the plastic box and he held it up to the sunlight, inspecting it with one eye bulging and the other eye shut.

'Have you always worked for the Committee?' asked Chess, resting her forearms on the table top.

'What a strange question,' said Lemuel, without actually answering it.

'What do you do for them?'

'Science.'

'You're a scientist?'

'Yes.'

'That's good,' said Chess who had never had a conversation with a scientist before and was unsure of what to say.

'Good?' laughed Lemuel, who swivelled his open eye in Chess's direction. 'That rather depends on the science.'

'Why? Is there bad science?' asked Chess.

'Oh yes. Most definitely, most emphatically, yes.' Lemuel sat down and grasped Chess's wrist with his free hand. She tried to pull her arm back but Lemuel held it tight. 'Very beautiful science, very powerful science, but very, very bad.'

Chess hesitated before asking, 'What kind of science do you do?'

Lemuel's head was bent over her thin wrist, admiring it. He uncurled his fingers from the translucent skin and ran their black tips along it. Chess could see the lobes of his brain and the delicate machinery working inside it.

'I try very hard to do good science,' said Lemuel. He was speaking unusually slowly and breathing unusually deeply. 'But it is very, very difficult to be good *all* the time.'

Chess saw the muscles in his jaw clenching. He stamped

his foot which made her jump in her chair. Then he looked up and laughed and he patted Chess's wrist. 'Now, for your blood.'

He pushed up the sleeve of her pullover and raised the hand with the ampoule high above the table. 'I only want a speck, a droplet, a mere cluster of cells. Such precious fluid.' He patted her wrist again and said, 'We are so close, you and I.'

Chess's eyes were trained on the glass capsule, pinched between Lemuel's forefinger and thumb.

'This won't hurt,' he assured her and she saw him squeeze the ampoule ever so slightly. When he did so, a needle of glass protruded downwards from its body. He kept squeezing, minutely, and the glass needle grew longer and longer but thinner and thinner until the tip extended to no more than a few millimetres above her forearm and was no thicker than a hair.

'You must keep absolutely still,' explained Lemuel. He leant over her arm, his hand still high above his own head. 'We must guide this in through a suitable pore.' He was concentrating so hard he barely breathed.

Chess saw the point of the needle dip into her skin. 'Aha,' chuckled Lemuel. 'We're in.'

As he said this, Chess felt a tickling sensation under the skin of her forearm. It was like having butterflies but in her arm rather than her stomach. Lemuel was rolling the ampoule slightly between finger and thumb.

'We need the right blood vessel. No sudden movements now. If the tip snapped off it would enter your blood stream, find your heart and pierce it. You would die.' He grinned at her, a humourless skull-like rictus. 'None of us want that to happen.'

Chess tried so hard to stay still that she started to tremble.

'Steady now,' said Lemuel. 'Steady. There!' A tinkle of laughter. 'We have it.'

For a moment, Chess saw the whole length of the needle flash red and then Lemuel relaxed his forefinger and thumb and the glass needle retracted into the ampoule instantaneously. He put it back inside the small plastic box, snapping the lid shut.

'Wonderful. A minute quantity of your blood has been taken and sealed immediately and perfectly, awaiting further analysis.' He tapped the top of the box with his finger. 'I designed this. I designed it for you, Chess. All that work, just to take a sample of your blood.'

'Thank you,' said Chess, rubbing her arm where the needle had entered it although there was no mark and no discomfort.

Lemuel waved his hand and laughed politely. 'Oh, don't thank me, Chess.' The whole of the bottom half of his face became a smile. 'You can't imagine what a pleasure this has been.'

'Thank you,' said Chess again, wishing she would stop saying "thank you" and wondering why Lemuel was becoming so excited.

'You know, if I wasn't in control of my faculties I don't know what I might do.' He began to laugh. The laughter broke up from his chest and out of his mouth in staccato bursts. He laughed so hard that there were tears in his eyes and then Chess thought that his eyes didn't look like they were laughing at all.

Why are you so unhappy? wondered Chess.

Lemuel banged both his fists on the table, stamped both of his slippered feet on the floor and shook his head from side to side with a groan. Then he ran from the table to the right-hand door that was at the far end of the room. He yanked it open, bolted into the room beyond and slammed the door shut behind him. Chess heard a key rattle in the lock.

She remained in the high-backed chair with her hands resting on the ebony table, not sure what she should do now. The sun poured in through the window, making her left side shine whilst her right side stayed in shadow. The sun wasn't hot. In fact, Chess felt quite cold.

There was a droning hum from the room in which Lemuel had locked himself. Chess didn't recognize the noise. She stood up with the idea that she might recognize it if she was closer to it but the noise which followed rooted her where she stood. It was a screeching electric whine; the kind made by circular saws that cut through concrete on building sites. It was so loud and so raw that it didn't just claw her ears; she could feel it in her joints and at the roots of her teeth. She pressed the heels of her palms against her ears to block it out but then it stopped. The far door swung open and Lemuel Sprazkin staggered out, unsteady on his feet as if he was drunk.

'Don't be alarmed,' he announced gaily. 'It's just my therapy. That's what I call it.' As he approached, Chess could see that now his eyes were bloodshot. 'It keeps me on the straight and narrow when I feel myself slipping: keeps my emotional and rational faculties healthy. Recalibrates my cognitive functions.' A peal of laughter. 'My *cog*-nitive functions.' More laughter. '*Cog*-nitive functions. Do you see?'

Chess was still standing. 'Shouldn't I go now?' she asked. She wanted to go.

'Definitely not,' declared Lemuel, taking the silver tray from the half-table and carrying it across to the French window. 'After all the hard work, we must refresh ourselves.' He put the tray down noisily, the stopper rattling in the neck of the decanter and the crystal glass rocking uncertainly. Two of the meringues toppled from the pile.

Lemuel threw himself into the chair opposite Chess, tossing one arm of billowing silk over the chair back and crossing his legs. He gestured with his free arm. 'Please, sit down.'

Chess looked at the door through which she had entered.

'Sit down,' repeated Lemuel firmly.

Chess sat.

'Tell me, Chess,' inquired Lemuel, 'do you enjoy Marsala wine?'

'I've never had it,' replied Chess.

'Never?'

Chess shook her head.

Lemuel smacked his dark lips and pulled the stopper out of the decanter. He poured a liberal measure of the toffee-coloured liquid into the crystal goblet. 'For all the science in all the worlds,' he mused, 'nothing equals humans' capacity to create pleasure.' He replaced the stopper and swirled the liquid in the goblet. It flickered yellow and then tan in the sunlight and Chess caught the scent of yeast and honey. 'I suppose it comes of having such short spans of life,' he surmised and he held the goblet towards Chess.

'No thank you,' she said. 'I don't drink alcohol.'

'Quite right,' agreed Lemuel. 'Alcohol, along with a desire for wealth and the relentless pursuit of pleasure has been the greatest undoing of your species.' He took a meringue from the pile, holding it in the same way that he had held the glass ampoule, and dipped it into the liquid in the goblet. 'I love it like this,' he said.

'You've got a sweet tooth,' remarked Chess.

'I've got a whole set of them,' said Lemuel and he grinned so that she could see them all. Then he extended his arm, holding the meringue to her lips. 'It is very, very sweet and very delicious,' he assured her.

Chess could smell sugar and honey and what she thought was flowers although she had never been close to many real flowers. It was a warm smell and a happy smell. Lemuel's grey eyes and beady pupils were fixed on her. She closed her eyes and opened her mouth.

'Lemuel!' It was Ethel. Chess thought she sounded angry and worried and she opened her eyes immediately. 'What are you doing?'

'Getting to know our guest,' explained Lemuel, perfectly calm. He set down the meringue and patted the grey box which was on the table, next to the silver tray. 'I have the blood sample.'

'You were meant to wait for me.'

Lemuel laughed. 'I just couldn't wait. I couldn't help

myself.' Chess thought that if he meant to sound apologetic he didn't.

'What have you given her to eat? To drink?'

'Nothing.' He looked across to Chess. 'Have I?'

Chess shook her head and remembered the taste of the meringue she had stolen.

'Although,' added Lemuel, 'I can offer her what I wish.' His eyes narrowed and all humour deserted his face. 'Ah, I see. You no longer trust me. I understand.' He looked at Chess. 'It is natural that old allegiances should be expected to weigh heavy at a time like this.'

'Nonsense,' said Ethel, 'I am just being . . .'

'Cautious?' suggested Lemuel.

'Do you blame me?' asked Ethel.

Lemuel laughed loudly. It was a hollow laugh and it made Chess uncomfortable.

'They need you downstairs, Lemuel,' said Ethel. 'Our agent has returned. She is in the operating theatre.'

'Dead?' asked Lemuel.

'Obviously.'

'Her skin is still intact? Undamaged?'

'Yes.'

Lemuel pulled on his frock-coat and marched to the door. 'Do not insult me, Mevrad,' he said as he passed her. 'We all have our limits.' He dropped the plastic box containing the blood sample into Ethel's palm. 'And mine are a good deal more unstable than most.' He laughed coldly and his laugh followed him down the corridor.

CHAPTER 12

With a scrape of chair legs, Chess stood up. She walked over to Ethel feeling guilty although she couldn't think of anything she had done wrong, unless stealing the meringue was wrong. But stealing a meringue didn't explain the tightness of Ethel's shrivelled lips or the frown that creased the grey skin of her forehead.

'What?' asked Chess.

Ethel shook her head and sighed. 'Your brothers don't seem to be able to stick with you, my love, and you don't seem to be able to stick with them.'

Chess shrugged. Ethel said, 'There are so many things that could go wrong right now. I can't help worrying.' She placed a cold, leathery hand on Chess's warm, soft cheek.

Chess looked back to the ebony table, silver-edged in the sunlight. 'Who is Lemuel?' she asked.

'*What* is Lemuel?' Ethel corrected her. 'Lemuel Sprazkin is a warp.'

Chess looked down at Ethel who was a little bit shorter than she was and raised her eyebrows in a way that showed that she had no idea what a warp was.

Ethel continued. 'Warps are genetically-engineered, chemically-enhanced intelligences. They are grown by the Twisted Symmetry.'

Chess's eyes widened. 'Why's he here?'

'It's all right,' Ethel assured her. 'He's on our side. He is here to help us.'

Chess didn't like the uncomfortable silence which followed so she asked, 'Was he grown, like a plant?'

'In a way,' said Ethel. 'Certainly more like a plant than an animal. But warps are made of flesh and blood.'

'What are they for?'

'The growing process is carefully controlled to produce an intelligence that is superior to any normal intelligence. This means that the warps can design the technology that the Symmetry need. They can design the most extraordinary devices and processes. But like everything that the Twisted Symmetry does, these devices and processes have one purpose.'

'Which is?'

'Pain, dear. The Twisted Symmetry feed on pain. They obtain energy from it.'

Chess thought about this and then asked, 'So why is he helping the Committee?'

'Lemuel Sprazkin was a primary warp; one of the Symmetry's highest intelligences. But he made a terrible enemy. He conducted an experiment on one of the Symmetry's most powerful and most bloodthirsty commanders. The experiment went wrong, as experiments are prone to do. Lemuel found he had no alternative but to desert the Twisted Symmetry if he wanted to escape the horrible revenge that his new enemy would doubtless have inflicted upon him. So he had to switch sides. He had to come to us, my love. But to do that, he had to change himself.'

Chess pictured Lemuel's brain and the machinery that she had seen working inside it. 'Is that why he has a weird head?'

'Yes dear, but it's not weird. It's very clever. Very logical. Lemuel knew that he could not survive with us unless he changed. Remember, he had been grown to be a warp. That meant that his mind was a cunning, treacherous thing, hungry for pain. So he had to change the way his mind worked.'

'You mean he had to become good?'

'That's a good way of putting it. He had to design a way of being good if he wanted to survive. And that's what he did. He can control his thoughts and emotions, directly, by re-calibrating his brain.'

Chess looked back down the long room to one of the doors at the far end; the door from which the noises had come. 'In there?' she asked, pointing. Ethel nodded. 'He sticks something into his brain to make himself be good?'

'Whenever he feels himself going wrong,' explained Ethel. Chess shuddered. 'It's horrible.'

'Not really, dear. He's just doing what a lot of people do, but in his case he does it with a machine and doesn't leave it to chance. Lemuel *has* to be good if he wants to survive.' Ethel chuckled. 'Funny, really; most people try to be good because they think they should but Lemuel does it because he has to. And it's just as well he does. His intelligence, his inventions have assisted the Committee very much.' Ethel looked into Chess's face. 'His designs have been essential.'

'But is he safe?' asked Chess.

Ethel sighed. 'Do you want the truth, dear?'

'Yes.'

'I don't know. That's the truth.' When Chess asked nothing more, Ethel said, 'Let's find your brothers, shall we?'

'Where are they?'

'Eating, of course.'

Chess was used to the dim, dank corridors of Committee HQ but she was sorry to leave the room full of sunlight. The bright doorway was behind her now, receding, and Ethel was taking her to the lift, sandals slapping on the cold floor. Chess's foot wasn't aching so much but the bandage was irritating because it was like walking on a lump constantly. As they walked, her thoughts drifted from her foot to her mouth, where a faint aftertaste of sugar lingered at the edge of her tongue.

Chess followed Ethel in silence until they had descended in the lift and entered a corridor that looked like the one which led to the storage tanks. As the lift hummed back upwards, Chess enquired, 'Why did you ask Lemuel if he'd given me anything to eat?'

'Because I'm taking no risks, dear. A devious genius like Lemuel is capable of a good deal of harm through something as innocent as, say, a meringue.'

Chess's guts lurched and then churned although she kept walking. 'But it doesn't mean that something bad would happen if I had eaten something like a meringue, does it?'

Ethel stopped by a set of double doors and looked at her. 'If we can trust him there is nothing to worry about.'

'You always say to trust no one,' muttered Chess gloomily.

'Well, there's your answer, dear. Are you all right? You look very pale.'

'I'm just hungry,' lied Chess, who suddenly felt very sick. Whether it was because of the meringue or because she was worrying about the meringue she didn't know.

'Then we've come to the right place,' said Ethel cheerily, and she led Chess through the double doors.

They entered a refectory where trestle tables were organized in rows beneath a low stone roof. A serving counter ran the length of one wall. On the other side of this counter was the clatter and competing smells of a large kitchen. There were thirty tables in the refectory and people were sitting at five of them.

Four of these tables were at one end of the room and their benches were occupied by men and women from the night patrols. On the floor around them were piled helmets and body armour, and utility belts that were laden with torches, water bottles, ammunition pouches and sheathed knives. Chess couldn't see any guns. Antennae bristled out of these piles like sticks and Chess could hear the crackle of transmissions from radios buried within the equipment.

The sharp bursts of radio speech mixed with the murmuring from the tables. The men and women talked quietly, relaxed, comfortable with each other; tired faces rested on palms and elbows leant on the tables. They drank slowly from steaming mugs that were filled with coffee strong enough for Chess to smell at the doorway.

At the other end of the room sat Box and Splinter. Chess was so glad to see them that she ran straight across to them.

She was watched by the night patrols, silent, dark eyes cool through the steaming coffee.

'You've had a lot,' said Chess, surveying the array of plates smeared with egg yolk, scattered with toast crumbs and dashed with tomato ketchup.

Box burped brazenly and guzzled the remaining wedge of toast. 'Always room for a bit more,' he said, licking his fingers. When Ethel appeared at Chess's shoulder he coughed to clear his throat. 'Sorry.'

'For what?' asked Chess.

'We shouldn't of left you,' he admitted, eyes drooping like a dog's. 'Again.'

'That doesn't matter,' said Chess, who sat down and decided that her stomach wasn't feeling so queasy now. The familiar ache of hunger was returning.

'It matters to *her*,' said Splinter, glaring at Ethel.

'Who's *her*?' asked Ethel. 'The cat's mother?'

'You tell me,' replied Splinter.

'There's no need to get all prickly, dear. Just because I gave you a ticking off for putting your belly before your sister.'

Chess noted a quick exchange of glances between Box and Splinter. Box raised his eyebrows slightly and nodded towards his brother. Splinter chewed his lip for a moment as if coming to a decision and then he pulled his hand out of his morning coat and slammed it down on the table top.

'Explain that, Ethel,' he demanded, revealing the dictaphone.

Ethel sighed and shook her head and she laughed weakly. 'You are very good, my love; very good at being bad.'

'I know what you didn't want us to hear,' announced

Splinter. He was talking more loudly than was normal for him and Chess noticed eyes glancing across from the tables at the other end of the refectory.

'I know that this computer brain is deadly to touch, I know that the air surrounding it will poison us and now I *know*,' Splinter was shouting now and his pale face was shot with white blotches of fury, 'I *know* that there *is* a squealer. The Twisted Symmetry have got someone inside Committee HQ and you don't want anyone to know.'

Splinter was on his feet, leaning towards Ethel with his knuckles resting on the table. There was a tiny fleck of spit on his chin and he rubbed it away brusquely with the back of his hand. On the other side of the room a bench screeched over stone. The tread of boots approached.

Ethel held up her hand, palm open. 'It's all right, sergeant,' she said quietly. 'Nothing to worry about. We're just having a disagreement.' The boots returned to the other side of the room.

'Have you told *her* who the double agent is?' asked Splinter, quietly now and indicating Chess. 'Because if you'd have been straight with us, this morning wouldn't have happened. Maybe we would have been careful to stick together, and maybe she wouldn't have gone off with Lemuel Sprazkin.'

'Is he the squealer?' gasped Chess, wide-eyed. 'Definitely?'

Splinter nodded and now the hint of a smile danced at the corners of his mouth.

'And Ethel knew?'

'Oh yes,' said Splinter triumphantly, 'she knew all right.'

Chess didn't see his satisfied grin because she was staring at Ethel in disbelief. 'You told me he was safe,' she cried.

'I said I didn't know,' explained Ethel defensively.

'She knows all right, according to this,' alleged Splinter, pointing to the dictaphone.

'I have *never* said that Lemuel Sprazkin betrayed us,' said Ethel icily and she raised a waxy pink finger to point at Splinter. 'Be careful, my love. In the circumstances, you are quite entitled to be angry with me but you are not entitled to tell lies. Telling lies to stir up trouble is dangerous, particularly when you obtain such obvious pleasure from it. It is a bad sign, Splinter. Be very, very careful. Do you understand?'

Splinter tried to outstare Ethel but he might as well have tried to outstare a basilisk. He sat back down and clenched his fists under the table. 'Yes,' he said and the word hissed from his lips like acid.

Ethel's faced softened and she sat down too. 'There are reasons for everything I do, my loves,' she said. 'It does appear that somebody here is feeding information to the Twisted Symmetry; information about you. And Lemuel Sprazkin is the obvious suspect though we can't be sure about him. Not yet. But I am on the same side as you, you know.' When Splinter didn't look convinced she asked, 'What would have happened to you if I hadn't been at the detention unit?'

'We'd have been slabbed,' admitted Box.

'Slabbed?' queried Ethel.

'On the slab; the mortuary slab,' explained Splinter. 'Dead.'

'Very picturesque, dear,' said Ethel. She took off her spectacles, wiped the lenses with the hem of her pleated skirt and put them back on. They slid the short distance to the tip of her nose and she looked at Chess, Box and Splinter over their rims. 'Trust no one, my loves, but you must trust me.'

Splinter made a final protest. 'Why have we got to steal something that is impossible to steal? Impossible to steal and live, that is.'

'It isn't impossible.'

'Yeah, I know, apparently *she* can touch it,' he said, jerking his head at Chess. 'But we'll all be poisoned by the air round the brain, if the Twisted Symmetry don't get us first.'

'I have planned this carefully, Splinter. It can be done. And there have been sacrifices to make this possible, my love. Painful sacrifices.' Ethel thought for a moment and then asked, 'Do grizzly scenes make you feel ill? Have you got strong stomachs?'

'I've got an empty stomach,' grumbled Chess, dejected.

'Fly head doesn't have a stomach, he's got a bin bag,' said Splinter.

'What kind of grizzly scene?' asked Box.

'Don't eat anything just yet, dear,' Ethel said to Chess, patting her hand. 'Better to watch what I'm going to show you with that stomach empty.' She stood up. 'Come with me.'

Box looked at Ethel dubiously. 'Whenever you say that, something weird happens.' But he followed her all the same.

Chess knew that Ethel was taking them to the operating theatre before they had stopped at the plate glass window that looked into it. This time the room was not in darkness. White light glared mercilessly from the lamps that hung in a cluster from the ceiling, illuminating the operating table across which a body was lying. A green sheet covered the whole of the body except for one leg which was bare.

Around the table stood three figures. Two of them wore gowns and face masks like surgeons. The third wore a long black frock-coat and a sharp, thin smile. A scalpel glinted between his gloved fingers. He bent over the prone body and prodded its exposed thigh with a rigid finger. The surgical lamps reflected in a small square of glass set in the top of the figure's head.

'What is that?' spat Splinter, disgusted.

'That's Lemuel Sprazkin,' said Chess softly.

'Of course,' considered Splinter. 'The traitor.'

'Funny you should use that word,' said Ethel. 'That's what the Twisted Symmetry call him.'

'He looks evil,' said Box.

'You're very impressed by appearances, aren't you, dear?' observed Ethel.

The scalpel flashed and set to work. Chess closed her eyes but Splinter's remained wide open.

'He's got a funny sort of coat,' said Box.

'It isn't a coat,' said Ethel.

'It looks like a coat,' insisted Box.

'Appearances, appearances,' tutted Ethel. 'It isn't a coat, it's a computer. Something Lemuel designed before he came to us. The warps do that; design things that improve their already remarkable abilities. That coat, as you call it, is a fully integrated bio-supercomputer. When he wears it, it functions like an extension of his brain.'

'Is it very powerful?' asked Splinter, not taking his eyes

from the dark line the scalpel had scored up the exposed thigh.

'Oh yes,' said Ethel. 'Huge memory and capable of three quadraflops.'

'Quadraflops?' asked Splinter.

'Sounds like a bad way of falling down,' quipped Box and he pretended to slip over. 'Look,' he laughed. 'I've quadraflopped.'

Nobody else laughed, and Ethel looked at Box as if he was a very silly boy indeed. 'Three quadraflops means that the computer can do a lot of things at once, if you subscribe to that system of measurement. Liquid metal cooled as well; see all the silver lines? They dissipate the heat the computer generates.'

'Wow,' said Box, serious.

'Yes, dear. "Wow" just about sums it up.'

'But the computer brain that we've got to steal from,' asked Splinter. 'Is that even more powerful?'

'Much more powerful, my love. The cerebral torus can calculate the probability of events happening across multiple universes. It makes Lemuel's coat look like an abacus.'

'Wow,' mouthed Splinter, begrudgingly impressed.

Chess hazarded a glimpse through one eye and saw Lemuel guiding the scalpel around the top of the thigh. 'What's he doing,' she gasped, closing her eye. Through the glass there was absolutely no noise but she could imagine little sucking noises as the blade slit flesh.

'This agent died for you,' said Ethel. Chess couldn't tell whether Ethel meant for her in particular or for all of them but she didn't care. She didn't like what was happening on the other side of the glass.

'It hasn't been easy to discover the layout of the complex where the Twisted Symmetry keep the cerebral torus,' Ethel was saying. 'It is well guarded with anti-surveillance devices that have prevented us from spying on them with technology. Spy technology cannot penetrate the complex and it cannot operate inside it. Just like here in fact; we have anti-spy measures in place. But it has been vital to investigate the layout of the complex if you are to be able to steal the program and escape with it. So we have had to use agents.' Ethel paused. 'No agent has returned to us alive.'

Lemuel shifted his position and began to draw the scalpel down the inside of the thigh. Splinter watched, fascinated. The thigh was a slightly yellow colour, like old wax. It appeared that a rectangle was being cut across the front and round the side. No blood came out of it. He knew that that was because this was a dead body.

'But the body of every agent who has entered the complex has been returned to us; after the Symmetry have finished with it.'

'So this agent was on a suicide mission?' asked Splinter. He resisted adding the words 'like us'.

'She didn't see it that way, dear,' replied Ethel. 'She had her reasons for volunteering.'

'I can't think of any,' said Splinter with a snort.

'You haven't seen someone you love destroyed by the Symmetry.'

'Love?' ridiculed Splinter. 'Love is stupid. It doesn't do anything.'

'Our agent was willing to make this sacrifice if it meant we come one step closer to defeating the enemy,' said Ethel. 'She had sufficient poison to make sure she was dead before the enemy had captured her.'

'But what was the point of dying like that?' demanded Chess, turning round so that her back was to the window.

'The enemy's practice of returning our dead agents to us will be their undoing, my love.' Ethel put a hand in her skirt pocket and pulled out something that looked very much like a cheap biro. They all looked at it, even Splinter.

Box opened his mouth to say that it looked like a pen and then, realizing that Ethel was bound to tell him that it wasn't what it looked like, he said nothing. But his mouth remained open.

'This is a scrip,' said Ethel. 'It is a small laser. It can be used to write inside skin.' She held the flat nib against the mottled back of her hand. 'If I activate it now, a fine beam of light would penetrate the thickness of my skin and burn its inner surface. It would burn it wherever I moved it.'

'So you can draw or write on the inside of your skin?' guessed Splinter. 'Like it was a piece of paper?'

'Correct,' nodded Ethel. 'Although I always think of it as a piece of parchment. When employed by an agent trained in its use it can record information very clearly. It is most effective to draw a map.'

'Did Lemuel design it?' asked Chess.

'Yes, dear. This agent was tasked with penetrating the Twisted Symmetry's complex and then mapping the routes into and away from the cerebral torus. The plan was for her to map them around the top of her left thigh. Lemuel is removing the skin now and then it will be treated to preserve it. The agents have to write the wrong way round for us to be able to read on the inside of their skin. Very clever.'

Even Chess turned round to look back through the window. Lemuel was working the scalpel back across the front of the thigh to the place above the knee where the first incision had been made.

'Our map should be on the inside of that large flap of skin. A map like that is called a dermacart, you know.' Ethel clicked a knob at the top of the scrip and dropped it on the floor. Chess saw its plastic casing shimmer wet as if it was sweating and then the plastic began to bubble.

'The scrip contains a tiny vial filled with acid. Cracking open the vial releases the acid and, hey presto, the scrip dissolves.' A tiny pool of liquid hissed and bubbled on the floor where the scrip had landed. 'No one would know what has happened. All evidence has been destroyed.' Then Ethel pointed through the window. 'Until the dermacart is revealed.'

Chess, Box and Splinter looked from the congealed fluid, still spitting on the floor, to the operating table. Using both gloved hands, Lemuel Sprazkin was peeling back the skin from the agent's thigh whilst one of his assistants aided with a long, flanged probe.

Chess screwed up her face.

'Aren't you glad you skipped the bacon and eggs, my love?'

'Don't you mind what's happening to her?' insisted Chess.

'This was her choice,' Ethel replied. 'It was necessary.'

'You're not a sweet old lady at all, are you?' said Box.

Ethel looked at him with eyes that were cracked by tiny

blood vessels. She smiled. She didn't have to remind him that things are not always as they seem because Box shook his head and said, 'I know, I know,' before she could speak.

Under a cold, white sky, an old lady sat on a bench in a park at the edge of the city. The bench was perched on the top of a hill, high enough to look back across the grid of glass and concrete which climbed so high and spread so wide that even the vast sweep of the river was impossible to see. The old lady and the bench were ink black against the blank sky.

The old lady was knitting and the clicking of her needles chipped the high silence of the hill. She worked fast and with determination. As she worked, a figure climbed the grey tarmac track that cut up the grass slope, leaning forwards slightly. The needles clicked and the old lady unwound the ball of wool in her lap until the figure had crested the hill, crossed to the wooden bench and sat beside her.

She put down her needles and pulled a tatty pink shawl around her. The man who sat beside her stuck out his brown corduroy-trousered legs and rested a sandwich bag full of bread crumbs on his lap. His cheeks glowed as red as his sweater.

The old lady looked askance at the sandwich bag. 'Were you expecting ducks, Captain Riley?' she asked.

The man laughed. 'I wanted to look as if I was, Ethel.'

'Ducks, on a hill, at the edge of the city and no pond in sight. Most unlikely.' Ethel snorted and wiped her nose with the tasselled edge of her shawl. Then she said, 'It is definitely the girl. We have tested her blood. The level of amarantium is uniquely high. I knew it was her anyway; to me she was unmistakable.'

The man nodded.

'So far, so good,' continued Ethel. 'But we have a problem.'

'A problem,' echoed Captain Riley and he raised his eyebrows.

'The Committee has been infiltrated,' said Ethel. 'The Twisted Symmetry suspect this is the girl. It seems that we have a double agent; an enemy spy amongst us. That's why we have to meet like this; away from eavesdroppers.'

Captain Riley looked up at the wide sky thoughtfully. 'Who?'

Ethel shrugged. 'Lemuel Sprazkin is the obvious suspect. But no one is beyond suspicion.'

'Professor Breslaw?' asked Riley.

'Everyone has their limits, their weaknesses, Captain. Even the Professor.'

'I can't see why the Professor would help the Twisted Symmetry.'

'Joachim Breslaw is dying and he doesn't want to. He has kept himself alive for decades but his ingenuity is almost exhausted. Temptation comes easily to a man in Professor Breslaw's position and the Twisted Symmetry are masters of that subtle art. People will do bad things for the promise of more life.' Ethel laughed cheerlessly. 'I have been around long enough to see that better than most.'

'But you are going ahead with the mission anyway?'

'Of course. We have no choice.' Ethel looked up and down

Captain Riley's athletic figure which was reclining with surprising comfort on the bench.

'You manage to look very . . .' she selected the most suitable word, '. . . conventional, my dear.'

'Good. The Charitable Operations Executive doesn't exist, officially. We can't draw attention to ourselves.' Riley laughed softly. 'All the effort; we joke about it, you know. The Committee select the best from the police and the armed forces, from every country, and after all the graft we can't tell anyone.'

'They wouldn't believe you if you did, Captain. I know. I've spent three days with the Tuesdays and they still think I'm making it all up.' She inspected her peeling finger nails. 'People never see what they don't expect to see and if they do see it, they don't believe it. It's just as well, I suppose. Can you imagine the pandemonium if people really knew what went on? You're a police officer, aren't you?'

'Officially.'

'They call you "the crashers". Did you know that?'

'Yes,' said Riley.

'Oh,' said Ethel. 'I didn't. Always new things to learn.' Then she clasped her hands, fixed her eyes on the far horizon and said, 'I'm sending them in early.'

'How early?'

'This evening.'

Captain Riley was a professional. He did not overreact. His surprise was registered by a short silence. Then he said, 'They won't be ready, Ethel. They need several weeks of treatment to prepare them for the atmosphere inside the complex. If you send them in now they will not be able to breathe.' He spoke in a calm, matter-of-fact way. 'Send them in now and they won't have a hope.'

'I have to send them in now. And there is an alternative to the treatment.'

Captain Riley's green eyes narrowed. 'The only alternative would be to use . . .'

'Roaches, Captain. Yes.'

'You can't, Ethel. It takes months of training to use a roach.'

'The Tuesdays are clever and adaptable and tough,' said Ethel.

'That's one way of putting it,' observed Riley, wryly. 'I've checked their criminal records; they've been a constant source of trouble for years, and very difficult to catch.'

'Excellent,' said Ethel. 'They have many talents; they just haven't been able to use them properly, until now. And they have lived difficult lives, Captain. They will be able to withstand more than you think.'

'Maybe so, but still, Ethel, roaches? It's bad science; to have one fixed to your face, to have its membranes in your nose, your mouth, your eyes?' Captain Riley shook his head. 'I hate warp technology.'

'I'm glad to hear it,' said Ethel. 'But we don't have months and we don't have weeks. We have to act now and I'll tell you why. Whoever is feeding our secrets to the Twisted Symmetry will be expecting the Tuesdays to be sent into the complex in about two weeks time, because I have told everyone that it will take two weeks of praetorisone injections to immunize Chess and her brothers against the poisonous atmosphere around the brain. Therefore the enemy won't be expecting Chess yet. If I can take the Tuesdays in now, without telling anyone, and if they can complete the mission swiftly, we can get them in and out without the Symmetry being warned by the double agent, whoever it is.'

Riley nodded. 'OK. How will you get them in?'

'Through the vortex.'

'And what about getting them out?'

'That's where I need the Charitable Operations Executive. I will arrange a rendezvous with the Tuesdays, somewhere close to the complex. They'll meet me there when the mission has been completed, at a time I give them. But before they meet me, I'll let everyone know about the rendezvous and the time that Chess, Box and Splinter will be there. Of course, I shan't say where they've been. I'll let it slip that I sent them on an errand.'

'In the dead of night?' questioned Riley.

'These aren't carol singers, Captain Riley. These are the Tuesdays. They do things in the dead of night.'

'An errand to do what?'

'I don't know,' huffed Ethel irritably, 'I'll think of something nearer the time. Anyway, that's not the point. What matters is this: our double agent will inform his masters of where Chess will be and when she'll be there and the Twisted Symmetry will come for her. But it is we who shall be waiting for them. We recover our thieves and their vital loot, we shall ambush and neutralize the enemy units that attend and we shall also discover the identity of our double agent. I will ensure that Lemuel Sprazkin and Joachim Breslaw are both with me at the rendezvous.'

'You plan to kill three birds with one stone?'

'That's one way of putting it, Captain.'

'All right,' said Riley, legs outstretched and re-crossing his ankles. 'My orders. Where, when and what do you need?'

'The Valley Stadium dog track, four a.m. tomorrow morning, three close quarter battle teams, four snipers and a helicopter gunship on standby.' Ethel paused and sucked her lower lip thoughtfully. 'I think perhaps another two close quarter battle teams in reserve: the more CQBs the better. The enemy won't attend in numbers because they will only expect Chess and her brothers but they won't be taking any chances either.'

'It will be difficult to get a helicopter gunship at such short notice, Ethel,' said Riley. 'We aren't meant to draw attention to ourselves. The COE doesn't exist, officially, remember?'

Ethel patted him on the hand. 'See what you can do, Captain, there's a dear.'

Captain Riley stood up, the sandwich bag full of breadcrumbs still in his hand.

'Snipers on the stadium towers, arcs of fire covering the routes in and out?' he asked.

'Just the ticket.' Ethel smiled and picked up her knitting needles. 'Meet me in the commentary box at four-thirty a.m. Everyone else in position from four a.m. I'll tell the Tuesdays to meet us there just before dawn, at five. We can expect the enemy to arrive at about the same time.'

'Will the children know about the COE? That this will be an ambush as well as a rescue operation?'

'They won't know anything about this arrangement. They will be expecting to meet only me.'

'This won't be easy.'

'Of course it won't. Nothing this important ever is.'

'We are playing for high stakes, aren't we, Ethel?'

'You have no idea how high,' said Ethel.

'Why is the girl so important?'

'Do you need to know that or is that just curiosity getting the better of you?' asked Ethel, wagging a knitting needle at him.

Riley smiled. 'Curiosity.'

'The time will come when everything will depend on Chess. Everything.'

Captain Riley nodded and turned to go but after taking only three steps he stopped and looked back at Ethel. 'How do you know you can trust *me*?' he asked.

'I don't trust anyone, Captain, but if I did, you'd be one of the few.'

'But why?'

Ethel rested her needles on her lap again. 'You know what the Twisted Symmetry do to children?'

'I've heard.'

'And you have children, Captain?'

'Yes. Two.'

'Do you love them?'

'Yes. I'd die for them.'

'Well, there's your answer.' Then Ethel bent her head and resumed her knitting. The needles tapped out time and Captain Riley walked down the hill, a stick figure against the big, white sky.

CHAPTER 13

Unusually, Chess had woken before her brothers. Even though there was always a faint glow in the storage tank, she knew that it was early evening. She lay on her bunk, listening to Splinter's quiet breathing and Box's snoring. Ethel had brought them here after they had watched Lemuel remove the dermacart. She told them they were to catch up on sleep. 'There won't be much time for sleeping over the next twenty-four hours,' she had said, full of mystery but with no explanations.

Chess listened to her brothers sleeping for as long as she could bear before climbing down to the wooden floor and padding out of the tank.

She hadn't meant to go very far from the wall where the round, white doors of the storage tanks were set in a row like huge metal shields but when she saw Lemuel Sprazkin striding up a connecting corridor in his long frock-coat, she decided to move further away. He saw her and waved with a wiggle of his black-tipped fingers but Chess acted as if she hadn't noticed him and she quickened her pace, hurrying away from him and away from the storage tanks.

She had hoped that he wouldn't come looking for her but she heard him call her name. She didn't want to run but she kept imagining his glass head and the scalpel between his fingers and she could hear the sounds that came from behind the locked door and then she realized that she was running. Her legs took her along passageways, past the operating theatre now in darkness, echoing up the stairwell and through the doors and corridors that led back to the room with the desk and the lamp and the windows behind metal cages.

As she pushed the door open, Professor Breslaw spun his wheelchair to face her. 'Chess,' he said. 'This is a pleasant surprise.' Then he observed her flushed cheeks and he heard how she was panting. 'What are you running from?'

'I was lost. I got lost.'

Professor Breslaw studied her through his one eye and pulled the end of his ginger moustache, thoughtfully. 'You look a little frightened.'

'Getting lost here is frightening.'

'Hmm. Well, it shouldn't be. Anyway, young lady, you are quite safe with me,' and he displayed his thick yellow teeth in a smile that was fringed by his drooping moustache. 'Come in, Chess, and close the door. Even in my coat I feel the draughts.'

Chess did as he asked, relieved to have got away from Lemuel and to have found the Professor. He seemed warm and safe despite his strange accent and the way in which he smiled at her like a horse.

The final flush of evening failed to penetrate the grimy windows. The Professor and his desk were illuminated by the yellow light of the hanging lamp. The stacks of papers were balanced precariously or had collapsed in mounds across the top of the desk. A ledger with brown covers lay on the floor on top of a crumpled fan of documents.

Now that Chess was standing beside Professor Breslaw, she couldn't stop her eyes from travelling along the sprouting tubes that connected him to his wheelchair.

'What do you think of my web?' he asked her.

'I've never seen so many tubes in one person,' replied Chess in a way that she hoped sounded polite.

Professor Breslaw rattled a phlegmy chuckle. 'I am like a big fat spider, no? Waiting in my web whilst everything goes on around me.' He jabbed a sausage of a finger towards Chess's tummy. 'And you must be a juicy little fly.'

'Buzz,' said Chess absently, looking at the papers on the desk and then realizing that she couldn't read what was written on them. Whether that was because she wasn't very good at reading or because they were written in a foreign language, she couldn't tell. It looked as if it might be a foreign language.

'Ah, it is good to see someone so young and fresh,' said the Professor. 'We are all so old here.'

'You don't look all that old.'

'I am one hundred and forty-three.'

When Chess opened her eyes wide with amazement, he laughed loudly and then began to cough so hard that his face turned cherry red. The tubes quivered and shook as he spasmed. Chess hesitated between slapping his back or going for help. With all the tubes, she couldn't see where to slap him but she didn't want to leave the room either. Then the coughing fit passed and the Professor cleared his throat.

'You see, inside I am falling apart,' he explained. 'All of this,' and he gestured to the chair and the tubes, 'is to keep me going. I have built it. Much of what should happen inside my body now has to happen outside my body. You could say I am living inside out.'

'Can't Lemuel help you?' asked Chess.

Professor Breslaw looked at her darkly and then shook his head. 'There is good science, Chess and there is bad science. So, I make my choice.'

'You're like Lemuel. He tries to do good science.'

'I am nothing like Lemuel,' he warned her.

'How old is Ethel?' asked Chess, to change the subject and because she wanted to know.

'Ethel, Mevrad, is very old but her spirit is not like mine. Mevrad's spirit is powerful, too powerful even for time to destroy.'

Chess thought about what that actually meant. 'She can live forever?'

'Her spirit can. The bodies change but the spirit does not.'

It sounded unbelievable but the Professor looked as if he meant what he said. 'Why?' asked Chess. 'Why is she like that?'

With a shake of cables, Joachim shrugged. 'That is not a question that a scientist can answer, Chess. The simple fact remains that some spirits extend across great reaches of time. The bodies die but the spirit does not. You have met Mevrad's friends, Argus and Sekhmet?'

'Yeah. They're not like other cats.' Chess recalled what had happened in Ethel's kitchen.

'Not in the least. Do you know who Argus and Sekhmet really are?'

Chess shook her head.

'You must brush up on your ancient Greek and Egyptian mythology. Then you will know. But it comes to the same thing; some spirits are stronger than others. Some spirits persist.'

Chess was wondering what Greek and Egyptian mythology was and what it had to do with cats and how she was meant to 'brush up on it' when she couldn't even read properly, when Professor Breslaw sighed and said, 'I wish I had a spirit like that. I do not want to die.'

'What matters is to do good things.' Chess thought this sounded the right sort of thing to say.

'Very wise,' said Joachim, 'and very young. Just think what you could do with a very long life. Think what you can do with a life of hundreds of years. Or thousands.' Professor Breslaw sighed again, more deeply than before.

'That would be useful, I suppose,' admitted Chess, idly pushing the light that hung above the desk with the tips of her fingers. It swung gently, the cone of yellow light traversing the desk to and fro like a pendulum. She noticed the marks her fingers made on the lamp shade and she blew at the dust.

'Useful!' Professor Breslaw chuckled with a crackling throat. 'You could not sound as if it mattered less. To the young these things do not matter. You think you will live forever, no?'

'No,' said Chess. 'No, I don't.' She stopped fiddling with

the lamp shade and looked at the Professor. 'But is that possible?'

'Is what possible?'

'To live forever, even if you're not someone like Ethel?'

'It is possible,' rumbled Joachim gravely. 'It is possible to open the dimensions and stop time: to make space and time collapse. To make them collapse into infinite nothingness. Then there is no time and therefore there is no ageing.'

'That must be hard to do,' said Chess uncertainly.

The Professor's good eye bulged and his mouth twitched but he managed not to laugh out loud. 'To collapse time and space requires more energy than you could imagine. But to live suspended in the nothingness that remained?' He shrugged. 'To me, that would not be living at all, even if I had sufficient energy to do it.'

'Energy?' Chess knew the word but she wasn't sure what the Professor meant by it.

'Power, force, strength to change things in the world around us,' he explained.

'Has anyone done it?' she asked. 'Has anyone stopped time so that they can live forever?'

'No,' said Professor Breslaw and he leant out of his chair and caught Chess's fingers in his broad hand. 'But they are trying. They are trying very hard.' He spoke urgently, jutting his chin forwards and jerking his head. His moustache was caught in a fine spray of spit where it hung over his upper lip. 'What they require is energy.' Then he let go of her wrist and said, 'I want you to come with me. I want to show you my laboratory. I think you would enjoy it.' There was a whisker of a smile about his mouth.

'All right,' said Chess, who had nothing else to do and liked the way that the Professor talked to her; as if she wasn't stupid, as if she could understand things. That made her ask him about something she had heard but hadn't understood. 'What's the Eternal?'

Professor Breslaw growled to clear his throat. 'Where did you hear about the Eternal?' The smile had vanished.

By eavesdropping on you when we first got here, thought Chess, but she didn't want to admit that. She stood still and felt her mouth go dry and wondered whether she had said something wrong. Joachim Breslaw was glowering at her and Chess didn't know what was worse; the eyeball that bored into her or the dead lump of the patch.

'Chess!' It was Box. He had entered the room behind her. 'What are you doing?' He was out of breath and he sounded irate. 'Ethel nearly slabbed us, you idiot. You're not meant to go wandering off.'

'You better go, Chess,' said Professor Breslaw and his face softened. 'Maybe you see my laboratory another time?'

'OK,' agreed Chess, to please him. But why wouldn't you tell me about the Eternal? she thought. What has it got to do with me?

Perhaps he could read her thoughts through her eyes because he said, 'There will be a time for answers, but not now. Now, you have to go.' He nodded at her kindly and looked behind her towards Box. 'Go on, your brother is waiting for you.'

Chess couldn't think of anything more to say. She walked over to Box.

'What were you doing?' he whispered.

'Come on. Let's go,' said Chess.

They left Professor Breslaw sitting by his desk in the middle of the otherwise empty room, his web of cables edged yellow and black beneath the hanging lamp.

Ethel was waiting for them in the storage tank. She had a hessian bag by one foot, a briefcase by the other and a scowl on her face. The top of the bag was tied shut with string.

'What is wrong with you lot?' she demanded, exasperated. 'You're like sheep, wandering all over the place and getting yourselves into trouble.'

'I was lying here for ages, doing nothing,' protested Chess. 'I was bored.'

'Really, dear? Well, I've got something here that should make things a little less boring for you,' and Ethel nudged the bag with the side of her plastic shoe.

'What have you got in there?' asked Box suspiciously.

'Sit down, all of you,' and Ethel pointed to one of the bottom bunks. When Chess, Box and Splinter had jostled into position and Splinter and Box had stopped arguing about who was taking up the most space, Ethel grasped the rough brown bag around its neck and held it up.

'Tonight,' she said, 'you will enter the place where the Twisted Symmetry keep the cerebral torus.' The bag swung above her head. Chess's eyes switched between the bag and Ethel's spectacles which glinted a hellish yellow in the glow of the storage tank.

'Tonight!' Box was astonished. 'Look at these two, they're covered in cuts and bruises and bandages.'

'It has to be tonight,' Ethel said. 'You must go before anyone has time to warn the enemy that you are coming.'

'Because of the squealer?' confirmed Splinter, glancing up at Ethel coldly from under his pale eyebrows. He pulled the bandage from his wrist and rubbed the skin which was still pink but no longer tender.

'Tonight,' continued Ethel, with the bag still held high, 'you will cut a section out of the brain and bring it to me. You will do this without being captured and without coming to harm. I know that you can do this.'

'But how will we do it if we can't even breathe near to the brain?' asked Splinter.

Ethel looked up at the bag swinging slowly above her head. Three other pairs of eyes followed hers. 'Roaches, my loves. You can do it with roaches.'

'What are roaches?' asked Box.

'Like gas masks. Very effective gas masks. But living gas masks.'

'Gas masks aren't alive,' declared Splinter.

'These ones are,' said Ethel.

'I knew she'd say that,' Box whispered in Chess's ear.

Ethel set the bag by her feet. She bent down and pulled the string that was wound around its neck. It undid easily and the bag flopped to one side and gaped open like a loose mouth.

'Now, don't worry yourselves overmuch,' Ethel warned, sticking her hand into the sack. There was a clicking and clattering as if she was stirring pebbles or shells. 'This looks worse than it is and feels worse than it looks but it will keep you alive.'

She pulled her hand out of the bag and held up what she had taken so that everyone could see it.

'Ugh!' gasped Chess.

'That's revolting,' said Box.

It looked as if Ethel was holding a clump of soft black seaweed that was studded with strips of dark shell. Thin strands dangled from her fist and trailed limply to halfway down her forearm. She extended her arm towards the bunk and opened her hand to reveal a flat, black, leathery pad that filled her open palm. The strands were all connected to this central pad, jutting out of it like legs from the underbelly of a beetle.

'This is a roach,' explained Ethel. 'It is a genetically engineered organism, designed by the Twisted Symmetry but grown for us courtesy of Lemuel Sprazkin. At the moment it is in its resting state but when it is activated it will attach itself to your face and allow you to breathe, even in the most poisonous atmospheres.'

'If you think I'm putting that on my face, you must be mad,' announced Splinter.

Box dared to prod it with his forefinger. 'It's dry,' he said, a little hoarsely, 'and a bit rubbery.'

'It is a very noble little organism, my love. When you breathe through it, it absorbs all the poison into its own body tissue and only the good air enters your lungs; so it dies and you live. It's a kind of filter; a living filter. Until it dies, that is.'

'How does it work?' Splinter was disgusted, but curious.

'You put your mouth over its body.' Ethel pointed to the central pad that was resting on her open hand. 'The roach's legs will fasten themselves over the top of your head and round the sides. The body will spread itself over your face and quickly line the inside of your throat, your nostrils and cover your eyeballs with its own membranes, which, incidentally, means you won't be able to blink. It will stay like that until you press your hand over the front of your face; then it will let go immediately. If you don't remove it yourself, it will help you to breathe for precisely fifteen minutes before the poison gas kills it. Then it will drop off automatically.'

'But what if I still need it to breathe after it drops off?' asked Splinter.

'Then you would die soon afterwards, dear. But ten minutes is all you need if you do this properly; if you work as a team.' Ethel smiled at them cheerily and advanced with the roach outstretched. 'So then, who's first?'

The legs swung and clicked against one another loosely like bead necklaces. Chess grimaced as they dangled under her nose. She thought it looked as if the roach was lying on Ethel's hand, already spent, with its limbs drooping from exhaustion.

'I'll give it a go,' she was surprised to hear Box say. 'If it's the only way to survive where we're going, it's the only choice we have.'

'Good lad,' said Ethel, who sounded as surprised as Chess felt. 'You are a plucky creature, aren't you?'

'Not really,' muttered Splinter. 'Just a very stupid one. A stupid, fly head sort of creature.'

'Now, now, dear,' said Ethel to Splinter. 'You can go next if you want to. I've got enough for one each in here.'

'I don't mind waiting,' Splinter replied. 'I'll watch the plucky creature stick his head in the noose first.'

'Here goes,' said Box and he took a deep breath. Then he pressed his face onto Ethel's hand hard enough to push her arm down.

There was no hesitation. In a flash, the legs flicked up and wrapped themselves hard round Box's head. His hair bristled in clumps in-between the tight black limbs and the body squeezed itself over the front of his head, spreading across his face.

Chess heard Box moan. He reached up to the legs that were gripping the side of his head and he leant back but he didn't press his hand onto the roach's body to make it release.

'That's it, dear,' Ethel encouraged him, holding his arms. 'Don't fight it. It won't hurt you. Try to breathe normally.'

Box grunted as the roach's body stretched over his eyes. Now the whole of his face looked as if it had been covered by a thin mask of rubber that had moulded itself perfectly over his features. As Chess watched, the mask began to whiten over Box's eyes, his nostrils and his mouth as if it was stretching to breaking point. The whitening patches stretched further and further and then, silently, they split open. Box's eyes looked out and his mouth gaped, lips coated by the roach. He gulped air like a swimmer breaking water.

After he had sworn vigorously he said, 'It stings; in my eyes and up my nose and down the back of my throat.'

'That's where the roach's membranes have lined your own respiratory surfaces. But it won't harm you,' Ethel assured him. 'You can see all right, can't you?'

'Yeah, fine, for someone with a spider strapped to his face.'

'What's it doing?' gasped Chess. All across the roach's body and along its legs, narrow lines of deep red had risen, following the gaps between the strips of exoskeleton. They began to pulse.

'What's it doing?' echoed Box, starting to panic because of the tone of Chess's voice.

Ethel took hold of the hand Box was raising towards his face. 'Relax,' she said. 'It's just breathing. It's breathing through your blood and its own circulation is working now.'

'Is my blood mixing with its?' Box was alarmed.

'Just think how it must be feeling, fly head,' observed Splinter. 'Nothing has ever got so close to your mash before and lived.'

'Only mixing a little,' said Ethel. 'It won't do you any harm, my love.'

Box nodded and stood up. He walked up and down the wooden floor of the storage tank. 'It feels a bit tight,' he said, 'and it doesn't feel very nice. It's sort of swamping my face and stinging my eyes and nose.'

'It will keep you alive, dear.'

'It's a cross between a massive beetle and a face mask,' said Chess, nose screwed up with revulsion. 'It looks disgusting.'

'Actually,' said Splinter, 'I'm starting to get used to it. It might even be an improvement.'

'Take it off,' prompted Ethel. 'Splinter can try next.'

Still standing, Box raised the flat of his hand to the front of his face and pressed. The legs relaxed so quickly and the body shrank so rapidly that when the roach slithered off his face he nearly dropped it on the floor. In moments, the pulsing red arteries had faded.

Box weighed the limp, black body in his palm. 'I'd prefer a smack in the face,' he said. With his free hand he ruffled out his thick curly hair and he scratched his head.

'Are you sure you haven't got nits, dear?' enquired Ethel.

'I'm not wearing his if he has,' said Splinter.

'Don't worry, my love; like I said, I've brought you one each.'

Splinter tried his next. Chess could tell that he hated it. She knew that he only put it on because everybody was watching him and because Box had already done it. His body shook as the roach fastened itself to his face. When he took the mask off his cheeks were tinged yellow.

'You look as if you're going to be sick, dear,' observed Ethel.

'I've felt better,' admitted Splinter.

'Your turn, my love.' Ethel took a third roach from the sacking and offered it to Chess. With a lump in her stomach, Chess took the creature from Ethel.

It weighed nothing and its legs swung lazily. She lifted it and taking a deep breath, pushed her nose and mouth into the cold body. She was startled by the strength of the little legs which worked their way into her hair and tightened so that the body was pulled hard against her face. Then there was darkness. Something spread inside her mouth and burrowed up her nostrils and this was followed by a burning sensation down the back of her throat, like when she had accidentally got water up her nose. At the same time she realized that she could see again but her eyes were stinging as if they had been filled with smoke.

'I don't like it very much.'

'Nobody does, dear. Take it off now.'

As soon as she pushed her palm against the roach it

collapsed into her hand. Her eyes felt warm and wet and she blinked with pleasure, long eyelashes flicking up and down.

'You really are extraordinary young people. Not exactly nice young people but very extraordinary ones.' Ethel gathered the roaches and placed them gently back in the bag, the shell-covered legs rattling against each other. Then she clicked open the briefcase.

'Now,' she announced. 'It is time for your briefing. Listen carefully to what I say. Your lives and the success of this mission will depend upon it.'

CHAPTER 14

The Tuesdays were sitting in a row, back on the bottom bunk. They watched in silence as Ethel reached into the briefcase, lifted out an artist's easel and erected it in the centre of the storage tank. Then she pulled out a rectangular wedge of plastic bound with a quick release strap. She undid the strap and the plastic flipped open, first downwards and then outwards until she was holding a large plastic board. She propped the board on the easel. Next she took a cylinder from the case. She upended it and a roll of documents slipped out and into her hand. She secured the unrolled documents to the board with aluminium clips.

Chess looked at the display. The first item was a large black and white photograph. It showed an aerial view of a group of buildings. The texture of the photograph was grainy, as if it had been taken through driving rain, and this combined with the unusual perspective made it difficult to define.

If the photograph was unclear, Chess found the two documents clipped alongside it impossible to decipher although with a bitter taste at the back of her mouth she knew what they were made from. They looked like yellowing sheets of parchment and both were covered with diagrams and notation in what appeared to be ochre ink. But Chess knew that this was not ink and she knew that these were not pieces of parchment. They were pieces of human skin, burnt by scrips. These were dermacarts.

Ethel was bent over, digging in the bottom of the briefcase. When she stood up she was holding a stick.

'A wand!' gasped Box. 'I knew it; you *are* a witch.'

'Not every old lady that looks like a witch *is* a witch,' muttered Splinter.

Without responding to either of them, Ethel shook the stick and it extended with a click so that now she was holding a long pointer. She swiped the pointer, cutting the air left and then right before thrusting it towards Box.

'En garde!' she declared, adopting the pose of a fencer, her powder-blue frock stretching taught between her scrawny thighs and her scraggy grey fringe flopping over her spectacles. Box shuffled backwards uncomfortably and so did Chess and Splinter. With a flourish of the pointer, Ethel sprang back to a standing position, her green cardigan slipping from her shoulders.

'Can't resist it, my loves. I've always wanted a rapier. Rather fancy myself as a swordswoman,' and she cut the air once more with a whipping slash.

'If she is a witch,' Splinter whispered in Box's ear, 'she's a mad one.'

The tip of the pointer twirled and rapped the plastic board. 'Pay attention,' ordered Ethel. Chess, Box and Splinter paid attention.

Ethel pointed to the aerial photograph. Although it was of poor quality and gave a bird's-eye view that was strange to him, Splinter recognized what it showed. There was a perimeter wall that ran in an oval with buildings inside it at either end. Across the middle of the oval, spanning from one side to the other was something that looked like the top of another wall, cutting the oval in two, but which Splinter knew to be an arch that overlooked the exercise yard below.

'That's the Riverside Prison,' he said.

'What's that got to do with anything?' said Box. 'It's been empty for years.'

'It isn't empty now, my loves,' said Ethel. She tapped the photograph with the tip of the pointer. 'The Twisted Symmetry are there. It's where they keep the cerebral torus.' She indicated the buildings to the left of the prison complex. 'Over here are the cell blocks, and over here ...' She slid the pointer to the other end of the oval '... are the workshops and the incinerator. Of course, the incinerator isn't working any more, but in here, inside the incinerator building, is where the Symmetry keep their brain.' Then she pointed to the arch that cut across the complex. 'I am going to take you here. This is where you will break in.'

'It's not like us to be breaking *into* a prison,' observed Box.

'How?' Splinter wanted to know. 'How are we going to break in?'

'Through the vortex.'

'Oh yeah,' he responded. 'Obviously. How silly of me not to guess.'

'From this arch you can see over the whole of the prison. On it are built offices and watch rooms. I will take you to the central watch room, here.' The pointer flicked the photograph at the centre of the arch. Then it traced a line going right. 'From that watch room there runs a walkway, an open gantry built from girders. You will cross that gantry and arrive at the incinerator chimney, here.'

Chess had noticed the dark circle in the centre of the buildings on the right side of the prison and wondered what it was. Now she knew that it was the view down the chimney.

'The gantry runs for fifty metres between the watch room and the incinerator chimney,' Ethel was saying. 'Where it meets the chimney there is a door. You will enter the chimney by that door.'

'How high is the gantry?' asked Box.

'About a hundred feet above the buildings and the incinerator shed.'

'So if we fall, we die.' Splinter confirmed.

'Unless you can bounce,' replied Ethel.

'Fly head might survive then,' he said thoughtfully, and then he asked, 'What about guards?'

'There are a large number of traders in the prison complex and there are hunters too but they are not located at the incinerator. There's no need for them there. Nothing can survive in the incinerator because the gas that feeds the brain is so poisonous. The traders and hunters are more concerned with this end of the operation,' and she slid the pointer back to the cell blocks.

'What's in there? I thought the prison was empty?' Chess leant forwards to scrutinize the photograph, as if she might be able to see what was inside the grainy, grey print.

'Children,' said Ethel. 'Lots of children. The Twisted

Symmetry have been collecting them there for weeks; bringing them in from other locations, we believe. However, the children are not your concern. Can we return to the chimney, dear?'

They should be our concern, thought Chess, wondering whether the street rats who had been taken from the wharf were being kept in the old cell blocks. But she listened silently as Ethel continued to explain their mission.

'The chimney rises about two hundred feet above the incinerator. You will enter about halfway up it, a hundred feet above the place where it meets the incinerator shed.'

Ethel lifted the pointer from the photograph and brought it down gently on the first dermacart. Now that Ethel had started to explain the layout of the prison complex, Chess understood what it depicted. It was a cutaway side view of the chimney and incinerator. The rust-red diagram showed how there was a large chamber below the chimney and in the centre of this chamber there was something that was shaped like an enormous lozenge.

'You will descend to where the chimney meets the top of the incinerator shed.' The pointer travelled down the dermacart. 'You will come to a narrow platform in the centre of which rotates a fan. The fan prevents the gas from here,' she indicated the chamber below the platform, 'from coming up here,' and she indicated the chimney. 'You put on the roaches and find the control box on the wall that allows you to turn off the fan and turn it off. From this point you will be working against time.' Ethel regarded them sternly. 'One mistake and you die.'

'If we're not dead already,' observed Splinter.

'You descend into the incinerator, down to the cerebral torus.' Ethel moved the pointer to the second dermacart. Chess could tell that this was an overhead plan of the computer brain. She wondered how many of the Committee's agents had looked down from the platform at the bottom of the chimney, burning what they saw into their skin, before this dermacart had been smuggled out of the Twisted Symmetry's control.

At the centre of the plan was a ring that looked like a giant doughnut, positioned within a rectangular box. Chess guessed that the box represented the walls of the incinerator.

'This is the cerebral torus, mounted on its base-frame, inside the incinerator,' explained Ethel.

'It must be huge!' exclaimed Chess.

'Judging by the measurements recorded by our agent,' Ethel pointed to some of the figures that were scrawled on the dermacart, 'its top is eleven feet above the ground and it is forty feet in diameter.'

Box whistled between his teeth. 'That's a lot of brain.'

'It has to do a lot of thinking, dear,' said Ethel. 'You will all descend to the floor in the centre of the computer. Be careful; the light is weak and the air is poison. An amarantium core runs through the brain. That is what enables it to calculate events at multiple times in multiple universes. Chess will use a specially weighted wire to cut through the brain. Only her body contains sufficient amarantium for her to handle the brain safely.'

'Why?' asked Chess.

'Coincidence,' said Splinter. 'There's nothing special about *you*.'

'Only Chess touches the brain,' warned Ethel. She looked at Chess. 'You will cut through it in two places, as close together as possible. Remove the section and the brain will heal perfectly. The slice you take will contain all the information that is necessary for us to reconstruct the computer and the program. Then we can predict where and when the Fat Gobster will strike.

'You will fold the section that you cut inside the wallet I give you. It's a big wallet and it's impregnated with amarantium to withstand the effects of the brain but not so much as to harm any of you. There are vacuum compression straps on the outside of the wallet. Once you have wrapped the slice of brain inside the wallet, pull the straps; it will shrink-wrap the brain, making it easier to handle, although it will still be quite heavy. Then you must all get out.'

Ethel pointed to three channels that led away from the incinerator shed, drawn in dark red lines; one to the left, one to the right and one straight down. 'Enter this,' she said, identifying the downwards channel. 'It will take you to the river, eventually.' She swung the pointer over to the aerial photograph and now Chess distinguished a narrow pipe leading down from out of the buildings on the right of the prison. The pipe appeared to go underground before it reached the perimeter wall.

'It's a drain. It passes under the wall and runs for thirty metres before it comes to the river.' Ethel indicated a position that was off the bottom of the photograph. 'Once inside the drain you can remove the roaches. The channel that heads right, out of the incinerator, acts as an extractor. It carries foul air away, but there's a large fan over the entrance that can't be stopped from inside the shed so you can't go down there even if you wanted.'

Then Ethel traced the route of the channel that led left from the incinerator. 'This is a ventilation shaft. It starts at the incinerator and ends near to the exercise yard. It won't take you out of the complex but it may take you into the arms of the enemy. Whatever you do, do not take that route.'

'Where do we go once we get out?' asked Box.

'Go to the old dog track. You know where that is?'

'Yes,' said Splinter. 'Not far from the prison. North of it, maybe half a mile.'

'Bang on,' said Ethel. 'Get there for five a.m. tomorrow. Come into the stadium, right in the centre of the track. I'll meet you there.'

'Everything you do happens at old places,' observed Box.

'Of course it does, dear. Humans build places and then abandon them. When the humans move out, other things move in. There are always powers waiting to occupy the places that no one watches.'

'What if we don't show?' asked Splinter. 'What if we don't get out?'

'If the Committee have to mount an operation to rescue you, they will, but that will be messy; far too lively, you might say. Just stay alive, try not to get captured and try to get out.' Ethel appeared to think something over. She coughed and scratched her capillary-webbed left cheek and then said, 'There are certain members of the Twisted Symmetry who you must never approach. Petryx Ark-turi is one of them.'

'Who's he?' enquired Splinter.

'*She* is a primary warp. *The* primary warp. She built the cerebral torus and has taken charge of the operation at the Riverside Prison for the time being.'

'Is she in charge of the Twisted Symmetry?' asked Box.

'No, dear. She is very powerful but she is certainly not in charge.'

'The Inquisitors are in charge of the Twisted Symmetry,' said Splinter, with relish.

'Yes, dear. That's right.' Ethel pursed her lips. 'I see you had no difficulty in remembering that little detail.'

'Might they be there?' asked Splinter. 'Might one of them be there?'

'If I thought for one moment that one of them was there, I would send you away; far away from this world.'

'Are they looking for us?' Chess's voice was very quiet. She fiddled with the saggy cuffs of her pullover.

'They are looking for *you*, dear,' and she jabbed a finger at Chess. 'Of course, they don't know for sure that you are you. They don't yet know what we know. If they knew that, and if they knew that you were here, they would come in force to fetch you. For now, they only suspect your identity. But they want you nevertheless. And when the time is right, we shall let them have you.' Ethel smiled at Chess's startled expression. 'But not now. For now, we have to steal some brain.'

'And stay away from Petryx whoever-she-is,' confirmed Box.

'Petryx Ark-turi,' Ethel clarified. 'One of the Inquisitors' most loyal and powerful servants.'

'Like Lemuel Sprazkin,' observed Splinter brightly.

'Like Lemuel Sprazkin *was*,' Ethel corrected him. 'Now,' she said, smacking the side of the pointer against her thigh and changing the subject. 'Equipment. You are the experts when it comes to skulduggery. What do you need?'

'Can we have anything?' gawped Box.

'I'd never agree to that, dear.'

'Do we get guns?' he asked hopefully.

'No, you don't get guns. Guns are silly. If everyone has guns, everyone starts shooting. If everyone starts shooting, everyone starts dying. So no guns.'

'Can we have rope?'

'Yes.'

'OK. We need rope, lots of rope.'

'About two hundred feet of it,' specified Splinter. 'And a grappling hook.' He closed his eyes, recalling the instructions that Ethel had given and then he studied the photograph and the two dermacarts, clipped up on the easel. 'Three pairs of rubber gloves, wire cutters, wrist watches, torches, a chisel, the roaches and the wallet for the slice of brain.'

'And the cutting wire, of course,' Ethel added. 'It has a heavy weight at one end,' she said to Chess. 'You throw it over the section of brain you want to cut and the weight pulls it down the other side like a cheese wire. Then you pull it through and repeat the exercise. That way you'll remove a whole slice of brain as easily as a wedge of cheese.'

'That's everything,' announced Splinter.

Ethel repeated the list back. 'You'll each need a backpack to carry your equipment. It won't all fit in your pockets.'

'And chocolate,' insisted Box. 'We need chocolate. An army marches on its stomach.'

'An army would struggle to march over yours,' Splinter commented.

Chess laughed. It felt good to laugh. It was a relief.

'Quite right. Chocolate,' agreed Ethel. 'I shall ensure that there are sufficient supplies inside the backpacks.'

'I hope they're big backpacks,' said Box.

'You must wait here whilst I get everything, my loves.' Ethel started packing the items back into the briefcase and she spoke as she dismantled the easel. 'I'm going to lock you inside this storage tank whilst I'm gone; to make sure no one distracts you and to make sure none of you wanders off.' She paused, collapsed easel in hand, to look at them and say, 'I've never known such ones for wandering off.'

She banged the tip of the pointer on a wooden floor slat and it retracted. 'I won't be long and then we'll be on our way.' She dropped the pointer into the briefcase and clicked the lid of the case shut. Then she brushed her hands over the front of her frock, as if beating away dust.

'Don't forget the chocolate,' Box reminded her.

'I won't forget the chocolate,' Ethel reassured him. She took the briefcase in one hand, the sack containing the roaches in the other and marched out of the storage tank. The door closed firmly behind her. Then there was a grinding clunk that made the door vibrate and the tank echo.

Splinter tested the door. The handle wouldn't move; the door was secured fast.

'Prisoners,' he stated.

'As usual,' said Box, lying on a bunk with his legs outstretched, most of his shins sticking out beyond the frayed woollen hems of his trousers. He slipped his hands under his braces and closed his eyes.

'Are you frightened, Splinter?' Chess was sitting on the bottom bunk opposite, picking at a hole in her jeans where her knee protruded.

'A bit,' said Splinter, pacing up and down the tank. He stopped and looked at her. 'Do you know something about all of this?'

Chess wrinkled her nose. 'What do you mean?'

'How come all of this has something to do with you?'

'I don't know, Splinter.'

'No. Neither do I. You're nothing special, Chess. Have you got that?'

She nodded.

'Just remember,' said Splinter, bringing his cold blue eyes so close to her big brown ones that Chess could feel the chill. 'I'm in charge.'

'I know you are, Splinter. You always are.' She wondered why he was being like that with her. She couldn't imagine him not being in charge. She wanted him to be in charge. He was quick and clever and always knew how to get things done. She looked at him, thin and dark by the door and she wished that she could think of a way to make him like her more.

Chess sat on a bunk and stared down at her feet and tried not to think about what Ethel meant when she had said that the Inquisitors would get her when the time was right. She hated knowing that so much was unknown; so much about her and so much about everything around her. It created an empty ache behind her ribs. She wanted the wharf and the ledge and nothing else. She tried to think of the voice, the singing voice, but the emptiness swallowed even that.

She looked across to Splinter again but he was still leaning against the circular entrance door, scowling into space. She looked over at Box. He was lying on the bunk opposite, chest rising and falling with each slow, deep breath, eyes closed. Chess closed her eyes and bit her lip. She had never been so close to her brothers but felt so far away. She had never felt so alone.

The door clunked open with the shock of a gunshot, banging Splinter's head which was resting against it and startling Chess. Box jolted awake and rolled off the bunk, landing with a thud on the floor.

'Caught you napping, did I?' asked Ethel with a lopsided smile, looking up and into the tank from where she stood on the steps outside. 'Nearly gave you another shiner, dear,' she said to Splinter who was rubbing the side of his forehead that wasn't already bruised.

Swift and vigorous, Ethel threw three backpacks through the doorway, one after the other. 'Your equipment, my loves,' she said. Chess noticed that Ethel looked back through the doorway as if checking that nobody was watching her, before pulling the door closed.

'I'll take this one,' said Box, tugging at the packs and then hoisting one of them on his arm. 'It's the heaviest.'

'It's got the grappling hook inside and one hundred feet of rope,' explained Ethel. 'Chess and Splinter each have fifty feet.'

'And there's plenty of chocolate,' announced Box, delighted with what he had found stuffed in the two side pockets of the pack. He snatched out a bar, tore off the wrapping and set to work with a great smacking of his lips.

'You are disgusting,' stated Splinter.

'Just keeping the energy levels up,' gurgled Box through a cloying brown mush of chocolate. He chewed and swallowed and cleared his mouth with his tongue. 'Ready for battle; unlike you, bean pole boy.'

'Pig butt,' replied Splinter.

'Bean butt,' retorted Box and he laughed at his own great wit.

Oblivious to her brothers' squabbling, Chess looked inside her backpack to check the equipment. It was half-filled by rope, with gloves and wire cutters tucked down one side and a long, coiled wire inside a clear plastic pouch resting on top. Her fingers rubbed against something rough, almost hairy, and she saw that underneath the transparent pouch which contained the cutting wire there was a wad of sacking. The roach would be inside that, lifeless until she let it fasten itself to her face. She swallowed hard and drew the pack shut.

'I've got the wallet,' said Splinter, who had found a plastic pad that concertinaed out to form a huge case, like a map case but much bigger. It stretched the width of his arms and from his chin to his toes. Four short straps were attached to one side and they dangled loosely.

'Those are the vacuum compression straps,' Ethel explained. 'Pull them once the brain is packed inside and it'll shrink-wrap it.'

Splinter folded the wallet until it was no bigger than a book. He slipped it back into his pack. 'I hope our slice of brain shrinks easily,' he observed.

'And doesn't turn to mush,' added Box.

'Like yours has done,' mumbled Splinter. He removed the rubber gloves from where they were tucked by the rope and stuffed them into one of the pockets of his morning coat. He did the same with the wire cutters. Then he took out a pencil-thin torch, tested it, nodded in approval at its piercing beam and slipped it into another pocket. 'Don't want to be digging about for this lot in the dark,' he said and he closed his backpack.

Ethel gave each of them a wristwatch. She helped Chess and Box to fasten theirs in place.

'I've never had a watch,' said Chess.

'You don't need one,' commented Splinter. 'You can't tell the time.'

'I can,' she insisted.

'OK, what time is it then?'

'It's nearly one in the morning,' said Ethel. 'Now, your watches are synchronized with mine. Remember, you meet me at the centre of the dog track in four hours time.'

Chess shook her hand and felt the plastic watch strap rub against her wrist, a little loosely. When she got the watch close to her face and blotted out the light from the tank with her fingers, she saw that the watch hands glowed.

'Nice,' she murmured.

'Time to go, my loves.' Ethel was standing at the other end of the storage tank in front of the lavatory door. She had taken a small box from her cardigan pocket and placed it on the wooden floor. The lid of the box was open and out of it curled a finger of mist.

'I'm not so sure about this bit,' muttered Box.

'You just put one foot in,' directed Ethel, 'and everything else will follow.' She noticed Splinter rubbing his injured wrist. 'The mortice-gate is open. Nothing will hurt you,' she assured him.

Splinter grunted dismissively to show what he thought of Ethel's assurances.

They shouldered their packs. The straps pulled the skin on Chess's collarbones but it didn't feel as heavy as she had expected. Her attention was fixed on the wooden casket opposite. Although it was very small, it loomed large before her eyes; everything else seemed to shrink away. Her legs felt heavy and weak at the same time. Then she felt something moving in her fingers and realized that it was Box's hand. She looked up and saw that he was grinning at her, eyes bright beneath his brilliantly black curls.

'Come on, Chess,' he said. 'Let's go together.'

'OK,' said Chess. 'Let's go.'

Box began to walk and Chess walked with him. Together, they approached the luminous opening of the portable vortex.

CHAPTER 15

Chess was standing in air; that was how it looked. Above her and below her and in every direction for as far as she could see there was nothingness. It wasn't white but it wasn't clear either. When she had stepped into the box it had been cold but now she was on the other side it wasn't cold or hot and her feet felt as if they were standing on something that wasn't hard or soft.

'We are in the vortex, my loves,' said Ethel. Chess had expected her voice to be swallowed by space like the way voices rose and faded when she used to play on the rooftops at the wharf and the street rats were shouting to one another. But Ethel's voice was surprisingly close, as if she was speaking in a small room.

'It's funny,' mused Chess, looking about.

'What's funny, dear?'

'I thought it would be . . . noisier than this.'

'It has its moments, dear, trust me. You must stay close to me and walk only where I walk.' She had been standing behind Chess, Box and Splinter who had been standing shoulder to shoulder. She walked round them with her hands in the pockets of her green cardigan and sniffed the air, head angled and the lenses of her spectacles white.

'Mist?' asked Splinter, also sniffing the air.

'No mist,' said Ethel. 'We are safe for the time being. But we must close the mortice-gate.' She turned to where they had come from. Chess saw her lips move but heard nothing. However, as soon as they stopped moving, a thick, metal grille slammed in from every direction, closing the way back.

The crash was ear-splitting and abrupt. Now, there was a gridiron that radiated up and down and outwards for as far as Chess could see and at its centre there was an aperture, no wider than a foxhole. The entire mortice-gate began to rotate slowly about this opening.

Splinter looked from his wrist to the wheeling gate. 'Could have had my arm off,' he grumbled.

'Lucky you didn't stick your head in first,' chuckled Ethel. 'Now, let's be on our way.'

Chess looked around. In one direction there was the boundless turning grid of the mortice-gate. In the other she saw nothing but nothingness.

'The vortex goes everywhere and in-between everywhere.' Ethel was feeling inside her pocket as she spoke. 'You can go to any time and any place from inside the vortex, but like I told you when we first met, it is very easy to get lost here. And once you are lost inside the vortex ...' She shrugged and waved an arm to indicate the endless emptiness.

'How do you know where to go?' asked Splinter.

'I have spent a lot of time in here, my love,' replied Ethel. 'I know many of the reachings; the ways that are safe to tread, ways that lead from one place to another or from one time to another.'

Box looked about. 'I can't see anything.'

'Reachings aren't like main roads, dear. You can't just see them. They're not signposted. You feel them. You're standing on one now.'

Chess tapped her white foot on the firm space beneath it and then slid it left and then right a short distance. Satisfied that she wasn't about to fall into infinity, she ventured to move it further away and suddenly found that the firmness had gone. To her horror, the ends of her toes began to blow away like a stream of dust. She snatched her foot back and felt her toes with her hand. They were as solid as they had always been.

'It's best not to wander from the reachings, my love. Eternity is a long time to be lost. Even though I know some of the ways, I don't take any risks. I use this.' Ethel held out her hand. Sitting on her wrinkled palm was a ball of sticks, closely meshed together.

'They look like matchsticks,' said Box, who gritted his teeth and stamped his foot in frustration because he realized that Ethel was bound to tell him they weren't matchsticks.

'They're not matchsticks,' said Ethel.

'Why do I keep doing that?' growled Box through his teeth.

'Because you are a very silly little fly head,' Splinter whispered in his ear.

'This is a tesseract,' said Ethel. She took it between the fingers of both hands and pulled it open. The sticks sprang apart to form a football-sized framework whose many sides were constructed of adjacent pentagons; the sticks of one pentagon also forming part of the neighbouring pentagons, like a spherical mesh.

'By looking through this, I can unravel all the dimensions inside the vortex and that lets me see where I'm going.' When she saw the blank faces looking back at her, Ethel said, 'You remember that I told you there is more space in the world than you can see?' Three heads nodded. 'Well, humans and creatures like you only experience four dimensions, four bits of space; up, down, across and forwards time, and I'm not so sure about time, it's a very slippery thing, more a matter of where than when.'

She frowned at Splinter. 'Don't look at me like that, dear, I didn't invent all of this. I find it hard to understand as well. Anyway, with a tesseract I can see into the spaces that are otherwise hidden. Very handy.' She patted it. 'This clever gizmo can help me find a way through the vortex and into the Riverside Prison without anybody seeing us.'

She slipped her fingers through the sticks and pulled her hands apart. The tesseract flattened and stretched and she put her face up to one of the many five-sided gaps between the sticks.

Chess could see straight through the tesseract but Ethel said, 'Aha! Just up and left a bit. The reachings in this part of the vortex have a habit of slipping. It's best to check they are where they're meant to be. Come on.' She collapsed the bundle of sticks but kept it in her hand.

'Just think what we could do with a tesseract and a portable vortex,' Splinter whispered to Box as they began to follow

Ethel through the emptiness. He sighed and answered his own question. 'We could do anything.'

'We'd probably end up lost,' said Box after a little thought.

'The problem with you, fly head,' stated Splinter, 'is you have no vision.'

Chess blinked as a dot of red appeared in the air before her. It was followed by another, its edges spattering outwards like the edges of a raindrop when it hits glass. Then there was a yellow dot and then a blue one and then the dots came more quickly, speckling wherever she looked. When she turned her head the brilliant dots moved with her, as if they were inside her eyes. Now the colours were bursting so rapidly that she couldn't see anything else. She screwed her eyelids tight and pools of colour ebbed in the darkness. She heard Box and Splinter calling to each other and then Ethel spoke.

'Stand still, all of you.' This time her voice dominated the space around it. It seemed to come from something far more powerful than the old lady's body. 'What you are experiencing is sound; extra-dimensional sound that you can't hear but which is so mighty you can see it. It will pass. Wait.'

Chess stood still with her eyes shut. As the colours began to fade, Box said, 'Why did that happen. I mean, how can we see sounds?'

'Why can't we see anything else?' added Splinter.

Chess opened her eyes and saw Ethel close by, shrivelled in her powder-blue frock and misshapen cardigan. When Ethel spoke her voice was small and close again.

'This is a strange place for you, my loves. You can only

experience bits of what is happening around you because you only exist in a tiny part of the vortex.' She pointed to a place above them. 'Look.'

They looked and saw a purple smudge in the nothingness; how far away, it was impossible to tell. The edges of the smudge sharpened and then dipped inwards at its centre to make a shape that Chess thought was a bit like a bowtie. As she watched, the right-hand side of the bow tie shrank, leaving a purple triangle that grew smaller and smaller until it had vanished altogether. Chess, Box and Splinter remained staring into the emptiness. Then Chess sensed something else; she had the most distant feeling that a vast iron echo had passed slowly over their heads.

'A cross-universal shipping lane passes through this sector of the vortex,' said Ethel. 'It's navigated by giant vessels that carry deep cargo; freight and raw materials in massive quantities which have to travel colossal distances, even between universes. What you saw then was a small part of the tail fin of the *Leviathan III*. What you heard on your eyeballs was one of its booster rockets firing.'

'I didn't really see anything,' pondered Box.

'You only see pieces, my loves, those pieces that are in your space. Think of your world as the surface of a pond. If I pushed a stick through that surface you would only see the little bit of wood that was on the surface. You wouldn't know anything about how much wood there was above or below the surface.'

'Great,' said Splinter, turning his back to where the shape had been. 'Now we're pond life.'

Chess stayed looking into space.

'What is it, dear?' asked Ethel. 'What can you see?'

How does she know that I can see anything? thought Chess. 'Nothing really. I mean nothing,' she said absently. I can only see a small bit of space, Chess reminded herself, only the bit I'm in. And when she stared into the void again she was sure that there was nothing to see.

Ethel had unfolded the tesseract and was scanning the vortex. Satisfied, she collapsed it and set off, her little body plodding through space. Chess followed, walking close behind her brothers. Splinter's morning coat and trousers looked blacker than ever in the emptiness and he walked with short, careful steps like a raven in snow. Box walked immediately behind him, taking care to put his feet only where he was sure Splinter had put his.

Chess didn't know how long they had been walking for; the vortex was so barren it was difficult to gauge the flow of time. Also, when she looked at her wristwatch the hands seemed to have gone the wrong way. She wasn't very good at telling the time because she had never been taught how to do so but she could tell the hours. According to her watch it wasn't yet one o'clock, which was odd because Ethel had said it was one o'clock when they had set off.

'We're just stopping here, my loves,' said Ethel. In front of her there was a movement, a drift of white like a ragged curtain of cloud. 'I've found a gap that takes us somewhere you might recognize.'

The Tuesdays drew close.

'Now, you wait here. Don't move an inch,' Ethel said.

'Don't worry, we won't,' said Box, looking at his feet as if whatever they were standing on might give way at any instant.

For a moment the cloud separated and through it, Chess saw night and a wet brick building, slashed orange by street lamps. There was a row of vans parked nose first against its walls.

'That's the back of the central post office,' said Splinter.

'It's like we're standing in the loading bay.' Box scratched his head, puzzled. 'But we're not; we're standing in here.'

'The vortex goes everywhere,' Ethel reminded him. 'It's just a matter of being able to open it up in the right place. We can see out but no one can see in. Could I borrow your knife, dear?'

Box pulled the lock knife out of his pocket and handed it to Ethel without wondering why she had asked for it.

'What do you want with that?' quizzed Splinter, who never liked to see a knife in a hand unless it was in his own.

'I'm going to hide something in the wall behind the rubbish bins.' She looked at Chess. 'Have you got that, dear?'

'Yes,' said Chess, wondering why Ethel was doing this and why she was looking at her so pointedly.

'I'm going to loosen a brick with this knife and put this mobile phone inside the wall.' Ethel held up a small silver phone that she had lifted out of her cardigan pocket.

'How many things do you keep in your pockets?' asked Splinter.

'Nearly as many as you do, dear,' said Ethel before she continued talking to Chess. 'This phone has one number stored in its memory. Just the one. With it you can contact Julius.'

'The man with the freaky eyes and the silver face?' interjected Splinter.

'You will need him, I think.' Ethel was concentrating on Chess, ignoring her brothers. 'Not now, but some time not very far into the future. You will be alone and in danger. He will be ready to help you.'

Why would he bother to help me? Chess told herself. I am nothing to him. But she couldn't stop a lurch of hope that somewhere, Julius might be thinking of her. However, she didn't speak about how she felt; she had learnt not to do that. 'When?' was all she asked. 'When will he help me?'

Ethel wrinkled her forehead and held up her hands. 'I don't know exactly when. I don't even know if this will happen. But I think it might, my love, and since it is something I can plan for, I'm planning for it.'

'But how do you know it might happen?' persisted Chess, realizing that she didn't want it *not* to happen. The danger wouldn't matter if it meant she was more than nothing to Julius.

'I know about a lot of things that might happen. I have calculated carefully, considered every move, looked at every possibility I can imagine. But it's difficult to be sure about anything.' She smiled at Chess kindly. 'So, we must settle for being ready for everything.' She weighed the mobile phone in her hand. 'It's nuclear-powered so it will be ready to use if the time comes. Remember, dear; a loose brick behind the rubbish bins at the central post office.'

'I'll remember,' said Chess, resolute.

Ethel walked through the drifting mist.

'Don't start thinking you're all important,' Splinter

warned Chess as Ethel and the rear of the post office vanished from view.

'I don't,' Chess assured him, as meekly as she could.

'She does some of these things just to impress us, you know. If she was so smart she wouldn't be running a scabby operation in the old bus depot whilst the Twisted Symmetry are busy taking over the universe.'

'Universes,' Box corrected him.

'And don't you start getting all technical, fly head.'

'It may *look* like a fly head, but actually it's an intergalactic warrior,' announced Box.

'Yeah, an intergalactic warrior with a blunt lock knife,' observed Splinter as Ethel stepped back into the vortex.

'Job done,' she said, folding the lock knife and handing it back to Box. 'Not far now,' and she walked away from the shifting cloud and into the blankness of the vortex. The Tuesdays followed.

Chess thought they hadn't travelled much further before Ethel said, 'We're here.' As soon as she said that, Chess felt a heaviness seep through her thigh muscles, like before she had entered the portable vortex but much worse. Her heart stung as it started to beat harder. She noticed that a little to her right, the vortex was stirring as it did where there was a gap from it into the world beyond.

Ethel was looking through the tesseract, twisting it a little, its stick frame skewing between her hands. 'Yes, yes. Good. This is the way in. It's dark, of course. Good. Very good. Nobody's there.' She pushed her hands together and the tesseract collapsed into a knot the size of a golf ball. Then she looked at the watch on her wrist. 'Just wait five minutes,' she said.

Splinter looked at his own watch and his brow knitted immediately. 'It's earlier than when we set off!' he exclaimed. He looked at Ethel, suspicious. 'How'd that happen?'

'Slippery thing, time,' Ethel reminded him. 'Time and space inside the vortex don't always do the same things as time and space outside the vortex. By my watch it's five minutes to one. It's safer to wait until a little past one o'clock before you leave the vortex, just to make sure that you don't arrive at the prison before the time that you actually set off to get there.'

All of them stood in silence. Chess kept glancing at the gap out of the vortex, trying not to think about what might be waiting for them on the other side. She felt nervous and without thinking of what she was doing she started to sing to herself, very quietly.

'*When I was on horseback, wasn't I pretty?*' Her voice sounded very small, the words swallowed at once by the yawning emptiness of the vortex.

'Don't sing that stupid song,' snapped Splinter.

'I like it,' said Chess. 'Mum sang it.'

'We don't have a mother. We don't have anything apart from each other and sometimes, I'm not sure about that.'

'You are a very unhappy boy,' Ethel said gently.

The muscles in Splinter's jaw clenched and unclenched and he stared at where the ground would normally have been. Then Ethel coughed to clear her throat.

'When you get in you must move quickly. Through the

door that leads to the gantry. It will take you over the buildings to the chimney.'

'We know,' said Splinter, whose hollow-cheeked face was hard as bone.

'Good. Very good. Well then,' and she gestured to the shifting vapours. 'Now is the time. In you go. And good luck.'

'Thanks,' said Box, glad to be doing something at last. Hands gripping the straps of his backpack, he stepped into the mist and was gone.

Splinter said nothing. He didn't even look at Ethel. Stooping slightly, he followed Box and was shrouded from view.

'You next, my love,' said Ethel, resting a hand on Chess's shoulder. 'You can do this, Chess.' She took hold of Chess's hand which was very cold and she squeezed it hard. Then she bent forwards and kissed her on the forehead. It made Chess feel warm and safe. She wanted to hug the scruffy old lady but she didn't know how.

'I know that you can do this, my love; all of this has happened before. You can do it. I know.'

Chess remained standing by Ethel's side.

'Go on,' said Ethel. 'It's time to go.'

Chess turned and took a deep breath. Then she walked the way her brothers had gone.

CHAPTER 16

Ethel and the vortex had vanished; Chess was in an unlit room, the size of a portacabin, with doors at either end. She recalled that this was the central watch room, located at the middle of the arch that spanned the prison. The long sides of the room were made of glass. A small hatch was set in one side, visible because of its thin metal frame. Through that window, Chess could see only night although she knew that beyond the hatch there would be a walkway that crossed one hundred feet above the prison to the incinerator chimney. Box and Splinter were standing at the other long window, faces pressed to the glass which was already clouding with their breath. They had to lean forwards to see out because running the length of the window were a row of steel lockers that came up to Splinter's hips.

'This is high,' marvelled Box. 'It's like looking out of a captain's window.'

'You mean the bridge of a ship?' asked Splinter, not moving his eyes from where they were riveted to the glass.

'Yeah, like the bridge of a ship.'

'Have you ever been on a ship, fly head?'

'No, but I'm using my imagination.'

'Well, imagine shutting up,' said Splinter.

In silence, Chess joined them and looked out. It took a little time to piece together all that she could see. The thick white beams that swung through the darkness were search lights. They were mounted at regular intervals on a high wall. Chess recognized that this was the outer wall of the prison. The bleak buildings opposite which looked like hospital units but with bars on their windows were the cell blocks. They were tall but even their rain-dreary rooftops were lower than the perimeter wall. The figures patrolling along the top of the wall and carrying rifles were hunters. Chess couldn't mistake their uniforms which made them look darker than the night except when they were caught for a moment in the arcing beams of the search lights. Then the silver death's-head insignia flashed and the jackboots glistened with rain.

Beneath her and stretching from the arch to the cell blocks was a huge, open yard. When Ethel had described the layout of the prison to them, Chess had imagined the yard empty. But it wasn't empty. It was full of children; thousands of children. They were sitting in closely packed rows with their hands on their heads and moving up and down the rows, cracking whips and kicking backs, were traders.

The search lights swung over the heads of the children, the bright beams dashed with rain, and where they stopped in circular pools at the prison gates to the right of where Chess was looking, she saw a fleet of cattle trucks parked in lines. Their tailgates hung open and between their high sides stalked more traders. Behind the cattle trucks leant a rank of black and chrome motorcycles. There stood hunters, helmets on their heads or tucked under their arms.

'Can you see any of ours?' asked Box.

'No. There's too many,' replied Splinter.

Chess rubbed the condensation from the glass with her fingertips. Rain ran down the big window in beads and poured into the yard, cascading white in the search beams like sleet. Yet the circles of light that dipped and swung over the heads in the exercise yard only made the rest of the darkness darker. The children looked wet and thin; more detail than that it was impossible to see. But Chess knew how cold they would be. She knew how rain chilled your skin, numbed your scalp, stung your eyes; how it made you shiver whilst your clothes stuck to you in squelching strips. She could imagine how the children's joints must be aching as they sat with their hands on their heads, clothes heavy, shoulders on fire. She saw how some of the children had trouble sitting up straight, how their hands slipped from their heads, how their bodies leant and then toppled sideways. And she saw how those cold, tired bodies were punished by the whips and boots of the traders who loomed over them, hair wild and black, eyes glinting savagely.

She wanted to tell Splinter how she felt but when she looked across to him she saw that he was transfixed, face pressed to the glass, eyes alight. She knew that Splinter only looked like that when he was fascinated by something; when it excited him.

'No, Splinter,' she meant to say, but all she did was croak drily and then cough. He jerked his head to look at her, angry at the interruption.

'Down!' exclaimed Box as a searchlight came out of nowhere and flashed across the watch room window. He ducked as quickly as Splinter and Chess did. The light passed but they stayed kneeling in the darkness. Chess balanced with her hands on the floor because the backpack made her unsteady.

The room flooded yellow again as a searchlight poured in through the long window. The lockers cast a shadow across the floor that slid sideways as the searchlight moved on. Then darkness once more.

'What are they doing?' asked Box.

'What are who doing?' replied Splinter.

'The children.'

'They're waiting,' said Splinter. 'Waiting to be taken somewhere. That's what all those trucks are for. They're going to be loaded onto the trucks.' He sighed. Images lingered before his eyes. 'The traders and hunters are in charge. The children are powerless.'

'Thanks for that last bit, Splinter,' ridiculed Box, and Chess noticed him glance at Splinter strangely, as if there was something about his brother that he didn't recognize. 'For a moment I thought the children were running the show.'

Chess leant her head on one side. A noise beyond the doors. Maybe voices. 'Someone's coming,' she whispered.

'Here we go again,' huffed Box. 'You're paranoid, Chess.'

'No, fly head. Not this time,' said Splinter. 'Someone is coming.'

There were voices on the other side of the door at the end of the room. They were muffled at first but they were getting louder, coming closer.

Splinter pulled open the door of the locker nearest to him. 'In here,' he hissed. 'Just get in and keep quiet.'

Box followed Splinter and Chess followed Box into the metal cupboard. She had to wriggle hard to get herself and her backpack into the narrow space. She found that if she lay on her side with her head on Box's shins, she could wedge herself into the coffin-like opening. Her left arm was pinned beneath her body but her right arm was free and she was able to pull the door shut, sealing herself and her brothers inside the locker.

Above her were strung bunches of cables. They ran in either direction for as far as she could feel. Chess realized that this was not a series of lockers but one continuous unit that was boxed in along the length of the room. It must have been part of a circuit that carried power cables over the arch from one side of the prison to the other.

A door handle ratcheted open abruptly and there were footsteps in the watch room. The voices which had risen and fallen vaguely as they had approached were suddenly clear. Chess's eyes had adjusted to the darkness inside the unit and she found that only inches from her face there were vents in the metal door through which she could look. Although it was night and the room was unlit, she could pick out the shapes and blurred features of the two people who had entered.

The first was very tall and wore a long thick coat. His hair was matted and tumbled from his big head in oil-black ringlets. He wore a plaited beard and his eyes glinted malevolently in the darkness. Chess recognized him as the trader who had driven the white van and caught her with his whip; the same whip that was jammed now into the thick belt he wore.

She would have recognized the second person even without his uniform and its silver insignia. She recognized his hatchet nose and his hard face, his sharp eyes and his tight mouth and she recognized his smell because it was the wrong smell for a human. It was a smell of dog.

I know those eyes, she thought, and for a moment she was back in the desolation that was the wharf, where a shadow on four legs prowled through the mist.

Then the Inspector spoke. 'We're early.'

'Petryx will be here soon,' said the trader in his clumsy growl. He spoke slowly, as if he had to struggle to produce each word.

There was a silence between them. Chess did not think it was a very comfortable silence. It was broken by the trader, who toyed with his beard thoughtfully and looked down at the Inspector with one bristling eyebrow raised and a wily wrinkling of his eye.

'Before I come to this world, I hear that three shipments of crystal have gone missing,' he said.

'That is no business of mine,' snapped the Inspector. 'I am posted to this part of this planet. My business is human children, not crystal.'

The trader continued to play with his beard and for the first time, Chess noticed the chunky jewelled rings on his thick fingers. 'I am not been here long,' he said. 'I do not know what little power you have.'

'The inquisitors need children, Jerkan. My work here is important.'

'Of course, yes,' smiled the trader. 'And yet, you lost the girl.'

'Just as you did, Jerkan. And you are meant to be a chieftain.'

'You make me angry,' growled the trader, letting go of his beard and tucking his thumbs into his belt. He glowered down at the Inspector who stared back up, unblinking, eyes lethal.

If it comes to a fight, thought Chess, the Inspector will win.

The door at the other end of the watch room opened. The Inspector and the trader turned to face the person who had just entered and Chess noticed that both backed away a little as this person approached. She knew that they had been waiting for Petryx Ark-turi and she guessed that it must be the Twisted Symmetry's primary warp who was here now. She angled her head to try to see her. It would have been difficult but for a flood of light as a searchlight passed across the window.

Through the vents she saw a figure who was taller than the Inspector but not nearly as tall as the trader. She wore a gown that brushed the floor and was criss-crossed with metal filaments, just like Lemuel's frock-coat. Her neck was long and her head was narrow and box-like, with sunken cheeks and hair that was shaved on the back and sides, but bristled thick and flat on top, the black flecked with grey. Her skin was paper-white and she wore a pair of pince-nez spectacles clamped to the bridge of her thin, chisel nose. Their small black lenses hid her eyes entirely. But what Chess looked at longest were her mouth and chin. They jutted forwards as if there was too much skull behind the tight, pale skin, or too many teeth.

I hope I am never alone in a room with you, thought Chess, immediately wishing she hadn't, because just thinking it seemed to make it possible.

The searchlight passed. Petryx Ark-turi stood in shadow again.

'This will be the culmination of a most fortuitous sequence of events,' she announced. She talked through her nose, stabbing each word as she spoke it. 'The cerebral torus has predicted many strikes but it is perfection that there should be one so close to this location.'

'Which is why we have worked so hard to bring so many captive children here,' observed the Inspector. 'We have been centralizing them for weeks.'

'You must have worked very hard.'

'The humans make good servants,' stated the Inspector. 'It has not taken many of us to infiltrate the hunters and control them. We have been amongst them for many years. We have guided them in the ways that best serve the Symmetry, but the humans have a capacity to be cruel to their own species that has made our work easy.'

'Nevertheless, I am sure your efforts have not gone unnoticed, Inspector,' said Petryx Ark-turi. 'How many children do we have, Jerkan?'

The trader paused, searching for the correct numbers inside his gnarled head. 'Seven thousand, two hundred thirty-two,' he grunted wrestling with each word.

'And how many have you already delivered to the airfield?'

'Eighteen thousand and six over the last three weeks,'

replied the Inspector. 'They have been kept secure. Waiting for now.'

'Twenty-five thousand, two hundred and thirty-eight children in total.' Petryx Ark-turi folded her arms. Chess could see her fingers which were long and thin like sticks. 'It is a modest number. It will not last long. The inquisitors' needs are vast and time is short; the fifth node is approaching. But if every strike across this planet could deliver the same quantity, our masters would be most content.'

The Inspector permitted himself a thin and clinical smile.

'All the arrangements have been made?' the warp asked him. Her head twitched slightly and she smelt the air with little sniffing noises. The Inspector waited until her attention had returned to him before he replied.

'The arrangements have been in place since the computer predicted this morning's strike at the Eastern Airfield,' he assured her. 'The children have been kept in disused hangars, under armed guard. At three a.m., the airport will be evacuated as part of a security measure. All flights will be directed elsewhere. All staff and members of the public will be clear of the airfield by three thirty a.m.'

'You are sure?'

The Inspector smiled. 'When you are the police, these things can be arranged. The convoy will leave this location at four a.m., precisely, escorted by outriders. Our safe passage has been guaranteed at the highest level.'

'Of course it has,' said Petryx. 'The Symmetry has many friends. There is no one who is beyond persuasion.'

Chess didn't like the way Petryx said "persuasion". She

twisted it with her nasal voice until it sounded more like a weapon than a word.

'From five a.m., all captives will be escorted into a holding area. Fences will be erected to contain them. No one will escape.'

'What happens should anyone try to do so?' queried Petryx. Her thin eyebrows knitted and she looked around the room as if distracted.

Chess's eyes were so used to the darkness now, and Petryx Ark-turi was standing so near to the locker door that Chess could see the black slits of her nostrils dilating, like a fish working its gills. The warp jerked her oblong head and skewed it at an angle on the end of her stalk of a neck. The nostrils flared.

She can smell us, Chess realized, and suddenly she felt so exposed that she might as well have been lying on the floor at the warp's feet. She wanted to warn Box and Splinter but even though she was so close that she was lying on Box's feet, she did not dare to make a sound. The smallest noise and they were bound to be discovered.

'Should anyone try to escape,' the Inspector was saying, 'my men have orders to shoot. We have found that this encourages other prisoners to cooperate. At five fifty-five a.m., all Symmetry forces will withdraw to a safe distance. The children will have been fenced in at the centre of the predicted strike zone. At six a.m., in accordance with the computer's calculations, the strike will happen. The children will be taken by the Fat Gobster.'

'Good. Very good, Inspector.' Petryx Ark-turi drew hard through her chisel nose and clenched her box jaw; smelling the air. 'And afterwards, you must find us more children; the Inquisitors are hungry. We expect strikes at a number of inconvenient locations in your sector of the planet over the next seven months. We have mounted operations at more convenient locations elsewhere for that period. But we expect the Fat Gobster to strike this city again in seven months. That gives both of you plenty of time to accumulate fresh supplies.'

'I only came to this planet for the girl,' Jerkan muttered into his beard.

'Then you may leave it when you have found her.' Petryx speared each word inside her nose before spitting it at the trader. She sniffed the air again and said, 'It is strange. Whilst my appetite for human children has never been as ravenous as the Traitor's was, I too find it difficult to control myself when their essence is so potent.'

The warp had turned to look out of the window. She was standing no more than six feet from the locker door. With her face pressed close to the vents, Chess could see her clearly.

'I smell their sweat. I smell their blood. I smell their fear. Strange though, how strong it is; as if they were here, in this room, so close that I can almost taste them.'

Chess bit her lips together to stop herself from gasping out loud. She held her breath because she knew that the room had become a room that was listening.

'Why so strong in here?' Petryx Ark-turi asked herself.

'There are many outside,' suggested the trader. 'Maybe that makes the smell strong.'

'No.' The word slid, sinewy, from the warp's sharp nose.

'This smell is nearer. I must smell my way. I must get close to it; as close as I can. I need a taste. Just a little taste.'

Nobody spoke. The silence was so intense that it ached in Chess's ears. Then in the silence there was a noise; a noise like an eggshell cracking but louder. Mixed with the cracking was the sound of something stretching, sticky and gelatinous. It came from Petryx but even with her eyes wide open and staring through the vents, Chess wasn't sure what was happening because the bottom of the warp's head appeared darker than before. It looked different.

Then Chess saw that the darkness wasn't shadow. The bottom of Petryx Ark-turi's face had changed. The spectacles remained clamped to her nose, but below them, Chess thought she saw a sheen of raw flesh and a dull blade of bone and movement; a wriggling, squirming movement as if a mass of something had come alive in the bottom of the warp's face where her jaws should have been.

Chess clasped a hand over her mouth to stop herself from screaming.

'Just a little taste,' drawled Petryx Ark-turi through the crawling wetness on the front of her face and she approached the locker where the Tuesdays were hiding.

CHAPTER 17

Petryx Ark-turi came towards the window slowly. Chess could see the straight edges of her gown silhouetted in the murk of the watch room. She knew that although the warp was thinking of the children in the exercise yard outside, she was bound to taste her way down to the place where she and her brothers were hiding. Chess was absolutely helpless and her heart was beating so hard she could feel the blood pulsing through her throat; blood that the warp could smell. Blood that was drawing her closer and closer.

She expected Petryx to bend down at any moment, pull open the metal door and discover her. But before Petryx reached the locker, the room vanished in pitch darkness. At that instant or maybe just before, Chess heard a tiny click from somewhere inside the locker and above her head.

'We've lost the lights,' snapped the Inspector. 'Something has happened to the lights.'

With a swish of gown, footsteps moved away from the locker and Chess dared to breathe out very slowly. 'What now?' Petryx Ark-turi snapped back. 'The lights are your responsibility, Inspector.'

Even though there had been no lights on in the watch room, the glow from the lights outside had been sufficient to illuminate the room dimly. Now the darkness was as thick as velvet.

A torch was clicked on and its beam pierced the night. 'There is a reserve power supply,' said the Inspector. 'I shall see to that. Then we'll trace the fault.'

'There should be no fault, Inspector.'

'Maybe it is a rat,' suggested the trader, his voice rumbling from the other side of the room.

'If it is a rat, it is no ordinary rat,' said Petryx Ark-turi.

The torch beam cut to the door through which the Inspector had entered. 'I need to deal with this quickly.' The Inspector was agitated. 'I want to check the electric circuits.'

'We shall come with you,' said Petryx. 'I am very interested to see if we have rats in the system. I might be able to make use of them. So many little creatures die in my experiments that I always need more.'

The fuzzy-edged beam of light swayed. A door opened. There were footsteps. The door clunked shut, footsteps receding on the other side. Then there was silence. Inside the locker nobody spoke; everyone knew to say nothing. Chess understood that the moment after danger had passed was the most dangerous moment of all. You thought you were safe, you relaxed, you started talking, you laughed. Then whatever had been waiting for you struck.

She looked at her watch. The luminous green hands seemed to wobble in the dark, even when she kept her arm as still as she could. She thought it was probably something after two o'clock but she couldn't be sure.

'Right,' whispered Box. 'I'm bored, I've got pins and needles all over and I've had enough of smelling Splinter's feet. Let's get out.'

'Go on then, Chess,' came Splinter's voice from somewhere beyond Chess's head. 'Open the door.'

Chess pushed the door with her fingers and sensed it swing open but she didn't begin to crawl out until she was satisfied that nothing was going to grab hold of her first. Then arms were freed, legs unbent, necks straightened, heads unjammed and swearing, grunting and heaving, Chess, Box and Splinter emerged from their hiding place. As they did so, the searchlights flashed back into life outside and suddenly the room seemed very well lit.

'That's the reserve power,' said Box.

'What happened?' whispered Chess, kneeling below the top of the locker.

'I happened,' said Splinter, 'as usual.' He raised his hands and displayed the rubber gloves that he was wearing with his fingers spread wide. 'I couldn't see what was going on but from what that Petryx Arch-lunatic was saying and where she was walking, I thought we'd be next on the menu. So I used these,' and he pulled the wire cutters from out of his morning coat. 'I'd noticed the wires when we got in there. We needed a distraction and cutting through a main power supply seemed a good way of doing it.'

'That was the click I heard,' marvelled Chess.

'Brilliant!' declared Box.

'She was a monster, Splinter,' said Chess earnestly. 'She did something horrible to the bottom of her face; it was all wet and moving.'

'Well, let's not hang about.' Splinter pulled off the gloves and replaced them and the wire cutters inside his coat. Then, digging out a box of matches from a different pocket, he crawled back into the locker.

'What are you doing now?' hissed Box.

'If they see these wires have been cut, they'll know for sure that something funny's going on.' Splinter's voice was muffled, like he was speaking through a blanket. 'If I burn the loose ends, they might think it was a short circuit or something.'

Box turned to Chess. 'He's very good,' he said.

'He is,' she agreed.

'Taught him everything he knows,' joked Box.

'Right,' said Splinter, sliding back into the room and looking at his wrist. 'Twenty past two. Time's getting short and before long they'll be checking these wires.' He pointed to the opposite window, where the hatch was. 'Let's go.'

A bolt on the top part of the frame released the glass hatch, allowing it to swing open and into the room. Cold air rushed through the opening and Chess felt tiny drops of rain speckle her face. Splinter was the first to crawl outside and Chess followed him.

Immediately in front of her were two iron girders, rough with rivets and wet with rain. They stretched ahead and into the darkness. They were shoulder width apart and several feet above them were two more girders, parallel with the bottom pair. Iron struts connected the lower girders at intervals like the rungs of a ladder. Chess's fingers were cold but she could feel that these struts were both gritty with rust and a little slippery. Between the upper and lower girders were crossbars that would make it impossible to avoid the slippery struts by sliding her feet along the thick metal beams.

Under the gantry there was a plunging drop to the zigzagging rooftops below. Their wet tiles were striped silver from the glow of the searchlights and black with shadow, but the rooms on the arch shielded the gantry from light. Chess could see only the sheen of metal leading into the drizzle ahead and beyond that, a black pillar that would be the incinerator chimney.

By shuffling over the struts on her hands and knees, Chess moved clear of the watch room giving Box space to emerge. Facing the opening in the window, he balanced with legs outspread, one foot on each of the lower joists. He wobbled a little as the wind gusted out of the darkness and over the walkway. Taking the lock knife from his pocket, he cut a strip of material from his trouser bottoms and he used this to wedge the hatch shut. Then Box turned to face the narrow metal bridge that linked the watch room to the chimney.

'No need to kneel,' he shouted, the wind catching his voice and hurling it into the darkness. Chess could tell that he was grinning even though she couldn't see his face. She could imagine his ruddy cheeks, his curly black hair beaded with water and his eyes alive with the rain, the wind, the darkness and the drop.

Reaching up to support herself with the top girders, Chess sprung to her feet. Now she could walk across the struts using the upper girders as handrails. Ahead, Splinter was doing the same thing and behind her so was Box. Leaning forwards to balance their backpacks across their shoulders the three of them edged along the walkway, above the rooftops and through the drizzling night.

The bandage that was wrapped around Chess's foot soaked up rain water. It became loose and began to slide as she walked on it. She tried to put her weight on her toes and then on her heel but found that this made it difficult to balance when she brought her other leg forward. She decided that the best thing would be to take the bandage off and it was as she thought this that she missed her step with her good foot. It slipped from a strut and into space.

Chess didn't cry out with shock. Her right hand didn't lose its grip, although her shoulder almost wrenched from its socket. She didn't hang helpless and then plummet to the roofs below although the fall was sudden. Chess was a street rat. She had scaled walls, stolen across rooftops, leapt between fire escapes and clung to her life by the strength of her fingers for as long as she had been despised and hunted.

Without having to think what to do, Chess's left arm shot down to take her weight on the bottom girder and her injured foot kicked across to jam itself against the bottom girder opposite. Only then did she look down and see the specks of rain glistening far below where they were caught by the searchlights that crept under the arch.

'Get up and stop messing about.' Box wasn't impressed.

'Sorry,' whispered Chess, hoisting herself back up. More carefully, she continued across the gantry. She concentrated on where she put her feet with such determination that it was only when she had passed through the small service door into the incinerator chimney that she realized the bandage had slipped from her foot.

Splinter was waiting in the shadows inside the chimney some distance below the door. 'There's rungs in the wall,' he said. Even though he spoke very quietly his voice echoed all the way up the metal chimney so that it sounded as if there were voices whispering high above Chess's head.

He switched on his torch.

'Not at me,' complained Chess as the beam flashed straight into her eyes. He pointed it at the wall and she saw that he was further down the shaft than she had expected and that between them both a series of metal rungs were fixed to the inner wall. She looked up and around. The chimney must have been at least fifteen feet across.

'No need for rope,' said Splinter. 'We can climb down to the platform on these.' The torch angled down. Maybe one hundred feet below there was a narrow ledge running the circumference of the chimney. At its centre the heavy blades of a large fan turned like a ship's propeller, humming through the air.

Box stuck his head through the doorway. 'Switch it off,' he hissed, angry. A click and the inside of the chimney was pitch dark apart from a feeble pink glow that flickered through the huge fan at its base.

'What d'you think you're doing?' Box demanded through gritted teeth. 'You may as well shine that torch straight out the door.'

'Well, get in and close it then.' Splinter's voice echoed up from inside the chimney,

'I'm just checking,' said Box.

'Checking what?' asked Chess.

'I don't know. What with you doing a jig out there and

him turning the place into a lighthouse it would be hard to miss us. And I thought I saw something moving, down on the roofs below us. Just before I got in here.' Chess heard the door close softly above her. 'OK,' sighed Box. 'Nothing. Nothing I could see anyway.'

In less than a minute all three of them were standing on the ledge at the bottom of the chimney. It wasn't much more than two feet wide, then there was a gap and then came the blades of the fan which filled the wide aperture and turned with a dull beat. Pale mauve light blinked between the blades from the chamber below.

We're standing where she was standing, thought Chess. With every flash of light from the fan blades she saw the flash of steel as the scalpel peeled the dermacart from the agent's thigh.

'This will be the control box,' Splinter was saying, patting a small metal case that was fixed to the chimney wall. On its top there was a dial switch and from its bottom a metal pipe ran down to the ledge. He unslung his backpack and kicked it to where the ledge met the chimney wall.

'When the fan stops, we can get between the blades and climb down. With the grappling hook in the bottom rung it'll be safe.'

'No,' said Box. 'Better to rest the hook on the edge of this platform.'

'Too dangerous,' objected Splinter. 'It could slip off.'

'Then whoever's up here has to hold it steady whilst the others climb down,' explained Box, 'and whoever goes last has to hope for the best. But I'm not leaving bits of rope stuck to that rung and hanging around because if anybody looks in here that's a dead give-away that something funny's going on. We have to be able to pull it off the ledge when we've finished. Always best to remove the evidence.'

'Well, I'm not going last,' said Splinter. 'Out of all of us, you're the only one who's built for bouncing.'

'Can we just get on with it?' asked Chess. Both her brothers looked at her. 'Please?'

'Splinter, then you, then me,' said Box. 'You two hold it steady whilst I come down. Keep some tension on it so it doesn't slip.' He shuffled the pack from his shoulders and knelt, taking care not to let his feet hang over the ledge where the blades were turning. 'We need to get this done and get back to Ethel.'

'We'll see,' said Splinter with a smile. Chess thought it was a strange thing to say and Box glanced up at his brother quizzically.

'See what?' he asked.

'Just an idea,' said Splinter innocently. 'Just something I'm thinking of.'

'Yeah? Well, less thinking and more doing.'

'OK, fly head, keep your hair on. This is where it gets lively.'

'Like it hasn't been lively enough already,' muttered Box, fastening a length of rope to the grappling hook.

'When I turn this switch the fan stops. When the fan stops turning the poison gas starts rising.' Splinter tugged a small sack out of his backpack. 'It's roach time.'

Box tugged two bars of chocolate from the side pocket of his pack. 'Not before I've stocked up on this. I'm not sharing it with some beetle that's strapped to the front of my face.'

'Just don't mash the beetle, pig boy.' Without further hesitation, Splinter yanked the limp roach from the sack and thrust his face into its body. The spindly legs jerked up and gripped his head. He grunted and then he looked up at Chess. Already the roach's body was pulsing with a network of red vessels. Splinter peered through the eyeholes in the creature's body. 'No time to waste, Chess. Beetle up.'

Letting the roach attach itself to her face didn't feel any better than it had the first time. Its legs crawled across her scalp, her nose and eyes burnt and she thought she was going to choke before she realized that she could see again and she was breathing easily. She looked at Box, now wearing his roach and he gave her a thumbs up. Then he tested the rope to check that it was fastened securely. Packs were swung back over shoulders.

Box looked at his wrist. 'Fifteen minutes and the clock's ticking,' he said. 'In we go.'

Splinter turned the switch. There was a squeal that resounded up the chimney and then a long groan as the blades of the fan slowed and shuddered to a halt. Box rested two prongs of the hook by the lip of the ledge and dropped the rope through a gap in the fan blades. It uncoiled into the chamber below and hit the floor with a slap.

Splinter was the first down the rope and when he was standing on the ground below, Chess sat on the ledge, caught the rope between her ankles and then lowered herself, hand under hand and feet clamped together. Box gripped the hooks above and Splinter held the end of the rope below. She slipped down with well-practised ease, observing the incinerator shed as she did so through stinging eyes.

Below her was the cerebral torus, a fleshy ring of bruise-purple material that almost filled the chamber, just as she had seen it on the dermacart. As she descended she saw that its outer skin was scored deep with wrinkles except for where iron buckles were clamped over it, biting into the soft tissue. These buckles fastened the torus to a metal platform whose struts and stanchions raised it nearly four feet above the floor.

The ring of brain was as thick as a car and looked tougher and more muscular than Chess had expected. It seemed to strain against the iron buckles, like a back bent double and trying to flex straight. It glistened with a sheen that Chess decided must have been deposited by the gas that billowed thick across the incinerator floor before drifting upwards in thinning trails. This gas was pink in the wan light. It issued from vents around the floor of the chamber, steaming from them with long slow hisses, like someone exhaling. Chess thought it sounded as if the room was breathing.

The rope dropped to the centre of the incinerator and into the middle of the cerebral torus. As she climbed down further she identified the three exits that had been mapped on the dermacart. Each of them was circular, about five feet in diameter and shrouded in vapour, like thick cobwebs. Beyond these openings Chess could see only darkness. She shuffled towards the end of the rope and the exits were hidden by the puce hulk of the brain.

When she was standing next to Splinter, the gas was so thick above the floor that she couldn't see her feet or her legs below the knee. It rolled across the room, licking up the platform and over the cerebral torus. She drew air into her lungs and saw the roach pulsing fiercely on Splinter's face. The air tasted normal, but now she was down here, Chess was in no doubt: without the creature that was clamped to her head and lining her nose, eyes and mouth with its own body tissue, the gas would have been deadly to her.

'Twelve minutes left,' said Splinter, looking up at the hole in the roof above. 'Fly head better shift his fat rump.' He wound the rope about his wrist and pulled it taut.

Box positioned the prongs of the grappling hook at the edge of the platform so that the rope ran straight down from the fastening eye to where Splinter was holding it. He had to inch over the ledge to make sure that the grapple didn't slip. Whilst he was counting on his weight pulling the hook down and secure onto the ledge, he knew that the slightest swing on the rope would cause it to slide the two inches into the gap. If that happened he would fall forty feet to the incinerator floor below.

'Don't move,' he called down to Splinter breathlessly.

'Don't tempt me,' came the reply.

Sliding down the rope quickly would have been too risky because he might have lost control and the hook might have slipped. So Box climbed down into the rising vapours slowly, shoulders burning with the effort of controlling the rope and holding his own weight, and all the time Chess kept looking up at her brother and then down at her watch and seeing how the minute hand was moving although she wasn't sure what time it was or how long they had left before the roaches died on their faces.

A little above Splinter's head, Box let go of the rope and dropped to the floor. Splinter pulled his arm away but not before Box had cracked his wrist with the heel of his foot.

'Fly head, you moron,' complained Splinter, rubbing his wrist. 'You could've said you were letting go.'

'Sorry,' said Box. He looked up the way he had come, towards the base of the chimney where the huge fan hung motionless. Now that he was on the floor of the incinerator it was difficult to get a clear view upwards. It was difficult to get a clear view in any direction.

'You nearly broke it.' Splinter inspected his wrist.

'You've got another,' said Box, distracted and peering up.

'It's all right for you,' continued Splinter, 'you can use both hands. This is my best hand.' Then he looked up to see what Box was looking at. 'What?'

'I don't know. I thought I heard something when I was on the rope. It sounded like someone was coming down the chimney.'

'You two are as bad as each other.' Splinter looked at his watch. 'Nine minutes.'

'Ssh!' Box put a finger to his lips and he mouthed, 'Listen.'

The three of them stood in the centre of the incinerator, encircled by the bulk of the cerebral torus, draped with the poisonous gas and they listened. Nothing at first, and then from high above, Chess heard a muffled clang of a boot on an iron rung. She looked at Box whose black mask was throbbing red with blood vessels. Her breathing sounded loud like it always did when she didn't want it to and the roach felt tight on her face.

'I knew we'd been seen crossing the bridge,' hissed Box. There was a long silence and then another faint ring of boot on metal.

'Someone's trying to creep up on us,' whispered Chess.

Splinter's mind was working. He had only seconds to consider the possibilities, evaluate the alternatives. His eyes flayed his surroundings until only the essential details remained. 'Lie down,' he hissed. 'All of us lie down in the gas. And wait.'

Chess did as Splinter commanded. Box and Splinter lay close by her. Now the gas rolled over her face. It was thick and luminous pink. Looking up was like looking up at evening clouds. For a moment she pretended that she was at the wharf, lying on a rooftop on a warm day, with Gemma lying next to her and seeing what shapes the clouds made for them. Then, with a slow sigh of gas, the room breathed and she heard Box say, 'The rope, Splinter. What about the rope?'

'Too late for that, fly head.'

Chess was staring up and through the gas. It swam over her and then it parted and through the shifting gap she saw something leaning over the ledge above her and looking down. It was a figure in a grey coat and it was kneeling at the edge of the platform.

'Trader,' breathed Box.

The trader's tangled hair sprouted in clumps between the straps of the mask he wore. The mask consisted of a pair of goggles with extended eyepieces and a mesh-fronted snout of a respirator that was strapped over his nose and mouth. He looked at the grappling hook beside him and then into the gas where the rope disappeared.

'He's alone,' whispered Splinter.

The trader leant further forwards, lowering his head until

it was level with the edge of the platform. Unsatisfied with the view, he placed one hand by his knees and with the other, took hold of the rope so that he could support himself whilst he lowered his head and shoulders into the incinerator shed.

'Keep absolutely still,' murmured Splinter. His clever fingers crawled across the floor until they found the end of the rope that hung from the ledge. 'That's it,' he crooned. 'You take a good look down here. Come on. Take a very good look. Take a very good, deep look.'

His fingers closed. The rope was pulled. The hook slid from the edge of the platform and the trader, who had been keeping his balance by holding the rope, fell.

With a yelp, he tried to catch a grip of the ledge with the hand that hadn't been holding the rope. His fingers did find metal and they splayed themselves over it, but the fall was too sudden to brake. However, his momentary grip on the ledge meant that he swung under it and then he was tumbling into the incinerator and towards the cerebral torus. He hit it boots first and the livid hulk of brain swallowed him up to his shoulders. He roared and shook and tried to pull his arms out of where they had plunged but Chess could see that the brain held him fast.

All of them stood and watched as the trader wrenched himself violently from side to side, trying to work his way out of the cerebral torus. He succeeded in freeing one arm and he flung this over the top of the brain, fingers clawing at the folded skin. He screamed.

The cerebral torus quivered and rippled, straining against the buckles and the gas hissed into the room. Now, as the trader struggled, Chess thought he was contorting strangely. His arm bent the wrong way and his neck stretched until his head was skewed at such an angle it was flat against the brain. His free hand slapped lamely and the clawed fingers started to pull away from one another; pull away as if they were separating from his hand.

For a moment, the trader stopped fighting and he stared at his hand. As it stretched wider and wider, holes began to appear in it, as if it was tearing apart. He began to scream again but this time Chess thought it sounded as if his voice was coming from further away.

Now his twisting neck bulged with knots of muscle and between these knots it split open but instead of flesh or blood, Chess saw space.

'It's like he's being pulled apart,' observed Splinter with cold fascination.

Chess couldn't say anything. Inside the roach, her mouth felt thick and dry. Through the tears in the trader's neck she could see the other side of the room.

'Pulled apart and disappearing at the same time,' concluded Splinter.

He was right. The trader's hand was so full of holes that it had almost vanished from sight and now the same thing was happening to his head and neck and even the mask he wore. They stretched and expanded and tore open to reveal space. The screaming had stopped, at least Chess couldn't hear any, but the gaping head and neck continued to turn and sheer. Piece by piece, the trader dissolved until Chess could see only a ghost of movement and then there was nothing.

Splinter was the first to speak. 'Anything that stupid deserves to die.'

'Being stupid doesn't mean you should die,' muttered Chess.

'Where's he gone?' asked Box.

Splinter shrugged. 'It's to do with the amarantium inside that thing, isn't it? The crystal. The stuff that's everywhere at once. It came into contact with him and now *he's* everywhere at once.' He laughed bleakly.

The room exhaled another billow of poison gas.

Box looked at his watch. 'Only about six minutes. We need to get this finished, Splinter.'

Splinter turned to Chess. 'You think you're so special,' he said. 'This is where you get to prove it.'

'I don't think I'm special,' said Chess. She stared at the slab of brain in front of her. Where the trader had been was now still and glistening. Moisture gathered in the deep folds. Then she looked at her hands which looked smaller than usual.

'I don't know why I have to do this,' she whispered. 'I don't want to do it, Splinter. You saw what happened to him.'

'The brain is waiting for you, Chess.' Splinter stared at her. Roach blood beat in a web across his face but his eyes were cold. 'It's time to start cutting.'

CHAPTER 18

Chess stood in front of the cerebral torus with the cutting wire hanging in her hand like a lasso. It was thin like cheesewire and about twenty feet long. A lump of metal was attached to one end. Chess had taken the roach bag out of her pack, ripped it apart and wrapped sacking pads around her hands so that the wire wouldn't cut into them as it ran through her fingers.

The brain loomed over her. Its surface was wrinkled with tiny creases as well as deep folds. It was impossible to tell how firm it was but the trader had sunk into it as easily as sinking into mud so she didn't think the weighted wire would have difficulty cutting through.

There was a long deep sigh and jets of poison gas streamed across the floor and into the air.

'Five minutes, Chess,' said Box gently.

'OK, OK,' said Chess. Now that she was close to the brain, she wasn't so confident about Ethel's assurance that she would be immune to its effects.

The roach was tight on her face but she was breathing easily, a faint pulse throbbing in her ears. She stepped away from the platform and swung the weight back and forth like a pendulum, gauging its momentum. Then she swung it up and forwards, letting the wire unravel and slide out of her hand as the weight arced over the slab of brain.

When she heard the lump of metal hit the floor on the other side of the torus, Chess wound the wire round her sacking-bound hands and yanked it hard. It came towards her and the weight clattered against the lower stanchions on the far side of the supporting platform as it was dragged forwards. Then the wire went taut and now, as she tugged on it, it began to bite into the brain.

There was a little resistance at first as it cut into the surface but almost at once the narrow metal cable was through and slipping into the body of the cerebral torus. It was held fast by the weight on the other side as Chess pulled. It cut down swift and smooth.

'That was easy,' said Box as the wire reached the bottom of the brain.

Chess had only to repeat the manoeuvre and there would be a slice of brain that she could ease from the mass and fold inside the large wallet that Splinter was already removing from his backpack.

'Come on,' urged Splinter. He stopped what he was doing to watch Chess who was pulling on the wire repeatedly. 'What now?' he snapped with a glance down at his watch.

'It's stuck,' complained Chess. 'The weight must have got snagged in the bars on the other side of the platform.'

'Brilliant,' muttered Splinter.

'I'll have to crawl through and untangle it,' said Chess. She squatted down to look through the swirling vapours at the struts and support bars that ran underneath the platform.

Box had walked over to her and now he took hold of the wire, having first taken the sack cloth wrappings from Chess to protect his hands. 'We don't have time for messing about,' he declared and as he said 'about' he heaved on the wire. Immediately he flew backwards and thudded onto the floor with the wire trailing loose from his fist.

'You idiot, fly head, you've snapped it.' Splinter was exasperated.

'It shouldn't of snapped,' complained Box, kneeling up. 'I nearly broke my shoulder.'

'The brain did it,' said Chess. She had picked up the broken end of the wire and was inspecting it. 'It must have eaten through the wire the same way it made the trader vanish.'

'Three and a half minutes and we start choking.' Splinter was looking around the chamber, eyeing the exits. Chess noticed how his gaze came to rest on the one that led to the exercise yard; the one that Ethel said they were not to take.

'You're going to have to cut the brain by hand, Chess,' he said. 'Or, we just don't bother and we get out whilst we still can.'

He eyeballed Chess through the black mask of the roach. It looked to Chess as if the creature's blood vessels were swelling and contracting erratically, as if it was finding it more difficult to filter the poison from the air that Splinter was breathing. She knew that in the same way, the roach would be dying slowly on her own face. But she didn't plan to leave until she had done what Ethel had asked her to do. This was her task; her chance, for once, to do something that mattered. Splinter's cool gaze was not going to make her back out, whatever the risk.

'We're going to have to leave it, Chess.' It was Box. 'It doesn't matter about the brain. Ethel will have to find another way.' He rested a hand on her shoulder. 'We're out of time. You can't do any more. Let's go.'

He's worried for me, Chess realized.

'Give me your knife,' she said.

'I'm not losing my knife inside that thing,' replied Box.

'Or mine,' added Splinter. 'We've got to go.'

'Give me a knife,' demanded Chess.

Box and Splinter shook their heads.

Chess's hand dropped to her jeans pocket and closed on a rough strip of metal. 'Fine,' she said, pulling out the nail file. 'I'll use this.'

'Don't, Chess,' pleaded Box. 'It isn't worth it.'

'Of course it is,' said Chess. 'We have to do this.'

Splinter said nothing.

Chess climbed up onto the platform, just to the left of the cut she had already made. Even standing on the metal shelf, the torus was taller than she was. She wedged her toes under the hulk of brain. To her surprise, it was warm. She rested the palm of her left hand lightly against the moist surface. In her right she held the nail file. She looked at the back of her left hand and it appeared normal. Her feet were exactly where they should have been.

'In this life you've got to use what you've got.' That's what Klinky Mallows had told her. The nail file felt no bigger than a claw but it was all she had and at least it would dig into the brain more neatly than her fingers.

At head height and no more than an inch from the first cut, Chess pushed the tip of the nail file into the cerebral torus. It broke through the surface easily and already, her hand was diving into the hot, wet body of the brain. She pulled it out, reached up so that her hand was level with the top of the brain and cut downwards and inwards until her arm was buried inside the livid mass up to her shoulder. The brain tissue parted with a long squelching noise.

'Two minutes,' shouted Splinter.

'Just leave it, Chess,' shouted Box.

Chess ignored her brothers. She drew in air and then pushed her head and upper body into the long, deep cut she had already made. The warm bulk of the brain smothered her and it was dark. She felt waves judder against her body as the cerebral torus convulsed. Pulse thumping and lungs starting to burn, Chess cut up and down and burrowed into the warm mass.

It would have been easy to panic, to strike out in any direction and simply chop her way out of the brain. But by concentrating all her thoughts on cutting as straight as possible, she was able to contain the sensation of being smothered by warm, churning darkness and she held back her exploding desire to breathe.

Now she was aware of an emptiness in her hand and a pulpy mush slipping between her fingers. The nail file had vanished and she was digging through the brain with her fingers alone, jabbing them forwards and sliding them up and down.

At least I'm still here, thought Chess, and then her flat hand broke out of the other side of the cerebral torus. Close behind it came her head and she gulped at the air, desperate to breathe.

Immediately she realized that the air tasted different; bitter and sulphurous. Her eyes and throat began to burn but this was not the burning sensation she had felt when the roach's membranes spread themselves over her eyes, up her nose and down her throat. This burning was hotter and deeper. As the air she had breathed filled her lungs she began to cough. The coughing ripped up from deep in her chest, making it ache. Each time she drew in breath, the burning increased and the coughing came harder.

'Chess! Chess!' Box was shouting to her. As the air scorched her eyes and throat his voice became distant, unimportant. Then she saw him standing below her and looking up. He must have crawled under the platform to see what she was doing on the other side.

'Your face, Chess, I can see your face.'

Chess put a hand to her face and touched the skin. The roach had vanished. Of course it had vanished; just as the nail file had vanished. The crystal core within the cerebral torus had dissolved it into nothingness.

At least my clothes are still on, thought Chess. It was a funny thought and it made her smile. Then she felt her lungs spasm and saw only darkness.

Box didn't understand why his sister was smiling as she toppled forwards from the platform. He didn't so much catch her as block her way to the floor and he sagged to his knees as she slumped into his arms, limp and with the breath rasping weakly between her lips.

'Listen, Splinter,' yelled Box, voice resounding off the

walls of the incinerator shed. 'Her roach has gone. I'm going to give her mine. Use the wallet to pull out the piece of brain and wrap it up. Meet me in the tunnel that leads out. And be quick. Even with the masks we've only got a minute.'

Box took a deep breath and pushed his face into his hand. Instantly, he felt the tension release from the back and sides of his head and then the dark body with its long legs dangling was prone in his palm. He cradled Chess's head, lifting it gently and he placed the black body of the roach against her face. The thin limbs jerked into life, digging into her hair which was damp. Box pulled his hand away so that the roach legs wouldn't strap it to Chess's hair.

She moaned and rolled her head from side to side. Box wasn't sure what damage the poison gas had done but he pushed that thought away, took Chess in his arms and stood up. His eyes were itching and he could feel the beginnings of the ache in his chest that sooner or later would make him open his mouth and breathe in the air.

'Change of plan,' shouted Splinter from the other side of the cerebral torus. 'We're taking a different route.'

By his unsteady tone, Box could tell that Splinter was grappling with the unwieldy slice of brain, pulling it from the mass and trying to roll it inside the wallet without letting it touch his skin

'We're going to take the tunnel that leads to the exercise yard,' his brother declared.

Are you mad? Box wanted to shout. The exercise yard would lead them to where the hunters and traders had gathered. But Box couldn't shout anything. He was finding it difficult to keep his eyes open, they were burning and watering so much. He certainly couldn't waste vital breath arguing with Splinter.

'Carry her through there before we all run out of time,' continued Splinter. 'I'm nearly done.'

Box stood his ground. 'No,' he risked yelping. 'Too lively.' Chess shivered in his arms.

'You go the way I say, fly head,' shouted Splinter. 'I'm going that way and I'm the one who'll get us out of here. I've got my reasons.' Splinter was panting, fastening the wallet tight about the slab of brain. Once it was secure he pulled each of the loose straps that dangled from the wallet. Air hissed and the wallet began to shrink, compressing the brain until it was the size of a small sleeping bag. He lifted it. It was heavier that he had expected. He took a lungful of air and shouted, 'We've got seconds, Box. Seconds.'

Box looked down at Chess. The roach was still pulsing on her face but it was obvious that the creature was labouring; the pulse was faint and spasmodic. The ache in his own chest was driving itself into his shoulders and down his thighs. His body wanted him to breathe. Hating Splinter, Box turned away from the cerebral torus and the sickly glow of the incinerator and carried Chess into the tunnel that led to the exercise yard.

As soon as he entered the tunnel he felt cool air rush over his face. It made his eyes water even more than the gas in the incinerator had done but it didn't sting them. The air was blasting down from between baffles in the arched roof above him. Once he had passed beneath them the rush of air stopped and Box guessed that it was designed to keep the poisonous gas out of the tunnel.

Instinctively, he ventured the slightest sniff. He was desperate to suck in a chestful but he didn't want to find that the air was still as corrosive as it had been in the incinerator. What he sniffed was cold and odourless. It didn't hurt his nose or his chest. That was good enough for Box who couldn't hold his breath any longer. He drank the air down and panted as if he would never get enough of it. As the stabbing in his lungs subsided, Chess's weight began to bear down on his arms but he didn't prop her against the curve of the tunnel wall until the entrance to the incinerator was only a coin-sized disc behind him.

The further that Box had gone into the cylindrical shaft, the narrower it had become. Where the tunnel left the incinerator it had been easy to walk but now the floor curved so deeply and the roof had dropped so low that he had to stoop to move forwards. He knelt down and pushed his hand against the roach on Chess's face. It released its grip and slithered to her tummy before flopping onto the floor of the tunnel where Box left it. He listened and heard Chess breathing, slowly but smoothly. He felt her forehead which was cool but not cold and held her hand which was limp but not lifeless. Satisfied that she was nearer to sleep than death, Box let out a long sigh, pulled off his pack and leant back against the wall opposite her.

It wasn't quite dark. Now that his eyes had adjusted to the murk he could pick out the pale sheen of Chess's face and the darker mass of her chestnut hair, black in the ventilation shaft. He could see narrow bars of light streaking the tunnel walls where they led away from him, towards the exercise yard. He could see his own hands as they worked at the side pocket of his backpack, pulling out a bar of chocolate. The silver wrapper flashed and then he closed his eyes as he bit. By the time that Splinter reached him, Box had devoured that bar and was waving a chunk from the next under Chess's nose.

Splinter watched him for several seconds before asking, 'What the hell are you doing, fly head?'

'Trying to bring her round,' explained Box.

'You are the only creature whose life can be sustained entirely by chocolate. She needs a doctor.'

'Rubbish,' said Box. 'Look.'

Chess coughed and licked her lips. Then she began to cough harder, a hacking cough that rattled up and down the tunnel.

'They'll hear us,' hissed Splinter.

'Too bad,' Box hissed back and then he glared at Splinter. 'You were the one who said we had to come this way. Moron.'

Splinter threw his roach at Box. It hit Box's shoulder and landed with a slap on the metal floor of the shaft. 'Don't question my thought processes, fly head,' he said. 'Just try to keep up with them.'

'Are you OK?' Box asked Chess whose open eyes glinted in the dark.

'Not really,' she said and coughed some more. 'I can't get my breath back and my eyes hurt.' There was a wet chewing noise. 'Thanks for the chocolate though.' More coughing. 'And thanks for getting me out of there. I thought I was dead.'

'Dead would be quieter,' said Splinter.

'Sorry, Splinter,' said Chess, trying not to cough which

only made her cough the more. She noticed light flash at the far end of the shaft. 'Where are we?'

'In the ventilation shaft,' answered Box and then pointedly and with another glare at Splinter. 'The ventilation shaft that leads to the exercise yard.'

'What!' choked Chess with another volley of coughing. She clamped her hand over her mouth to contain the noise. 'Why?'

'We're going to see what happens,' announced Splinter. 'We're going to see the Fat Gobster.'

Both Chess and Box knew his voice well enough to know that he was smiling at them in the darkness.

'You have got to be off your head,' stated Box, his face inches from Splinter's. 'We have to *get away*.'

Splinter pressed the tips of his fingers against Box's chest. He didn't push him but Box knew that the least touch from Splinter was a danger signal. 'Listen, fly head. Don't you want to find out what's happening to the others?'

'What others?'

'Our others. From the wharf. Remember? Or is that too long ago for your goldfish brain to handle? We might even be able to help them.'

Chess wanted to know what had happened to the others but she wasn't sure that Splinter was serious about helping them. The only person that Splinter was ever serious about helping was Splinter.

'And also,' continued Splinter, 'the really clever thing is not to follow Ethel's plan. She's trying to outsmart the squealer, right? But there's a danger that someone will discover her plan, or follow her to the dog track or something

266

like that. Now, if we do something that even she isn't expecting, the Twisted Symmetry will never catch us. By *not* sticking to her plan we make ourselves a lot safer.'

Chess realized that what Splinter said was perfectly logical but she knew also that he wasn't changing the plan to make them safer. She knew that because Splinter hadn't called Ethel an old lady or old witch or old hag. He had called her Ethel which meant that he was trying to sound nice and reasonable. There was nothing that made Chess more suspicious of Splinter than when he tried to sound nice and reasonable.

'He's got a point, Chess,' said Box.

'See, Chess,' said Splinter. 'Even fly head says I've got a point.'

She could sense Splinter's excitement in the spark of his eyes, the tremor of his voice and the electric tension of his body, taut as a bowstring.

You just want to watch what happens to the children, thought Chess. You just want to see what the suck worm does to them.

'How can we find out what happens to the others?' she asked. 'We can't just walk up and watch, you know.' It wasn't the same as refusing to do it but it struck her as a big enough problem to prevent Splinter pursuing his new plan.

'Very simple, Chess. We just carry on going down this tunnel. We open the grating at the end and we hitch a lift with everybody else.'

'It doesn't sound all that easy,' observed Box.

'It's quarter past three now. At four o'clock the convoy leaves for the airfield. The exercise yard will be packed with people coming and going and loads of vehicles. It won't be difficult for us to sneak a lift. How many times have we done that? You two leave your backpacks here; travel light. We only need the wallet now so I'll leave everything else and just carry that in my pack. We get on the back of a wagon, it carries us out of the prison and we get out when it stops at the airfield. Big deal. Once we've seen what happens, we can go to the dog track and find the old bird; keep her waiting for us for once.'

'We might be seen,' objected Chess, spluttering into her hand although the tightness in her chest was easing.

'We're street rats, Chess. Are we usually seen? Even when the crashers are after us, are we usually seen?' Splinter, sounding reasonable again.

'No,' said Box and he grinned. 'Not usually.'

'Well then. And this lot won't be expecting us. However much they're looking for us, the last place they'll expect us is in their own back yard. Not even Ethel or the Committee expect us to be there.' He held his backpack upside down, shook it and let the contents fall out; rope, wallet, chocolate.

'Let's keep the chocolate, Splinter. And mine and Chess's,' pleaded Box.

'You're such a pig, fly head,' said Splinter, but he did stuff all the chocolate bars into the side pockets of his pack. He pushed the large wallet, thick with brain, back into place and slipped his arms through the straps. 'This weighs a ton,' he complained. Then he began to crawl forwards, towards the flashes from the searchlights at the end of the shaft. He stopped once to look back and speak.

'No one sees what they don't expect to see; isn't that what

the old lady says? The last place the Twisted Symmetry would expect to see us is under their noses. It doesn't matter what the squealer tells them; we couldn't be safer.'

It was shortly before six o'clock that morning when Ethel realized she had made a mistake.

She was standing in the commentary box at the old dog track, looking out of the wide window at the rutted race circuit, the decrepit stadium with its mouldering towers and beyond the towers, a blazing pink streak of dawn. Beside her stood Captain Riley, corduroy trousers and red sweater replaced by black combats and body armour. Slung behind his back was a snub-nosed sub-machine gun. Grenades, a torch, a holstered pistol and a radio were strapped to his chest webbing and ammunition pouches, karabiners and a gas mask hung on his belt. On the left shoulder of his jacket was the patch displaying a grey star in a purple circle that was worn by agents of the Charitable Operations Executive.

Behind her sat Joachim Breslaw, a thick travel rug draped over his legs and tucked between the rigid cables that ran from the chair and into his limbs, and at the back of the room, leaning against the wall with arms crossed, was Lemuel Sprazkin. He wore a heavy black ulster coat and he glared at his boots without speaking. He had not spoken from the moment that two armed agents of the COE had appeared at his rooms at Committee HQ in the early hours of that morning and told him that they were escorting him to the city dog track on Ethel's orders.

'The snipers must be getting cold,' said Ethel, observing a

stick figure change its position on one of the stadium towers.

'They have been in position for nearly two hours,' said Riley. 'They are trained to hold a location for two months. Don't worry about the snipers, Ethel.'

'And the CQB teams?'

'Two are deployed around the stadium,' said Riley.

Two CQB teams meant eight men or women. Ethel strained her bloodshot eyes to survey the seating and penetrate the entrance tunnels but could see no one. 'Very good,' she murmured. 'They are very good, Captain.'

'They're the best.'

'And three more teams in reserve?' confirmed Ethel.

'Yes.' He turned from the window to look at Ethel and frowned slightly. She knew this; she had asked him the same questions twice during the past half hour. Captain Riley began to calculate; agents, ammunition, vehicles, communications. He had to be ready to adapt his plans to what was going to happen. He had to be ready to do this because he knew that Ethel's repeated questions meant that something had gone wrong.

'But we have no helicopter gunship?'

'We have two light transport helicopters,' said Riley. 'Like I told you earlier; that's the best I could do at such short notice.'

'No, that's fine, that's fine, Captain.' Ethel hummed aimlessly for several seconds and then smoothed her hands down the front of her skirt. Without turning her face from the window, she said, 'I think, perhaps, transport helicopters are what we will need.'

Joachim Breslaw cleared his throat. 'What is wrong, Mevrad?'

Ethel turned round and looked at Joachim Breslaw and then at Lemuel Sprazkin. 'I owe both of you an apology; an apology and an explanation.' Then she took off her spectacles, rubbed her face wearily and replaced them. 'I have made a mistake. A bad mistake.'

'Last night you told both of us that the Tuesday children would be here, at the stadium this morning, yes?' said Joachim. Ethel nodded. Joachim knitted his bristly, ginger eyebrows. 'You thought to tell us that so that one or other of us might tell the enemy? You thought to see which one of us was an enemy spy?'

'That is what I thought,' admitted Ethel.

Joachim gave a bleak half-laugh that was full of phlegm and empty of humour. 'You are astonishing, Mevrad. You really do trust no one.'

Ethel said nothing. Her attention was on Lemuel. His eyes remained fixed on his feet and his face was frost white and hard.

'Lemuel, I am sorry,' Ethel said gently. 'I am so sorry.'

When Lemuel did look up and speak his voice was deliberate as a scalpel. 'You have already discussed with Joachim the possibility that I might be working for the Symmetry?'

'I have,' admitted Ethel.

'You thought I had betrayed you?'

Ethel hesitated and then said carefully, 'I thought it was a possibility.'

'I see. Well, since it is agreed that I have not in fact

betrayed the Committee, have you asked yourself, Mevrad, how the Symmetry knew where to find the children when they were with *you*?'

Ethel turned away and looked through the window. The stark first light had been swallowed by low, undulating clouds. The morning was already turning grey. She closed her eyes and saw Chess in the detention unit when they had first met, saw the Inspector releasing her from her chains and saw how he had grasped her wrist and twisted the skin hard enough to hurt her. She knew that that was when the Symmetry had been one move ahead of her.

'They tagged her,' said Ethel. She shook her head to herself. 'So obvious. Why didn't I realize?'

'Everyone is fallible,' said Joachim, voice grating but soft. 'Not just humans. Everyone.'

Ethel wasn't listening. 'They inserted a tagging chip into her wrist whilst she was in the detention centre. They can monitor where the chip goes and wherever it goes, they know that Chess is there. When she was with me they knew where she was and they just had to observe my flat and wait for the right moment to send in the rippers. The only time they would have lost her would have been at Committee HQ and in their own complex at the prison where spy technology like a tag won't work.'

Captain Riley spoke. 'That means the moment the children leave the Riverside Prison, the Twisted Symmetry will know where they are.'

'But if they come here we are ready for the enemy just the same.' Joachim attempted to sound positive.

'They aren't coming here.' Ethel stared out of the window. 'Something has happened.'

'The Symmetry have taken them?' Joachim leant forwards, cables jerking.

'Who can say?' replied Ethel.

'What do you want to do?' asked Riley.

'We must be ready to help them if they have not already been captured. Now, if they have succeeded in taking the brain sample, and if they have evaded capture but could not come here, I think I know where they will try to go. Are your men ready to move?'

'On your command.'

'We will need those helicopters. You're also going to have to rustle up some assault craft to travel down the river. We must move fast.'

Captain Riley was already speaking into his radio; crisp, precise orders for his agents to withdraw, to make ready the helicopters, to commandeer the assault craft.

Ethel saw that the pinpoint pupils of Lemuel's grey eyes were fixed on her like drills. 'I am sorry,' she repeated softly.

'I have made such sacrifices,' he said haltingly, 'and face excruciating torment if ever my former comrades should have the opportunity.'

'I know, Lemuel, I know.'

'I could have betrayed you, Mevrad. I could have given the girl to the Symmetry. They would have welcomed me back for that. No agonies for me then.'

'I know that, Lemuel.'

'But I didn't do that. Do you understand, Mevrad? I didn't have to help you this time. This time I *chose* to do the right thing.' His voice cracked as he struggled to speak calmly. 'Just remember this, Mevrad: when it came to the test, it wasn't *my* loyalty to *you* that failed.'

Although Lemuel was glaring hatefully, Ethel saw the moisture glistening on his eyelashes. His mouth was rigid and his jaws clenched. 'This is your problem now,' he said, before turning away and marching from the room, letting the door swing shut slowly behind him.

CHAPTER 19

The same streak of pink sky burnished the woods at the edge of the eastern airfield. Between the woods and the first grey concrete taxiway there was a wind-buffeted strip of rough grassland, twenty metres wide. Normally it was deserted but this morning the grass was hidden beneath a fleet of lorries and motor bikes. Their engines had been silent for nearly two hours but the morning air was still thick with the fumes of oil and diesel.

At the far end of the taxiway, some distance from where the convoy had drawn up, there was a low, grassy embankment. Just below the crest of the embankment, lying side by side on their bellies and with heads just high enough to watch what was happening on the airfield was Box, then Chess and then Splinter.

A couple of hours earlier they had ghosted through the shadows of the exercise yard whilst all about, traders had been occupied with cracking whips and bellowing commands at cowering children who were being driven onto the lorries. Most went silently. Any who complained or moved too slowly were dragged from the lines and dealt with by whips and boots and fists. All the time, patrolling the high walls were hunters, and more hunters were assembling at the motor bikes.

Splinter had spotted an old, canvas-roofed truck whose rear was stacked with fencing and wooden spars. It was parked to one side of the yard and near to the entrance gates. With Box and Chess slinking behind him, he had worked his way round to the truck and was up and over its tailgate in a blink.

They wedged themselves horizontally in the narrow spaces between the canvas walls of the truck and its metal sides and, hidden in this way, they had been carried to the airfield as part of the convoy. It hadn't been a long journey but it had been cold and rough and more than once, Chess had been sure she would slip through the bottom of the canvas where it was lashed at intervals to brackets on the side of the truck.

The convoy had arrived whilst night was still deep. The smell of crushed grass and churned earth was sweet and the early morning air was so cold it made her want to shiver although she kept rigid. She could see nothing but she could hear traders close to the truck, stomping by its side and talking with their gruff voices in a language she didn't understand. Twice, someone had come to the back of the wagon to haul out a length of fencing.

They hadn't left their hiding place until half an hour after the last voice had trailed away. By that time the noise and activity around the vehicles had ceased although the shouting of orders and the growl of motor bike engines still drifted across the airfield. As night dissolved into morning with a whisper of mist, the Tuesdays had slipped out of the truck and snaked their way through the stationary convoy and into the wood line out of which they had spirited once they had passed behind the embankment at the far corner of the airfield.

To their left and behind them were the woods. To their right and distant was the airfield terminal, the control towers and masts flattened beneath the wide sky. Ahead of them stretched the runways and at the opposite end of these criss-crossing lanes were a row of hangars. Between the hangars and the embankment, in the centre of the airfield, was a compound built of high metal fences that were set in concrete crash barriers and guarded by hunters.

Whilst they had been hidden in the truck, Chess had heard the compound being built. There had been the rattle of iron mesh taken from the lorries and the revving of engines as the concrete stands were manoeuvred into place. Then there came the hiss of whips and barking of orders by the traders as the children were herded from the vehicles.

Chess thought that the compound looked about half the size of a football pitch. It was packed so tightly with children that those on the outside were jammed against the wire of the fencing. Petryx Ark-turi had said that there were over twenty-five thousand captives; Chess could imagine what the squeeze would be like for those at the centre.

Most of the captives would be nice children, jack children; children who were used to three meals a day, who were bought clothes and shoes, who had families; children who had never before lived with the terror of being hunted and beaten. Amongst them would be a few hundred street rats from the wharf, and maybe other rats who had been picked up in the city.

Chess looked for faces she knew, but there were so many children and they were so far away from her that it was impossible to see any of them clearly. They were all the same now; crushed together, waiting for whatever the Twisted Symmetry had planned for them. It didn't matter who was a street rat, who was a jack.

She and her brothers had arrived at the embankment as the last group of children from the hangars were being marched to the fenced enclosure by a team of traders. Chess guessed that there were as many as a thousand. They walked slowly, feet dragging over the runway, heads hanging. Chess knew what it was to be weak with hunger but these children had been weakened by more than hunger. She wondered for how long they had been stolen, not knowing what was going to happen to them, how long they had been kept in their thousands in the darkness of the hangars and what had been done to them as hour upon hour had passed under the brute tyranny of the traders. She saw how their wild-headed, towering guards roared at them and how they were generous with the lashes and blows they delivered.

With these last thousand children crammed into the compound, the entrance was sealed by more fencing. The traders returned to the hangars and although some others were still clustered in knots around the vehicles and on the runways, it was obvious that the operation was now entirely under the control of the hunters.

Hunters stood guard all around the fencing with rifles cradled in their arms. Eight jeeps mounted with heavy machine guns circled the compound, chunky tyres grumbling over the concrete runway. Beyond the circuit the jeeps were following sat a hunter at a table on which was mounted a console the size of a small television. Chess could see the blue glow of dials on the front of the apparatus. In the gloom of the morning they were luminous. Red lights flashed in lines along its top.

Next to the table stood another hunter, holding a cellphone. Chess could tell this because from time to time he put his hand to the side of his head and spoke. At other times he exchanged words with the hunter who was sitting at his elbow or signalled commands to the other units. This hunter was directing the operation. Despite the identical black uniforms and silver badges worn by the hunters, Chess recognized him. She recognized his shape and she recognized the way he moved and she knew that had she been closer, she would have recognized his smell.

The Tuesdays spoke in whispers. Their voices could barely be heard above the wind which moaned over the airfield and the drone of traffic which hummed from the far side of the woods where the motorway ran above the river and towards the east side of the city.

'My feet are cold,' complained Chess. The dew was seeping into her jeans and pullover. When nobody responded she said tentatively, 'Ethel was right after all; I was able to touch the brain.'

That prompted a reply from Splinter. 'Coincidence,' he muttered, without looking away from the scene in front of him. 'Don't be fooled by all that stuff about a blood test. They can't have done a blood test to see who you are. Think about it. You do a blood test by comparing a new sample of blood with an old sample of blood.'

'Maybe they had an old sample of Chess's blood,' suggested Box.

'How, fly head? We've only just met this lot, remember? The Committee have had nothing to do with us before. They can't have an old sample of Chess's blood to compare. So going on about testing Chess's blood to see if she is who they think she is, to see if she is someone special, is rubbish.'

Everyone was quiet. Behind them the trees stirred.

'What are they doing now?' asked Box.

The Inspector had been talking on his cellphone earnestly. The console operator held up a thumb and the Inspector circled his arm above his head and then held it out, his flat hand directed towards the hangars. As one, the sentries who had been guarding the compound turned from the wire and started to jog towards the far side of the airfield, where the hangars were. They were joined by a stream of hunters and traders who were leaving the centre of the airfield for the furthermost side. The jeeps continued to circle the children and were joined by a detachment of twenty outriders who peeled off to take up positions around the fencing, motor bike engines revving hard although the bikes were stationary.

'It must be time,' said Splinter and he looked at his wristwatch. 'Five minutes to go.'

'How is watching this meant to help the children?' grumbled Chess.

'Just shut up and keep watching,' replied Splinter. Chess saw that his face was transfixed in rapt fascination exactly as it had been when he had been watching the children from the watch room at the Riverside Prison.

Box rolled onto his side and looked back towards the trees.

'What now?' asked Splinter.

Box's eyes worked along the edge of the wood, searching the dark spaces between the tree trunks. Directly behind him was a track that divided the wood. Its floor was orange with leaf mould and rutted with shallow troughs and mounds of earth topped by bracken.

'Just checking,' said Box.

'Checking what?' Splinter began to glower at him.

'A feeling,' explained Box uncertainly. 'Thought I heard something.'

Splinter stared at him until Box said, 'OK, forget it. There's nothing.'

'Trust me, fly head,' Splinter assured him. 'This is the safest we've been for days. Right now, no one knows where we are.'

A cold wind scythed over their heads and howled through the convoy.

'Where's our suck worm?' pondered Splinter. He looked left to right across the airfield. 'No sign yet.'

'The wind's changed direction,' said Box. 'It was blowing at us. Now it's blowing behind us.'

Chess's feet were suddenly very cold. The wind was rushing out of the woods behind her and buffeting the embankment where she lay. When she looked over the crest of the hillock, her hair whipped forwards on either side of her face. The corners of her eyes started to water in the gusting air.

'Weird wind,' decided Box, almost having to shout although Chess was lying next to him and Splinter was lying on her other side. A chain of leaves spiralled by his head and went dancing across the airfield. The leaves were followed by a thin branch that stung his ear as it flew past. The leaves and the stick were joined by more debris that swirled over the grass and the concrete of the runways, coming from all directions until it was blown up against the fencing.

Chess also thought that the way in which the wind was blowing was strange and then it struck her what was wrong. Leaves and sticks and pieces of rubbish were blowing from all about the airfield but from every point they were blowing inwards, towards its centre; towards the compound, as if they were being sucked there.

'Shouldn't we move?' shouted Box as a branch the size of an arm shattered against the earth on his left side.

'Where to?' Splinter shouted back. He was watching the centre of the airfield. He saw the Inspector nodding and then taking the cellphone from his ear and putting it in a chest pocket of his jacket. He waved his arm and one by one the jeeps stopped circling the children and raced towards the hangars. The final jeep pulled up by the Inspector. Table and console were handed up to be stowed in its rear and then the Inspector and the console operator climbed on board before the jeep sped across the runways to join the others which were now entering the hangars.

The motor bikes remained but the scream of their engines was feeble beneath the rushing air. Splinter noticed how one of the remaining hunters looked up from his motor bike, dark glasses turning skywards. Splinter followed the hunter's gaze and saw how leaves and sticks were swirling up and into the air from all about the compound. They formed a dark trail that twisted into the sky; a charcoal sky that was moving in a way that Splinter had never seen before. Over the whole of the airfield the clouds had started to churn and bubble as if they were boiling. At the same time they were streaming inwards, coursing through the sky in rags to gather over the compound.

The hunter opened the throttle of his motor bike and sent the rear wheel into a spin. Splinter couldn't hear the squeal but he saw the puff of black smoke from the back tyre before the bike reared up. Then the front wheel slammed back down and the bike shot forwards, speeding from the compound. Behind it hurtled the remaining hunters, motor bikes weaving to avoid the debris that came flying towards them.

Chess thought she could hear screaming from inside the fences but she couldn't be sure because her ears were full of rushing air. The air pounded her face with such force that it was difficult to draw breath. Splinter was pointing up at the sky. When she looked she saw that directly above the compound, the clouds were churning and banking into a vast tube. The rim of the tube was formed by the waves of cloud that were drawn into it and as more cloud boiled inwards, the tube began to stretch downwards, out of the sky and towards the centre of the enclosure.

The only screaming that Chess could hear now was the screaming of the wind as it tore out of the woods and over her head. But even though she could not hear the children, she could feel how terrified they must have been and for an instant a bright disc flashed in front of her eyes and swirling towards the disc were tree branches and clothing and all about her was heat and fear, and the press of bodies and then there was a shriek, a human shriek and she was looking across to the compound and now there were children in the air, spinning and rolling and falling upwards; falling into the sky.

The vast churning tube yawned open and surged downwards. It engulfed one end of the compound, swallowing children and wire fence panels. Those who were at the other end were wrenched from the earth in a tumbling mass, streaking through the air or else scudding over the ground without stopping until they had disappeared within the ravenous maw of the suck worm. Chess saw how hundreds of children clung to the fences only to be picked off as the Fat Gobster's strength overcame the grip of their fingers or merely ripped the fencing from the concrete stands, consuming it and the children who were still clinging to the wire.

Her eyes had been shut tight long before the suck worm began to retract. Even then the blustering air thumped her face so hard she pushed it into the turf in front of her to escape its blast. She lifted her head only as the wind eased. When she peeped over the top of the embankment she saw that the centre of the airfield had been picked bare of any item that was not made of concrete or rooted to the earth. The compound had been torn apart. Some of the fence panels remained in their bases but many of the bases were empty now and the panels had gone. There were no children; there was no sign that any children had ever been there. The clouds were rippling as water does after a stone has hit it, rolling away in every direction from a point directly above where the fenced enclosure had been. As the suck worm withdrew it released the sky which settled back into a low, brooding blanket of grey.

Chess was aware of Box and Splinter gazing out over the airfield in mute astonishment. The air was absolutely still. Splinter spoke only after a woodpecker had broken the silent aftermath.

'That was amazing!' he said.

'That was horrible,' said Chess.

'That was the biggest vacuum cleaner I've ever seen,' said Box.

'What do you know about vacuum cleaners?' scoffed Splinter.

'I know they suck stuff up.'

'They don't suck up children,' observed Splinter. He rolled onto his back with difficulty because of the pack he was wearing. 'Amazing. Just amazing.' He looked sideways at Chess. 'It was impressive, wasn't it?'

'I didn't like it,' was all she could say to describe what she had felt as the suck worm had struck. But what she had felt had been vivid and terrifying. Even now, if she closed her eyes, she could see the suck worm's mouth descending; as if she had been right under it, as if she had been in the compound.

'You don't understand the way the world works, Chess,' explained Splinter. 'You have to have power. Look at what the Twisted Symmetry can do. It's no wonder . . .'

'We know,' groaned Box, bored with Splinter. 'It's no wonder they are *so* great and the Committee are *so* rubbish.'

'You said it,' said Splinter, smiling up at the sky.

Chess felt colder than ever. 'We should go now,' she said. 'Before it's too late.'

'OK, OK,' grumbled Splinter. 'Don't wet your pants.'

Box started and sat bolt upright. He swore once. 'It's too late.'

Splinter rolled over and next to him, Chess sat up. 'No,' she mouthed.

Standing over them were five hunters carrying rifles. Chess realized that they had come out of the woods below the embankment. Their eyes were hidden behind dark glasses but their mouths were grim. They raised the rifles towards Chess and her brothers.

'How?' was all Splinter could say and he kept saying it. There was no way the hunters should have found them. They hadn't been seen by anyone and nobody knew that they were going to be at the airfield.

Out on the runway, engines coughed into life. Chess looked over her shoulder and saw four motor bikes riding towards them and behind the motor bikes came a big white van with rusty wheel arches.

CHAPTER 20

The white van stopped on the taxiway at the foot of the embankment. The motor bikes pulled up behind it and the hunters dismounted with a clatter of boots. Three of them drew stun sticks which they slapped against their gloved palms whilst the fourth stood with his arms folded.

'Down,' ordered a hunter with a rifle, jabbing its muzzle in the direction of the van. Box stood up, slapping grass from his jeans and T-shirt. Splinter stood up more slowly. The elbows of his morning coat were muddy and so were the knees of his black trousers. He shook his shoulders to position the backpack. Then he took a long look at the five hunters with the rifles before turning to study the hunters waiting at the bottom of the other side of the bank.

'Nine of you and armed,' he said. 'I'm flattered.'

'Down,' repeated the hunter.

'Come on,' said Splinter.

As Chess followed him the van's front doors opened with a squeal and a clunk. Long legs emerged from the driver's side and from the passenger's side and behind the legs followed short, stout bodies and craggy heads streaming ragged coils of black hair. The passenger slammed a huge arm over the roof of the van to help wrench himself out of the compartment. Chess saw the chunks of ring on his forefingers and after he had pulled the hair out of his eyes and looked up the embankment, she recognized him. He stepped out of the van, stood to his full height and stroked his plaited beard.

'Girl,' grunted the trader who had clambered out of the driver's side. Chess recognized him as well.

'Again,' said the trader with the beard. 'This time we beat you all and make you sleep. Then you come peacefully.' He looked across to the hunters with the stun sticks. 'If you kill the boys by accident that is OK. You must beat them very long. But the girl must live.'

'I don't mind Chess being special,' muttered Box, walking down the bank very slowly. 'but I'm sick of everyone wanting to kill you and me because of it.'

'The driver,' whispered Splinter. 'What's he got in his hands?'

Box looked. He looked harder. The driver had nothing in his hands. Then he looked back at Splinter and barely nodded.

'Move it,' snapped a voice from behind and he felt something jab the small of his back.

The traders had walked over to the hunters at the foot of the embankment and were waiting with them. The hunters had removed their crash helmets in preparation for the hot work ahead, but the dark glasses remained. Fingers flexed on stun sticks. One of them had started to smile.

As they stopped in front of the hunters, Splinter said very calmly, 'Now.'

Box broke left, sprinting around the front of the van. As he did so, Splinter grabbed Chess from behind with his forearm round her neck, pulling her head almost in front of his own. The attack came from nowhere and she fell backwards, against Splinter's body.

'Go on,' screamed Splinter. 'Go on. Shoot. Shoot me. Shoot me and kill her. Kill your precious girl. Kill her.'

The hunters with the rifles took aim whilst the others hung back, uncertain of what to do.

'Let go, Splinter. Let me go,' gasped Chess, beginning to struggle. She was finding it hard to breathe and now Splinter had the tip of his knife against her neck, just below the ear.

'Do it,' he screeched, wild. 'Come on. You shoot and you kill her. You try to touch me and I'll kill her. I don't care.' The knife was jerking dangerously against her neck as he dragged her backwards.

There was a cough and a rumble and the van engine shook into life. 'Come on,' yelled Box. 'Cut the dramatics and get in.'

Splinter had reached the open passenger door. He backed in and let go of Chess's neck. 'In. Now,' he hissed. The doorway was blocked by Chess's body. He gripped the back of her jeans to hoist her into the van.

Box was in the driver's seat. The keys were where the driver had left them; in the ignition. The van started with a shake but when he went to pull the door shut, the trader without the beard was there. He reached in and grabbed Box's wrist. Box drove his heel into the trader's throat. That worked because the grip on his wrist was released but as Box went for his jeans pocket with his other hand, the trader sprang back, thrusting his wild head into the van. His long, thick fingers fastened on Box's neck and he began to crush. Box could feel his windpipe crunching.

'Kill,' grunted his attacker, stubs of teeth grinding in Box's face.

'This ... belongs ... to ... you,' gasped Box, pushing the end of the extendable cosh under the trader's slab of jaw. Box pressed the release button and the cosh extended by a foot and a half immediately. The trader toppled backwards like a pillar, with the handle of the cosh under his chin and its tip protruding from the back of his head.

'Strawberry jam,' said Box, grimacing at the crimson spatters down the inside of the window as he pulled the door shut.

'Drive,' shouted Splinter as Chess swung her feet clear of the door he was slamming.

Box rammed the van into first gear and stamped on the accelerator. The van lurched forwards, shuddered and then lurched forwards again. He eased on the pedal and the engine coughed but the van travelled smoothly. He steered off the concrete of the taxiway and onto the grass, aiming for the gap in the trees behind the embankment.

'What did you do that for!' Chess was yelling at Splinter. 'You nearly strangled me.'

'I was getting us out of there,' Splinter shouted back.

'And you nearly stabbed me!'

'I wish I had, you ungrateful little cow.'

'Heads down,' shouted Box. Looking left he had seen two

hunters kneeling on the bank, rifles trained on the van. There were two sharp cracks and he heard the bullets slam into the left side of the van around the front wheel arch.

'They're aiming for the tyres,' he shouted and he drove faster at the trees, feeling the van jolt as the wheels thumped into the rough ground on the edge of the wood. In his shaking side mirrors he could see motor bikes in pursuit.

'You wouldn't of minded if they had shot me,' shouted Chess.

'I'd have paid them to do it,' Splinter shouted back.

'I hate you.'

'Good.'

As the first rank of branches lashed the front of the van and whipped across the windscreen, Box turned on the radio. The wheels hit a shallow trench in the soft earth and the van slew right, the steering wheel spinning in Box's hand. He wrenched it round, pulling the van out of the skid.

'What are you doing?' Splinter shouted at him.

'Finding something to shut you two up.' Box twisted the dial through crackles and voices and an orchestra before finding music that was thrashing out loudly enough to satisfy him. He turned the volume as high as it would go and smiled across to Splinter and Chess. 'Hold on,' he cried.

The track was about twice the width of the van. It was flanked by pine trees that were planted too densely to enter. He gripped the wheel and tried to avoid the worst of the ruts and mounds but it wasn't easy. The track ran downhill and Box was driving as fast as he could which meant that they were going quicker and quicker. Every time he skidded by one boggy trench, he would plough into the next or prang into a lump of earth that hit the wheels like a boulder and made the suspension groan. He threw the van left and right and bulldozed through earth and vegetation, heading for the motorway that he knew was on the other side of the wood.

'They're following us,' shouted Chess who had spotted the motor bikes in the wing mirror.

'Four of them,' replied Box. He had been watching the bikes as they scrambled after him, jumping the mounds in a way the van couldn't. They were gaining on him gradually. There were two bikes on his left, one to his right and one immediately behind. He noticed the hunter on the right gesture to the two on the left.

'They're catching up,' yelled Chess, voice competing with the screaming of the van's engine and the roaring music.

The front wheels were rammed to their rims by the edge of a shallow trench and the front of the van flipped up to crash back down with a bone-snapping jolt. Splinter had to stick out both hands to stop himself from being hurled onto the dashboard. He shouted at Box to be careful. Box laughed very loudly.

'What's this worth?' Box yelled.

'For stealing a vehicle and escaping from the crashers?' Splinter yelled back. 'Five shocks and three months in gaol.'

'I didn't get any shocks last time they caught me for this,' boasted Box. 'I had a good lawyer.' The music roared and the suspension sang horribly. 'I'd like to be a lawyer.'

'I'd like to be a judge,' shouted Splinter. 'I'd like to judge people and find them guilty.'

'Of what?'

'Of being weak.'

It sounded as if someone had just smashed the rear windows with a lump hammer.

'That wasn't aimed at the wheel arches,' cried Splinter. More glass shattered in the back and this time they heard the crack of a gun. With the grimy rear windows shot out, Box could see who was behind them in his rear-view mirror. This hunter had dropped back a little and was holding a pistol in one hand whilst he controlled the bike with the other. He raised the pistol and snatched another shot.

'Down!' shouted Box as the bullet struck his side of the van with a thump.

Chess glanced out of her window and then across to Box. 'They're right next to us,' she cried.

Splinter looked around the cab and saw a large plastic container in the footwell. Engine oil. He picked it up and shook it. It was half full. 'Just as well the engine isn't in good nick,' he shouted, unscrewing the cap and handing the container to Chess. 'Use this.'

It was difficult to keep steady as they cannoned over the track but with Splinter holding the back of her jeans, Chess wound down the passenger window and leant out. One hunter was almost close enough to touch and the other was on his tail. The steel front forks and black fairings of the bikes were streaked with mud. The engines were screaming.

Chess lobbed the contents of the bottle over the face of the hunter nearest to her. The oil glooped out in a long, syrupy tongue, coating the hunter's goggles. He lifted a hand to wipe the goggles clear, his front wheel struck a rut, the handlebars spun out of his grip and the motor bike boomeranged across the track. The hunter behind drove straight into it. His bike flipped into the air, wheels spinning, and catapulting him into the trees.

Box slowed down, closing the gap between the van and the motor bike that was directly behind it. The hunter sped up, readying himself for a shot at the back of Box's head. As he raised the pistol in his black-gloved hand, Box stamped on the brake pedal. The van halted with a lurch, a skid and an eruption of earth and bracken. The hunter slammed into the rear of the van like a fly hitting a windscreen.

The bike to Box's right raced ahead. The rider looked back to see what had happened and then looked forwards in time to see a tree that appeared to be coming straight at him. The bike powered into the tree trunk hard enough to smash it down before its mangled frame bounced to a standstill.

The air smelt of pine resin and engine oil. Box put a hand to his forehead, felt the wetness where his head had struck the steering wheel when he had braked and saw the blood on his fingers. The radio was playing but the woods were silent. He turned the radio off and leant back in the seat.

'I could get used to the countryside,' he said. 'It's peaceful.' He shut his eyes and took a deep breath.

With curses and groans, Splinter and then Chess crawled back onto the seat from the footwell where they had been thrown. Splinter was furious. 'Fly head, you nobwit, you nearly killed us.'

Box said nothing.

'You deserve that,' Splinter said when he saw the gash on Box's head.

'Thanks very much,' said Box, opening his eyes. He turned

the key in the ignition. The engine coughed, the van shook and then it began to roll forwards.

'They're going to come after us,' said Splinter.

The van bumped over the track and now they could see where the tree line ended and the belt of tarmac that was the motorway began. Vehicles flashed right to left below them.

'It won't be difficult,' he continued. 'Only three of us and stuck in this heap of junk; they'll get us now. We were lucky just then.'

Box threw a sideways glance at his brother. As far as he was concerned, luck had nothing to do with it; it had been his quick thinking.

'We need to go somewhere they don't expect to find us. Throw them off our trail.' Splinter rubbed his sharp chin. 'I'll think of something. Leave it to me. And I'll see if I can think of something that doesn't nearly get us killed, fly head.'

Box was silent. He gripped the wheel and focused on where the track ended and a steep bank dropped to the motorway. Without slowing, he let the van coast over the edge of the bank and rattle down the stony slope. It hit the road with a crunch and a fountain of sparks from the front bumper. With vehicles swerving in front and behind, Box drove across the carriageway, crashed through the barrier on the central reservation and entered the carriageway that led towards the city, missing a juggernaut that thundered past them so closely that the van doors shook.

'Fly head, you moron,' screeched Splinter.

Box pulled the van round to join the flow of traffic. A loud grating came from the rear. 'We've got a flat tyre;

hardly surprising,' was all he said. He pursed his lips and concentrated on driving the vehicle in a straight line, which wasn't easy. He taxied across to the slow lane where the van crawled forwards. Traffic began to bank up behind them.

'You drive like a maniac through the woods,' complained Splinter, 'and now you're driving like an old woman.'

'We're lucky this thing is driving at all,' Box said. 'Something's broken somewhere. It won't go any faster.'

'We should go back to the wharf.' This was the first time that Chess had spoken since they had escaped the hunters.

Splinter looked at her with contempt. 'You are as stupid as he is. That's the first place they'll look for us. It's obvious we'd go there.'

'They'll find us wherever we go,' said Chess, 'but at least Ethel will be at the wharf.'

'Why?'

'Because she knows that's where we'll go,' insisted Chess. 'It's obvious, like you said. And she's the only person that can help us.'

'What can she do?' Splinter lashed back.

'Something. Anything.' Chess rubbed her knee which had been sore ever since she had been thrown into the footwell. 'I don't know what she'll do but we need to be with her.' She hadn't meant to shout but her knee was really hurting and she knew that they were on their own and she knew that there was nothing they could do if the Twisted Symmetry came for them now. She was frightened.

'Rubbish,' Splinter shouted back. 'She's useless. I'm in charge. I'll decide what we're doing and we're not going to the wharf.'

'Shut up, Splinter,' said Box. 'I'm driving and I decide where we're going. You got us into this mess; I'm getting us out of it. We're going to the wharf.'

Splinter hesitated. 'But they know we'll go there,' he wheedled, trying to sound reasonable.

'I'm not bothered,' said Box. 'If I go down, I'm going down fighting, and if I'm going down fighting it's going to be on *my* territory.'

'Very impressive,' snorted Splinter, folding his arms. 'It will achieve nothing.'

'It's better than running away. And maybe Chess is right. Maybe Ethel will be there.'

'So what?' sneered Splinter. 'What'll she do? Fight them off with her knitting needles?'

Box shrugged. Someone sounded a horn behind them. 'She can do magic,' he said.

'It's not magic, you idiot; it's science.'

'Magic, science; same thing to me,' said Box

Far to their left and below them was the river. Ahead of them the motorway dipped down to the vast spread of the city, glass towers wraith-like behind fingers of morning smog. Between the city and the river there was a long ridge and as the motorway curled alongside this ridge, the outlying shacks and alleys and chicken coups and chained dogs and thin children and filth of the Pit began.

'We're going in there,' explained Box. 'We'll ditch the van, go through the Pit and head for the wharf. We're not staying out here any longer. Far too lively.'

Traffic was snaking behind the van and horns were blaring as if it was a carnival. In his rear-view mirror, Box had spotted a pack of hunters working their way through the bank of traffic, the chrome of their motor bikes and the black uniforms weaving in and out of the stream of cars and lorries. The drone of motor bike engines grew louder, as if a swarm of wasps was approaching.

'We're sitting ducks here; we need to get off,' he said. 'Now!' He yanked the steering wheel left and with its chassis grinding, the van rolled off the motorway and onto the rough ground where the Pit began. The land sloped gently towards the first row of ramshackle huts. It was littered with stones, pallets and oil drums. The van lurched and groaned. Two hundred metres back, eight motor bikes had pulled out of the traffic. They growled and leapt after the van, closing on it gradually.

'As soon as we reach the Pit, we leg it,' shouted Box, above the desperate knocking and rattling of the engine. 'We don't starburst; we stick together and head downhill. They won't be able to follow us in there and we can cut through quicker than they can drive round.'

'And then?' asked Splinter.

'Then we head for the wharf.'

The van stopped.

'What've you stopped for?' Splinter looked out of the broken rear windows to see the mud churning cavalcade that was screaming towards them.

'It's had enough,' said Box. 'The van's dead.' He looked at Chess and Splinter, oblivious to the dark brown streaks of blood that crusted his forehead and he grinned. 'Here we go!'

They were out of the van and sprinting. Chess knew that

unless she fell badly or broke an ankle, she would be into the Pit before the hunters could ride her down. Her thick brown hair streaked behind her as she ran and her feet thumped across the mud. She felt strong and fast. Box and Splinter were only a body length in front of her. She heard the sudden bang of a gun, saw mud kick up to the left of Box's feet and then all of them had made it into the Pit. It enclosed them in its vast knot of slum shacks and alleyways.

They kept running; through washing lines, over crates, under lean-tos, into beggars. They ran through beaten yards where old women sitting on car panels rolled dice for children's teeth, across culverts where little girls played hopscotch over filth that ran like treacle, along ginnels where the only light to penetrate the gloom came from candles that burnt inside chipboard hovels. They ran fast, they ran without stopping and all the time they ran downhill. When they burst out of the last row of dwellings at the bottom of the Pit, Box and Chess collapsed on the earth, even though it was hard to tell what was mud and what was waste.

Splinter was bent double, wheezing, desperate for air. 'This lump of brain,' he gasped, 'is killing me.'

Chess rolled onto her hands and knees and waited for the pounding in her head to stop. Not far from where she was kneeling were the cesspools. She closed her mouth to keep the stench off her tongue. On the other side of the pools and to her right were the remaining warehouses, an island in the wreckage of the wharf. Beyond that was the flat drift of the river.

She saw that there were duckboards across the ground close by and where they came to the lip of the cesspools, a bridge had been constructed out of loose planks of wood. It was an improvement on a single joist. Crossing the pool would be easy. She allowed herself to hope that they would be all right.

Then she saw the dogs.

There were three, loping towards them with a light, energetic tread. Two of the dogs were Rottweilers; thick set, powerful shoulders, broad muzzles, black and tan; the type of dogs used by the hunters. The third was leaner, sharper and pure black. Chess stared at it and it stared back. She had seen this dog before, when it had come at her out of the smoke on their last visit to the wharf. She knew its eyes and she knew its smell.

'You again,' she said, almost to herself. The dog lowered its head and the whites of its eyes narrowed as it drew back its lips and growled. The Rottweilers began to bark, hackles bristling over their stout backs.

Box was on his feet. 'Not more running,' he groaned.

The black dog snarled and leapt towards them.

'Run,' yelled Splinter.

This was hard. Chess's legs were aching as soon as they started to work and once she and her brothers had made it over the cesspool, the shattered remains of the wharf were merciless on their bare feet. But the dogs were behind them, barking and snarling and bounding over the rubble with a clatter of claws. They were close enough for Chess to hear their panting, huge chests working like bellows. She switched off from the pain in her feet and followed her brothers as they headed for the outcrop of the warehouse ruins.

Even as they rounded the edge of the side wall, it seemed to Chess that the dogs were slowing down. As she caught up with Box and Splinter and they scrambled round the gaping frontage of the warehouses, she realized what the dogs had been doing.

You were driving us here, she thought. You were making sure we came to this place.

'I don't believe it,' despaired Box, coming to a standstill and heaving in air.

'Believe it, fly head,' said Splinter. 'This was your plan.'

Across from them was the place where they had sat with Pacer and Hex two days earlier. Pacer and Hex were still there and so was Gemma but they were not alone. Standing with them were six traders, armed with whips and coshes. The traders had hold of them in the gloom at the back of the warehouse.

'Yo, Chess!' shouted Pacer, who was bleeding from a cut to his bottom lip. A fist was driven into his back hard enough to make him drop to his knees.

On either side of the tent where Chess had sat with Gemma, and separated by the narrow metal girder that supported its plastic roof, stood two hunters, jackboots dashed with mud, dark glasses above hard mouths. One of them rested his hand on the pistol butt that jutted from his holster. The other was holding what appeared to be a pile of dark clothing. From across the scattered debris of the wharf came the rumble of motor bike engines and the crunch of boots.

The Rottweilers advanced, growling. The Tuesdays walked slowly into the high-roofed shell of the warehouse, drops of water echoing as they smacked onto the floor from the skylights and cracked roofs.

When Chess, Box and Splinter were inside the warehouse and close to the tent, the Rottweilers jogged over to the hunters and sat by their sides. They licked their lips and looked up at their masters who ignored them. Then the black dog walked round Chess and her brothers, looking up at her as it did so. Its lips drew back down one side of its vicious muzzle revealing sharp teeth, but Chess knew that this wasn't meant to be a snarl.

It's smiling at me, she realized.

The dog turned its head away and padded past her, towards the hunters. As it did so, it changed. The hair on its body began to bristle and recede, vanishing altogether in some places and revealing the tough, pig-coloured skin beneath. Its legs twisted and thickened and grew long, paws spreading and splaying open into fingers and toes. Its head twitched and shook, snout shortening, tongue hanging out and then curling into its flat face. Then it stood on its hind legs, stretched its shoulders, flexed its arms and with a loud snapping of sinews and a cracking of joints, what had been a dog was now a man.

He had his back to Chess, Box and Splinter. Taking the clothes from the hunter, he stepped into his trousers, pulled on his jacket and boots and strapped on his belt.

'So that's what they wear under their uniforms,' Box said to Splinter, sidelong.

A chain of motor bikes drew up between the river and the

buildings, engines growling. The riders dismounted. A squad of hunters came running across the rubble and into the warehouse. There was a crashing of boots, a rattle of rifles unslung, the click of safety catches flicked off. Silence.

The man turned round as he was handed his glasses and looked straight at Chess with the same eyes that she had seen in the dog's face. They were empty, hungry eyes and she wasn't sure whether this was a man with the eyes of a dog or a dog with the eyes of a man. But she knew the eyes and she knew the smell and she recognized the cruel slash of mouth.

'Hello, Chess,' said the Inspector. Then he looked over to where the traders were gathered and he pointed. Chess saw that he was pointing at Gemma. 'Bring me that one.' He pulled a knife from his belt and he looked back at Chess. 'Mess me about this time and I kill your friend.'

CHAPTER 21

'Don't worry, Chess,' said Gemma as she was marched to the Inspector by one of the traders. 'I'm not frightened.'

'Shut up,' snapped the Inspector and he slapped her across the face with the back of his hand, knocking her to the floor so hard that her spectacles spun to the ground. She looked up at the Inspector, blinking in surprise, blond hair in her eyes. She opened her hand to push it away and the leaf that she had been clutching spiralled to the floor.

A wave of anger prickled Chess's skin.

The Inspector gripped Gemma by the back of her neck and dragged her to her feet.

'Don't touch her,' said Chess.

'I am touching her, little girl,' said the hunter and he shook Gemma hard enough to make her head jerk.

'Don't hurt her,' said Chess, stepping forwards. She spoke clearly and calmly although she could feel a tremor in her legs.

'I am hurting her, little girl.' The Inspector squeezed the back of Gemma's neck and she gasped and would have fallen forwards had she not been gripped so tightly. 'The only way to stop her hurting is for you to come with us.'

Chess's thin arms stuck out of the sleeves of her baggy purple pullover and her fists were clenched. 'Ethel will make you leave her alone.'

'Ethel isn't here,' said the Inspector. 'You're on your own. Nobody is coming to help you.'

'Ethel will come,' stated Chess.

'Well done, fly head,' muttered Splinter. 'We've really had it now.'

Box looked about. 'Oh, I don't know about that,' he said. 'You take that puny looking one over there and I'll deal with the other twenty-nine.'

'Shut up,' roared the Inspector, pulling the glasses from his face, and for a moment it snouted forwards, black and furred with lips ripped back and teeth sharp. Gemma gasped and then shut her mouth tight to stop herself from crying out.

Chess dug her nails into the palms of her hands but stayed where she was. When the Inspector's face had become human again she repeated slowly, 'Ethel will come.'

Silver glinted in the hunter's hand and the slim blade of a knife was under Gemma's chin. 'I don't think so, little girl. Now, you come to me.'

Gemma's blue eyes were fixed on Chess's brown ones. She didn't speak but Chess felt Gemma's fear, felt her confusion and felt the cold as the breeze lifted off the river and drifted through her tattered blue dress. The knife was pressed harder into Gemma's skin and for an instant, Chess felt the sharp tip against her own skin. She blinked. The sensation vanished but the hot anger remained.

Box couldn't understand why the hunters didn't just come for them. There were so many hunters and they were all armed and there were the traders too. And yet he could tell that everything was waiting on Chess. Everyone was watching her. She stood in front of him and Splinter; between them and the Inspector, and she seemed so small and thin and so easy to hurt. Box's hand crept towards his trouser pocket; if they were going to hurt Chess, they would have to hurt him first.

From somewhere distant there came a low, thumping vibration. It was too far away for Box to be sure what it was but it seemed to be growing louder, as if it was coming closer. At the same time, there was a revving drone of engines at high pitch, skirling up the river. The thumping became a beating and then Box recognized it.

'Helicopters?' he whispered to Splinter. 'How many more of them do they need?'

Splinter was watching the Inspector, watching every twitch of his face. He heard the crackle of voices over the radio that was buckled to the chest of one of the hunters by the tent, saw that hunter say something in the Inspector's ear and observed a tightening of the Inspector's mouth.

'It's not more of them, fly head,' whispered Splinter. 'Someone else is coming.'

The helicopter rotors were hammering over the wharf now, resounding from the slopes of the Pit to the factories on the other side of the water. Their whining and drumming was joined by the scream of the two boats that Box could see powering up the river. They were long, flat-faced vessels that looked like military assault craft. Their grey metal hulls smashed the river into a creamy spray as they skimmed over the water. He could see figures in the craft but couldn't tell yet who they were.

The Inspector still had his grip on Gemma's neck and the knife to her throat. 'Listen up,' he shouted. His voice was surprisingly sharp and loud, even over the cacophony of engines and rotor blades. 'We have COE units inbound. Engage the assault craft with automatic fire; single shot only inside the buildings. Do *not* harm the girl and nobody tackles the old lady. I repeat; do *not* harm the girl and do *not* approach the old lady.'

From all around the warehouses there was the clatter of firearms being cocked and breaches filling with ammunition. With a scuffling of boots, hunters took up positions in a line that overlooked the riverbank, kneeling behind the motor bikes to use them for cover or lying flat in the rubble. Their weapons were trained on the approaching assault craft. Other hunters squatted about the warehouse walls, watching the sky above.

Satisfied with his force's deployment, the Inspector turned to face Chess who remained standing between him and her brothers.

'Last chance, little girl,' he said. 'You come with me or death will gorge himself today.'

The wind caught Chess's hair just as it had caught Gemma's dress. It blew the thick, chestnut curls across her face and into her eyes but she didn't push it away. She didn't look towards the river. She didn't look at anything apart from Gemma's eyes and then the Inspector's granite face.

'Let her go,' she said.

A blaze of gunfire and the river erupted in jets of spray as the hunters opened fire on the assault craft. Undeterred, the assault craft rocketed towards the riverbank. Box couldn't see anyone in them because they were staying low, protected by the armour-plated sides. Then, as the two boats covered the final fifty metres towards the wharf, machine guns nosed their way over the prows and there was a crackle of gunfire from across the water.

The hunters intensified their fire, throwing down a wall of bullets to block the approaching vessels but incoming rounds rattled though the motor bikes and raked the river bank. Sparks danced on metal, bricks shattered into dust and Box saw two hunters reel backwards and hit the ground, motionless.

The assault craft cut their engines and crashed over the final stretch of water and onto the bank. As they did so, the hunters concentrated their fire. Two men stood in one boat, sub-machine guns coughing from their hips. Another stood behind them and he threw two objects towards the bikes. One of the machine gunners jerked backwards, dropping his gun before falling. Then there were two sharp bangs and the riverbank swirled thick with smoke; hunters and assault craft vanishing within its rolling clouds. There was shouting, gunfire rattled up and down the water's edge and the air was sharp with the smell of explosive.

At the same time, Box noticed a surge of activity at the back of the warehouse. Pacer and Hex had chosen this moment to try to break away from the traders. They hadn't succeeded but Box could see a flurry of fists and his friends hopelessly outnumbered.

'It's too lively out here,' he yelled to Splinter as a bullet hummed past his head to bury itself in a concrete pillar. 'We might as well make ourselves useful.' He pointed to the scuffle in the shadows to their right. Snatching a piece of brick from the floor he shouted, 'Come on,' and charged towards the traders.

Splinter hesitated. To his left the smoke was clearing and he saw flashes of gunfire and bodies running. In front of him, Chess stood facing the Inspector, the two of them oblivious to the surrounding mayhem or the bullets that sang through the air. And to his right, armed only with a lock knife and a piece of brick, was his brother, hurling himself towards six traders.

Splinter picked up a lump of wood and hefted it left and right. It was light but hard; it would make a good weapon. He pushed reason and cunning to the back of his mind and let them be replaced by animal aggression. Screaming and with his coat tails racing behind him, Splinter launched himself towards the traders.

Box was hit across the shins by a cosh. White pain jolted up to his knees and he was on the ground.

Never go down; that was a basic rule. And if you do go down, get up.

He rolled away, vaguely aware of an incoming boot but ready to take its impact if it meant he could stagger to his feet. He was up with a trader bearing down on him. Box's lunge with his knife was blocked but he could use both hands equally well and the trader was not expecting the blow from the brick which shattered his elbow. He howled with pain and Box would have been upon him but for a boot that came from his side and struck his ribs so hard he thought his lungs had burst.

That's the trouble with being outnumbered, thought Box as he careered into a wall; you can still fight the enemy but it's difficult to keep an eye on them all.

Out of the corner of his eye, a knife was coming. He made ready to dive away but a long arm took him round the stomach, his feet left the floor and the blade was still driving towards him. But before it made contact, there was a shout and a length of wood cracked over a wrist and the knife was on the floor and already Splinter was swinging the wood with both hands up at the side of the head of the trader who had grabbed Box.

'Nice one,' cried Box as he broke free. Then Splinter was on the floor, clutching his hip where it had been rammed by an extending cosh and Box, Hex and Pacer were still fighting for their lives.

Ethel stood erect near the front of one of the assault craft. Beside her sat Joachim Breslaw, the travel rug draped over his legs. He was holding a hip flask and he took a swig, licked his lips and then wiped his mouth and moustache with the back of his hand. Bullets whined about them and sang off the armoured gunwales of the vessel.

'Thank you for coming, Joachim,' said Ethel, surveying the fighting with weary eyes. A bullet smacked the side of the craft. 'The risks are very great, I know.'

'I do not want to die, Mevrad,' growled the Professor. 'But I'm not frightened of dying.'

'Sadly, Joachim, not enough humans are.'

Around her, the COE agents were pinned down by the

hunters. There was no way they could break out of the boats and there were more hunters waiting around the warehouses. Some of them were sniping at the helicopters that hovered with rotors thumping over the warehouse roofs. Others were joining their comrades near the river, preparing to assault the landing craft. But Captain Riley was talking clearly and calmly into his radio as he knelt in the boat, beside Ethel. From time to time he looked across to the two helicopters that waited over the wharf.

Ethel did not watch the gun battle. She did not observe how the hunters were calling up reinforcements from the warehouse or how they were preparing to storm the boats. Her eyes were trained on Chess who was standing very close to the Inspector, almost blocking him from view.

'We have to end this, Captain,' she said. 'We have to get Chess out. Now.'

Two hunters scrambled from the end of the wall of motor bikes and charged at the boat.

'Two hunters, coming straight at us,' she announced helpfully.

Captain Riley tore open his chest holster, snatched out the pistol and standing clear of the protection of the walls, emptied a clip of ammunition with ferocious speed. The hunters were sprawling on the rubble before their jackboots had covered the short distance to the river.

'You don't mess about, do you?' observed Ethel.

Riley released the spent magazine, slid in a fresh one and knelt down. 'Make ready,' he said into the radio. 'On my command.' He looked over to where the hunters were massing along the riverbank, preparing to board the boats. 'Go!'

Splinter was down, Hex was down and Box and Pacer were trying to stay alive. Only by scrambling over the broken walls, swinging under joists and sliding over stone that rubbed their hands and elbows raw had they evaded the boots and coshes. But now they had been forced into a corner and four straggle-headed traders with hands powerful enough to crush bone were coming for them. Beyond them, Box could see hunters swarming across the warehouse front and in their midst, Chess facing the Inspector.

'This is it,' shouted Pacer, a link chain wrapped round his fist.

'There's so many of them,' yelled Box, knife ready, arm held out, preparing to make one last effort to break past the traders and get to Chess.

The traders roared and charged.

And then there was a cracking and a smashing and the air was full of glass; thousands of pieces of glass cascading down from the high roof and descending with the glass were men and women in black combats and body armour and wearing the shoulder patches of the COE. They swooped down, belts linked to ropes that trailed from the helicopters and their machine guns blazed with a fury that sent hunters spinning and crashing to the floor before they had realized what was happening.

They were met by fire from the hunters who were kneeling by the walls and two of them hung limp on their ropes before their boots hit the ground. But the large body of hunters near the river had not expected this, and were caught now between the fire from the warehouse and a sudden volley of gunshots from the boats.

The fighting was desperate. There were fewer COE agents than hunters, but they had surprise on their side and they had trapped the hunters in a savage crossfire. Everywhere, guns were crackling and bullets were singing and hunters and agents were falling.

'Everyone starts shooting,' whispered Ethel. 'Everyone starts dying.'

The Inspector was barking commands to the hunters on either side of him who transmitted his orders to the rest of his force over their radios. He gripped Gemma as effortlessly as a sack of rags, wrenching her from side to side as he snatched glances at the chaos around him and gave his orders. But he kept his eyes on Chess. About her, men and women were fighting, weapons hurling out fire at point blank range and all the time, she kept her eyes on the Inspector.

He swung back to face her, bullets hissing between them. He dug his gloved fingers into Gemma's hair to pull her head back and even though she didn't want to, Gemma screamed. The scream seared through Chess. She felt the freezing terror in Gemma's body but felt it turn into a white hot rage inside her own. It pulsed through her nerves, throbbing behind her eyes, tingling in her fingers.

'No more waiting,' growled the Inspector. 'You come to me now or your friend dies, now.'

Chess felt the air catch her hair just above her shoulder and then directly ahead of her she saw the ricocheting bullet bury itself behind the dark glasses of the hunter standing by the Inspector's right shoulder. The hunter slid down the wall, streaking it red with the back of his skull. The dog that had been sitting by his side looked at where he lay with astonishment and then bounded away, pursued by the other Rottweiler.

Neither Chess nor the Inspector moved.

'I count to five,' said the Inspector. 'Then I kill her anyway.'

'Please,' screamed Gemma. 'No.' Her cry cut through the smoking air, reaching even the boats.

'We have to get her out,' said Ethel, talking about Chess. 'Any longer and she's going to be hit. Your agents have got to pull her out.'

Riley was standing by Ethel. He ratcheted back the top cover of the pistol, then slid it forwards, cocking it.

'What are you doing?' she snapped.

'My units are locked with the enemy. They can't extract her safely.' He raised the pistol with both arms outstretched, his left hand cupping his right. He could still hear the squeal that had come from the little girl in the blue dress. He closed one eye and sighted over the short barrel with the other.

'I'm not standing here and watching him kill that girl,' stated Riley. 'If I neutralize the Inspector his units will lose control and then we can get Chess out.' He moved his head. Chess was positioned in front of the Inspector. Riley wasn't sure whether he could get a clear shot without hitting Chess or the girl in the blue dress.

'I understand, Captain, and I know you are a fine marksman,' said Ethel, 'but Chess is blocking the Inspector. If you hit her, it will be a catastrophe beyond your imagining.'

Rounds hammered along the panel of the boat in front of

Captain Riley's thighs. He didn't flinch but he lowered the pistol slightly and looked at Ethel. 'Are you ordering me not to open fire?' he asked. By his side, an agent braced her machine gun on the edge of the landing craft wall, squeezed the trigger and pumped out a stream of bullets that scythed down the hunters who had been firing at her commander.

'I'm not ordering you to do anything, dear,' insisted Ethel. 'You just have to do the *right* thing.'

Captain Riley nodded, mouth grim. 'Children don't die on my watch,' he said. He raised his pistol and took aim. The distance was beyond the safe range and every time he thought he had a clear shot, Chess or the Inspector moved slightly. But he knew this was possible. He just needed Chess to keep her head still.

Chess closed her eyes. All around her was gunfire, shouting, crashing boots. The Inspector was counting, slowly. She opened her eyes and focused back on where Gemma was being held but it was difficult to see clearly. Her eyes were burning and her head was bursting and her nerves screamed fear and rage.

'Two.'

The knife was rising. She couldn't see it move but she could feel it; she could feel the point pressing up, digging into the soft tissue beneath her tongue, ready almost to burst through the skin and into her throat: into Gemma's throat. Chess shook her head.

'Let her go,' she shouted.

'Three,' counted the Inspector, the corners of his lips drawing back.

Chess couldn't understand why her body shook like it did.

Fear and anger were pumping through her muscles and her head, and when she opened her mouth to shout, she felt her body falling away like it had melted. Only the fury and the heat remained.

'Four.'

'Let ... her ... GO!'

As Chess screamed GO, Captain Riley pulled the trigger of his pistol and her head was filled with a brilliant flash of white.

CHAPTER 22

Box heard the pistol fire and saw Chess's body stiffen. Her spine arched, her fingers splayed and her head and neck jolted back. Then she dropped to her knees as if something had just let go of her. But at the same time, the Inspector was blasted backwards. He dropped Gemma and the knife, his jackboots left the floor and his body was flung towards the warehouse wall behind him. It hit the wall with a dull thud but didn't fall. The Inspector remained suspended, legs twitching, with the narrow girder that had supported the tent roof thrusting out of the front of his chest. A dark stream of blood dribbled noisily from the iron girder onto the plastic sheeting below.

Almost at once, confusion spread through the hunters. Their commander was dead and there was no one to coordinate their fighting. The men and women of the COE intensified their assault, pushing out of the warehouse and out of the boats. The hunters were surrounded and were battling to escape. They retreated along the riverbank, men falling as they did so. When the final half dozen had fought back to the shattered walls of the old harbour offices and the gunfire had dwindled to sniping shots, Captain Riley ordered his agents to cease firing. The hunters staggered from the ruins and scurried across the wasted remnants of the wharf until the only thing to be seen were six ant-sized figures that vanished into the bottom of the Pit. Then the COE began the work of counting how many of their comrades had fallen.

'I thought you'd been shot,' said Box when he had walked over to Chess. She was standing bolt upright and staring straight ahead at the Inspector. Hex and Splinter were sitting against a pile of stones at the back of the warehouse and comparing grazes and debating who was the most badly injured.

'You looked like you'd been shot,' said Pacer. He shook her shoulder gently. 'Are you all right?'

She nodded. 'You OK?' she mumbled distantly.

'Traders nearly slabbed me. Otherwise, fine,' he laughed weakly.

'They legged it out the back of the warehouse as soon as the roof came down,' added Box. Then he looked where Chess was looking.

He didn't linger over the mess where the girder jutted through the Inspector's ribcage but he spent a long time looking at the Inspector's head. It lolled to one side and although it was the size of a human head it no longer had a human face. The cheekbones had widened and they stretched to a sharp snout. The lower jaw hung open in a frozen snarl, lips and long teeth stained crimson by the Inspector's own blood which dripped thick and slow from his nostrils. Short black fur coated most of his skull and face but there were patches of human skin over his jowls and along one temple as if the fur had been rubbed away. His eyes stared crazily at nothing.

'What a shot!' exclaimed Pacer with a whistle of admiration. 'Is it a man or a dog?'

Box thought for a moment before saying, 'Who cares? He's dead. That's all that matters.'

'You two have been hanging out with some weird people,' said Pacer. He put his arm round Chess's shoulders and turned her away from the Inspector. 'Come on. Wait over here for your wrinkly friend. And look out for the glass; it's everywhere.'

As Ethel and Captain Riley walked over from where the grim work of laying out the dead was taking place, Chess, Box, Splinter, Pacer and Hex were sitting on the rubble at the back of the warehouse. They sat close to one another. Hex was cradling his right forearm in his left hand and Splinter was leaning to one side, nursing his hip. None of them were talking; all of them were watching. The five pairs of eyes were set like round, bright jewels in the gaunt, dirt-streaked faces of the street rats and Ethel could see that they were trained on her and Riley.

'I don't understand,' said Riley, when they had stopped opposite the Inspector.

'Keep your voice down,' said Ethel. 'They mustn't hear what you're about to say,' and she indicated the ragged band of street rats with a sideways glance.

'I shot high,' insisted Riley, as quietly as he could. 'The girl's head moved at the last moment; it moved right in front of my aim and I shot high to avoid her.' He pointed to the wall above where the Inspector was impaled. 'You look in those bricks, you'll find a nine-millimetre round from my pistol.'

'There's no need to conduct a ballistic examination, dear,' said Ethel. 'I believe you.'

'Ugly, isn't he?' commented Riley.

'I'd say average, for his breed,' observed Ethel. 'You aren't seeing him at his best.'

Riley returned to what concerned him. 'But how did this happen? If I didn't hit him, what blew him off his feet? That's not a gunshot, Ethel. A bullet is never going to do that to him.' He shook his head. 'What did?'

Ethel looked over to where Chess was sitting, between Box and Pacer and then looked back to Riley. 'She did,' she said.

Riley raised an eyebrow and flicked his eyes from Chess to the gory corpse. 'How?'

'You saw it,' said Ethel. 'That's how.' Then her little hand closed on Riley's arm with a grip of steel and she turned her cracked old eyes on him like beacons. 'But you say nothing, do you understand?'

'Yes, I understand.'

'She mustn't know. None of them must know. Absolutely no one. Not yet.'

'I understand, Ethel,' Captain Riley assured her.

Ethel patted his arm gently, where she had been holding it. 'I know you do. There's a dear.' Then she looked from Riley to the Inspector, to the figures who were coming and going along the water's edge with heads bent and finally back to where the street rats were sitting on the stones, watching her.

'This is how it begins,' she said.

Chess awoke to the clicking of needles. She lay motionless, warm, muscles so relaxed she seemed to sink into the bedding, thoughts drifting. When eventually she opened her eyes, she saw a metal bed frame above her head and everything was bathed in a pale yellow light. She was lying in a bunk in the bulk storage tank in Committee HQ. Her brothers were asleep on the bunks across from her and sitting on a stool near to her feet, in front of the entrance door, was Ethel.

Ethel's head was bent over her knitting. The unkempt grey hair flopped forwards over her forehead and spectacles, and her knobbly knees were pressed together, supporting a ball of purple wool.

Without looking up, Ethel said, 'That was a good sleep, my love.'

Without sitting up, Chess said, 'Have I been sleeping long?'

'It's evening now. You've been asleep since we got back from the wharf yesterday morning.'

Chess's thoughts began to catch up with where she was. She remembered the final minutes at the wharf; the captain putting his arm around her waist to help her to the helicopter, Box and Splinter staggering behind her, men and women gaunt as wraiths and standing amongst the ruins like sentinels, the chopping beat of the rotor blades and then her eyes closing as the broken ground fell away and she and her brothers swung skywards.

'Gemma!' The name burst from her and she sat up suddenly. 'Where's Gemma?'

Box snorted loudly, knelt up with a start, banged his head on the frame of the bunk above and swore before collapsing back on the mattress. Splinter rolled onto his side and groaned.

Ethel had put down her knitting and was standing by Chess at once. She pressed a hand on her shoulder. 'Gemma's all right. She's with Hex and Pacer. They've been treated by the medics and given food and blankets. They wouldn't leave the wharf, dear. They said you know where to find them if you need them.'

Chess slumped back. Ethel sat on the bed beside her. Box groaned and rubbed his head.

'I spent a little time talking with Gemma,' she said. 'She's a very special sort of person, isn't she?'

Chess's head lay on the pillow but she nodded.

'She's a friend. A good friend, isn't she, dear?'

Chess's eyes prickled and she nodded again. Her throat felt too tight to speak.

'She asked me to give you this and to say thank you.'

Ethel took Chess's arm and put a dry leaf into her hand. Chess looked at the leaf and asked, 'Why did she want to thank me?'

'For saving her life, dear.'

'I didn't save her life,' said Chess. 'The captain did. Box and Splinter saw it.'

'Yes,' agreed Ethel and she curled Chess's fingers round the leaf and patted the back of her hand. 'That is certainly how it appeared.'

'I don't feel too bad, considering.' With a glance at the bunk above, Box sat up slowly before digging his fingers into his thick, curly hair and scratching vigorously with both hands.

'Head lice, I'm sure of it,' declared Ethel.

'Wood worm,' murmured Splinter.

'Anyway, you've all been patched up; wounds dressed and sticking plasters stuck. And we got that nasty tag out of your wrist,' Ethel said to Chess 'so the Symmetry can't find you so easily.'

'So there wasn't a squealer?' enquired Splinter, lying on his back and smiling at the bunk above.

'No, dear,' and then, before Splinter could beat her to it, she admitted, 'I was wrong about that.'

Splinter kept smiling and said nothing.

'You do look a bit of a state, mind.' Ethel's gaze settled on Chess. 'I'm knitting you a new jumper.'

'Thanks,' said Chess, 'but I like the one I'm wearing.'

'It's in danger of becoming part of you, dear. Do you realize, that's why the brain didn't destroy it? It's so impregnated with your body cells, it was immune to the crystal.'

'You know about what happened with the brain?' Splinter propped his head on an elbow, frowning.

'Of course. Don't look so surprised. Finding out about things after they happen is easy. It's finding out about them before they happen that keeps me awake at night.'

'What happened to the others?' Chess thought of all the children crammed in the compound and of what she had seen as the suck worm descended.

'Others, dear?'

'The other children. The one's that were taken by the Fat Gobster?'

'Do you want the truth?'

Chess didn't like the answers she got when Ethel promised to tell her the truth but she nodded anyway.

'The truth is, we can't be sure. But one thing we know; they will be with the Twisted Symmetry now.' Ethel shook her head. 'We fear for them.'

Chess knew from the silence that her brothers were thinking the same thing that she was thinking, but it was Box who asked the question. 'What happens next?'

'Not that it matters,' added Splinter. 'Since we've done what you wanted us to do.'

Ethel answered Box's question. 'Next, we use the brain you stole to construct our own universal quantum computer. Then we can calculate for ourselves where the Fat Gobster will strike.'

'And then?' enquired Box cautiously.

'Then we can find out what happens at the other end.'

'Good luck,' said Splinter.

Chess put the leaf under her pillow and sat up, combing her fingers through her thick, chestnut hair. Her feet were sore and so were her ribs but her mind was on something else; something that she still had no answer to.

'What's the Eternal?' she asked.

Ethel sighed, clasped her hands across her tummy and shook her head. 'The Eternal is a weapon,' she said. 'It's short for Eternal Core Decelerator.' She paused and then she added, 'There aren't many people who can control the Eternal.'

'Is that why the Twisted Symmetry wanted me?' asked Chess, looking at her intently.

'Wanted, dear?' Chess noticed how Ethel smiled sadly but she was so keen to have an answer to her question that she didn't listen to her say, under her breath, 'Want, my love, not wanted.'

'Is it because I can control the Eternal? Because of the crystal inside me?'

'In a way dear, yes.' Ethel stood up and cleared her dewlapped throat with a crackling hack. 'Now, that's enough post-match analysis. I sent Professor Breslaw shopping, to get something special for you all. We must go and find him.'

They trooped out of the storage tank, unsteady on their feet because they were all still a little drunk with sleep. At the bottom of the steps, Splinter turned to Chess and spoke in a nagging whine. 'Oh Ethel, am I special because of the crystal inside me?'

'That's not what I was saying.'

'Not much,' scoffed Splinter and he caught up with Box, leaving Chess to wonder what she had done wrong.

They walked in silence until they came to the doors that led into the refectory. Ethel smiled at them. 'Let's see if the Professor is ready.' She pushed open the doors.

Box entered first, followed by Chess and then Splinter. As soon as they did so, there was a loud scraping of benches on stone. The men and women of the night patrols who had been sitting at one end of the dining hall were standing and all of them were staring at the Tuesdays. The Tuesdays stood still and stared back. Then somebody started to clap and that person was joined by someone else and then the clapping swelled until all the men and women were clapping;

eyes solemn, mouths unbroken by smiles but clapping hard at Chess and Box and Splinter.

Ethel was standing behind Chess. She and her brothers shrunk back, closer to Ethel. They looked at the floor and suddenly each of them felt no more than they were; thin, ragged, dirty street rats, bare feet sticking out of the bottoms of their trousers, eyes big with hunger. But the clapping continued. It grew louder and then Box felt something different; a feeling that there wasn't such a distance between him and the men and women facing him, a feeling that they were with him and he was with them, that they were all in the same team and that it was the right team to be in. He looked up and although nobody was smiling and nobody said anything, he met their eyes and they met his and they were clapping. Box nodded.

'Come on,' said Ethel kindly. 'Professor Breslaw is waiting.' She steered Chess, Box and Splinter towards the other end of the refectory. Behind them the clapping died away, the night patrols returned to their seats and the low ripple of conversations filled the room.

Joachim Breslaw was sitting in his wheelchair. In his hands he held a plastic shopping bag. He greeted the Tuesdays with a nod and a friendly twitch of his ginger moustache. They gathered by the table where he sat.

'We had a quick whip-round,' explained Ethel.

'I've been to the supermarket,' said Professor Breslaw and his eye twinkled with delight. 'I have something that I am reliably informed you will enjoy.'

He pulled three metal spoons from the breast pocket of his long, multi-coloured coat and he placed them on the trestle table. Then, from out of the shopping bag he produced a yellow cardboard box and out of the box he slid something circular and spongy and brown that was topped with cream and was filled with a dark, sticky-looking sauce. It sat on a plastic tray which Professor Breslaw placed on the table beside the spoons.

Box leant forwards and sniffed. His mouth began to water but he ignored that. Instead, he stepped back and looked at Ethel, suspicious.

'What is it?' he asked.

'What do you think it is, dear?' replied Ethel. 'It's exactly what it looks like. It's a cake. A chocolate cake.'

Box opened his mouth to say that not everything that looks like a cake *is* a cake, but once his mouth was open he couldn't stop it from doing what it most wanted to do. Box picked up a spoon and began to eat.

ABOUT THE AUTHOR

Benjamin J. Myers studied philosophy and psychology at the University of Leeds before serving in the army as a troop commander in the Royal Artillery. He is now a barrister, specializing in criminal and human rights law. He enjoys fishing, camping, playing water polo and playing the piano. He lives in North Cheshire with his wife and three children.

Twisted Symmetry is the first in a six-part series and is his first published novel. He has wanted to be writer since he was young and all his life has enjoyed books and films of adventure, science fiction and fantasy. He's always been interested in why people do the things they do: is it right to do a good thing for the wrong reason? Is it wrong to do a bad thing for a good reason?

If you asked him where the ideas come from for the Bad Tuesdays books, he'd say they come from seeing how extraordinary events and people in every day life are treated often as if they are quite ordinary, until no one really notices them at all. But, then again, he'd say there's no such thing as ordinary.

Chess, Box and Splinter's story continues in ...

STRANGE ENERGY

What has happened to the children stolen by
the Twisted Symmetry?

The Committee is determined to find out – and enlists the
help of Chess and her brothers.

Is this a desperate gamble by the Committee, or a calculated
move in a deadly game?

What will happen when the Tuesdays journey to the heart
of the very power that is hunting them?